# Seer of the Stones

## The Stone Guild: Book 2

### J. R. Geraci

In a Nutshell Inc.

Cover art by Kate Ferrio.

Map art by Rena Violet.

ISBN: 979-8-218-42350-6

# Acknowledgments

First, I need to thank my marketing team: Joey Geraci and Tori Geraci. These two dedicated countless hours to generating incredible marketing material. Their ideas and creativity helped bring the world in these pages to life. *Joey, you can stop reading now.*

I wouldn't have survived the last year without my extremely underpaid personal assistant, Danielle Clements. She helped me meet deadlines, track finances, brainstorm ideas, and step away from ledges.

My beta readers were essential in making sure my story was where it needed to be. This amazing team included: Barbara Huber, Naseem Tarmohamed, Keerti Goorah, Andrew Dilworth, Danielle Clements, and Laura Geraci. Special thanks to Keerti Goorah for rereading to help me catch lingering errors (she didn't edit this section, so don't blame her for any missing commas here).

Three fantastic editors tackled the drafts of this book, but I am especially grateful for my very talented editor Sam Weiss (Wise Cat Editing). Her opinions, attention to detail, expertise, and sense of humor were invaluable to me. Also, if you're a fan of fantasy/horror, check out her book *The Afterlife Experiment*!

The gorgeous cover art was once again created by the incredibly talented Kate Ferrio. She perfectly captured the feel of book two. Truly honored to have her art represent my words.

As always, huge thanks to my entire family for their endless support. Extra thanks have to go to the Ferrio family. Hanging with them is like walking directly into a medieval pub crowded by a drunk Greg and all of his brothers. Thank you to the Ferrio men—Doug, Jamie, Brandon, Andy, Chris, Jeff—for the endless inspiration and laughter. Thank you especially to the Ferrio women—Eliza, Meghan, Kate, Zara, Ann—for keeping the boys out of trouble using an abundance of wit and grace.

Finally, I want to thank every single person who read the first book, cheered me on, left a review, or bought a book just to support me. It has meant everything to me.

Now, it's time to close this chapter and move on to the next. I hope you'll do it all with me again.

# Contents

LAND OF THE STONE GODS
NORA
KAMEN MOUNTAINS
KRAJ SEA
VIRIDIS
OGRE TERRITORY
OGRE ROAD
WINDSOR
RED FOREST PORT
MOTSU
GOVINDA
HOT SPRINGS
RED PALACE
LANDOW
RED FOREST
TRADE BRIDGE
WAY OF LIGHT
MORSKI
VIRIDIS RIVER
THE ENDLESS SEA
HARKIN
VIOLET FIELDS
TWELVE POOLS
WISTERIA
LISANTHUS
BRAZEN WAY
VERBENA
HEATHER
WOODPINE HALLOWS
PLUM
BELLFLOWER
ASTER
CLEMATIS
UMEKO
PAMUK
IRIS
MORADO
COTTON FIELDS
THE WASTELANDS

# Chapter I

## The Queen's Men

Quinn's eye twitched as Mae swung her hair for what felt like the thousandth time that morning. The siren appeared to be gliding through the Violet Fields rather than walking, which wasn't helping Quinn's mood.

"Who are you even trying to impress?" she asked, as Mae's straight black hair fell back into place. "There's no one here."

The siren twirled, revealing a wide smile. "You're here," she said. The purple stones in her hair sparkled against the backdrop of tall lavender and wild grass surrounding them.

A soft growl signaled to Quinn that Pima was circling back. Before she could react, the bear cub leapt through a patch of lavender and collided with her.

Quinn cried out as she fell backward onto the ground, and Mae burst into a fit of laughter. Kit, who'd been fast asleep in the bag on Quinn's back, scurried out in alarm. The fox's ears perked up, and his small head cocked to one side.

"*Pima*, you giant lump!" Quinn propped herself up on her hands. "You don't always have to live up to your namesake."

The dire bear's growing fangs appeared as she growled again. This time, Quinn knew the sound was meant to antagonize her. Kit seemed to sense what was coming and scurried to Mae's side. Without hesitating, Quinn dove toward Pima, barely wrapping one arm around her as the cub tried to dodge her. The two tumbled over the tufts of lavender, snarling at one another. Quinn managed to trap the bear under one arm. Panting, she leaned her elbow into Pima's thick, dark fur.

"I win," she said, between quick inhales.

Pima pushed her nose into Quinn's cheek and sniffed.

"Stop that!" She pulled herself off the bear, swiping at the snot now on her cheek. Next to them, Mae shook her head and continued walking. Quinn made sure the siren wasn't looking back before pulling a strip of jerky from her bag and tossing it to Pima, who caught it with her mouth.

"You're getting soft," Mae sang over her shoulder.

Quinn mumbled a curse under her breath. Did the siren have eyes in the back of her head?

Kit found his way to his new favorite resting place on Pima's back, and the two vanished into the lavender. Quinn dragged her feet after them. They'd been traveling for a week, and she was already bored of walking.

After they had snuck beyond the city walls of Viridis, they followed Pima's nose south toward the Trade Bridge. Although they'd decided to focus on finding Jaxon, Quinn couldn't help dwelling on why he had vanished. Did he run because he was afraid they'd reveal he was the prince of Twelve Pools? This didn't feel right to Quinn. As timid as Jaxon was, she couldn't imagine him running. Not when he'd been so focused on helping her protect Annabel. Then again, did Quinn really know him? Part of her was still angry that he had lied to them about who he was. It was difficult to even imagine that the scrawny, nervous boy with the disheveled dark hair was a prince.

She had plenty of time to contemplate this as they moved south. Staying off the main road had nearly doubled their travel time, but Quinn knew they needed to be far away from anywhere Viridis soldiers might spot them. So, they moved tactfully and slowly. The pace was enough to make Quinn want to pull out her hair.

She had dreaded crossing the Trade Bridge. Guards from each of the three kingdoms manned the northside of the bridge, monitoring trade and traffic. But Mae's charm worked easily on the men there. She was able to use her stones to dull any suspicion and convince them that the dire bear was being transported south as a gift for the Twelve Pools queen.

Quinn would never admit it, but she was thankful for Mae's voice. She was sure that by now, King Edward had posters everywhere with Mae's face plastered on them. Quinn wasn't sure if her face graced those posters too. Would her father be looking for her? Her mother had shielded her from his rage in the past, but helping a siren escape the dungeons and running away from home was far more severe than anything she'd ever done.

Worse was the thought of Lady Gwen. Her disappointment was palpable even from afar; Quinn could easily picture the glowering look the silver-haired knight would give her the next time they crossed paths. A shiver of guilt ran through her. Gwen had forgiven Quinn for a lot of rule-breaking in the years she'd spent training her—would she forgive her for this too? Or was Gwen too busy grappling with her own guilt to care about Quinn's treachery? Princess Annabel was supposed to be under Gwen's care, and she had failed to protect her. Just as Gwen had once failed to protect Annabel's mother. Quinn, on the other hand, knew the only person to blame for Annabel's kidnapping was herself.

*Don't think about him*, she thought fiercely as her lips burned in protest. An image of Prince Jonathan's dark unruly curls and mocking grin flashed in her head anyway. Her heart beat a little faster. She shook her head angrily and stared hard at the ground.

As she focused on her footsteps, Quinn realized every-thing was a little too quiet. She glanced back to find the siren standing still, her head tilted to one side. It reminded Quinn of the way Kit tilted his head when he was trying to understand her.

"I know that look," Quinn whispered. "What now?"

"Pima's distressed." The stones on Mae's head lit up purple.

"*Kit.*" Quinn's voice shook. "Kit's with her." She moved to run after them, but Mae caught her wrist.

"We could be walking into—"

"Does it matter?" Quinn yanked her arm away. "Pima may be able to handle herself, but I'm not abandoning Kit." She ran in the direction Pima had gone, Mae follow-ing close behind.

Quinn pushed through the last of the lavender and emerged on Brazen Way. The road was blocked by three sol-diers and one scared dire bear. Heart racing, Quinn quickly scanned the soldiers as she unsheathed her sword, noting their purple garb—the distinctive mark of Twelve Pools.

"They're scared and confused." Mae's head was shroud-ed in purple light as she called again on her stones.

"You don't say." Quinn snapped. She caught sight of the splotch of auburn in the midst of Pima's dark fur. *Kit.* Her stomach leapt to her throat. *Get out of there!* But the fox merely looked up from his spot on Pima's back and squeaked.

The men pointed their swords from the bear to the humans and back again, as if unsure which problem to handle first.

"Tell Pima to back away," Quinn said to Mae.

"Already on it."

Pima snarled at the soldiers, but she was retreating. As Mae worked her magic, Quinn moved forward to block the siren from view. One of the soldier's belts lit up red as he called on the power of his stones. Quinn tightened her hand on her sword.

"Let the bear go." Her voice was clear and loud. The soldier standing across from her took a step forward, closing the distance between them. Red light from his belt flickered against his brown skin.

"What do you want with the bear, little girl?" he spat. "We found her; we get to eat her."

"I'm afraid no one will be eating Pima today, or any day for that matter."

She itched to move, to attack, but Gwen's voice was in her head, drowning out her own and reminding her to be patient.

"You named the creature?" The man laughed.

"I'm getting bored," Quinn hissed. Confusion wrinkled the soldier's face, but the words hadn't been meant for him.

"I'm ready when you are," Mae answered.

The soldier glanced back at the others. "I think these wenches burned their brains out with those purple—" He cut off, yelling in alarm as Quinn's sword made contact with his plated arm. The impact sent his sword flying from his hand. A brown blur obscured Quinn's vision as Pima tackled the now swordless soldier, slashing into his newly exposed belly with long claws. His frantic screams pierced the air and then became whimpers.

Another soldier moved to attack Pima, but Quinn blocked his blade with her own and then slammed her shoulder into him. He stumbled back into the third soldier, who shoved him forward again, nearly impaling him with Quinn's outstretched sword. The man scrambled to swat away her blade.

"Tristan, you idiot, help me!" he screamed. But Tristan had backed up even more, fixated on the bear that was making a meal of the man who'd promised to eat her. Quinn guessed Mae was using her stones to cloud Tristan's head with fear because seconds later he was running.

Quinn smiled through the flashes of metal as the last soldier standing backed away from her swings. He glanced in the direction Tristan had run, ready to bolt. Quinn called on her stones and reached for the air behind his legs, tugging hard. He staggered back as the gust of wind made him lose his balance. She jabbed her blade forward one last time, knocking him to the ground. He had managed to hold onto his sword, but Quinn pressed a foot on his hand, forcing him to loosen his grip around the hilt. She picked it up and then pushed both swords against his plated chest.

Mae moved closer and placed her hands on either side of the soldier's head. Quinn watched as his widened eyes fluttered and then closed. The slowing of his chest was punctured by a snore as loud as Pima's growl.

Something tugged on Quinn's dress. Kit had found her. She smiled as the fox made his way onto her shoulder and then climbed up between the red buns atop Quinn's head. He lingered there for a moment, surveying the scene from up high, before determining the danger had passed and returning to the pack on Quinn's back.

"We made a mess." Mae gestured back at Pima's blood-covered snout. "We should have waited; I could've used my voice before they saw us."

"They were already agitated from attacking the bear. You always say it's harder to seduce them if they're alert."

Mae's lips thinned. "We should've tried." Her head glowed purple again. "Give me a second to read him. Drag Pima's dinner into the field, won't you?"

As Quinn backed away, she brushed accidentally against Mae. The siren's eyebrows furrowed together in alarm before she refocused on the sleeping soldier. Quinn stiffened. Mae must have accidentally read her. What had she seen? Trying not to think about it, Quinn took the dead soldier's wrists and tugged, dragging him into the lavender. Pima followed, sniffing the man's feet as they disappeared into the tall, thick whisps of green and purple.

Quinn dropped the body and surveyed the trail she had created leading to the road. Pima rolled across it, deepening the marks in the ground, before flopping belly up. Quinn raised her eyebrows at the bear.

"This is your fault," she said. Her stones glowed red as she shifted the rock at her feet, pulling it across the dirt to disguise the trail.

"Quinn." Mae's sharp tone was a stark contrast to the usual, whimsical way she spoke. Chest tight, Quinn returned to her side, leaving Pima belly up in the sun. Kit moved around in his bag and poked his head out to squeak at the bear, before returning to his resting place.

"I pushed his memory of us as deep into his brain as I could." Mae was still crouched over the man, but her stones had returned to their normal color. "If he remembers us, he'll probably think it was a dream."

She paused before her violet eyes met Quinn's blue ones.

"Jaxon's there," she said. "He's with the queen in Twelve Pools. At the castle on the lake."

Quinn felt some of the weight on her chest dissipate. They were heading in the right direction; they were going to find Jaxon, and they were going to convince him to help get Annabel back. "That's good, isn't it?"

"I think he's being watched closely." She stood, brushing the dirt off her knees. "There's someone trailing his every movement . . . and whoever it is, they're not small. This one was terrified of him." She indicated the soldier with her boot, using it to push his head in the other direction. "I picked up on something else. These soldiers were on their way to the Trade Bridge to set up camp and wait. The queen is positioning others there in the coming weeks. This won't be the last group we see if we stay on Brazen Way."

"Why is she sending soldiers to the bridge?" Quinn didn't know much about Queen Jasmine, but she did know that the young queen rarely concerned herself with matters north of Twelve Pools.

"I'm not sure," Mae admitted. "I don't think he knows. But I could feel the sickening excitement in the pit of his stomach. He thinks there'll be bloodshed."

Quinn spat on the soldier's unconscious body. "Let's get out of here."

# CHAPTER 2

# The Hidden Prince

J axon folded and unfolded the piece of parchment as though the contents might change. The same map stared back at him. Princess Annabel's roughly drawn sketch had lost some of the shine of its fresh ink. He guessed burying the note in his pocket every day hadn't helped.

The first time he unfolded it, he had hoped to see words that held the key to curing Lux Pox. Annabel seemed confident that she had figured it out and that this paper somehow contained the answer. If it did, Jaxon thought, it was written in invisible ink. Four stars decorated parts of the map, but there was nothing else. He studied them again. One star in Viridis, one in the Red Forest, one in Twelve Pools, and another near Windsor, close to the Endless Sea. Jaxon stared harder at the paper, willing it to speak to him.

A soft exhale startled him from his thoughts. He was in one of the private rooms in the sick ward, where Jasmine kept their brother hidden. In the bed at his side, Lukas lay still. His skin was taut and paler than ever. Jaxon could remember not long ago when it had a sun-soaked glow about it. Now he could barely stand to look at how much fat had gone from Lukas, how thin and ragged his small frame was.

Lukas was ten now, but he looked even younger than he had a year ago when the Lux Pox began to take him. His symptoms had only worsened when he fell into the coma months later. His dark hair had lost its color and faded to white. It matched the patches across his body that marked the Lux Pox, which had widened and grown. One of the marks had spread across his face, covering the area around his right eye. The patch reminded Jaxon of the white fur around Kit's eye.

He tried to shake away thoughts of Kit, but it was too late. Images of Quinn, as she watched her best friend disappear with the Windsor princes, bombarded him. Jaxon wasn't sure what haunted him most from that night, Annabel's limp frame in Prince Liam's arms or the manic look in Quinn's eyes and the rage he knew she felt—would still be feeling. Had she forgiven him yet for keeping secrets from her? Or was she somewhere, shooting arrows at a drawing of his face? Most likely, he knew, she'd be on her way to Windsor, ready to battle the entire army to save her best friend.

He called on his stone for what felt like the thousandth time in the week he'd been home. The room filled with soft green light. With his eyes closed, he held his hands over Lukas's chest and searched for whatever was broken inside him. But his magic detected nothing. His brother's blood flowed normally, his heart beat the same as anyone's, and his organs worked as they should.

As Jaxon pulled away, something in his stone's magic seemed to catch a little. The sensation felt familiar, but Jaxon couldn't quite place what was familiar about it. He hadn't noticed it before. He held his hands back over Lukas's chest to check again.

"You can only keep him alive for so long, Alexander."

A tall, striking woman was standing in the doorframe. Her deep indigo dress looked almost black in the dim light of the room. A golden crown sat on her head. Purple stones were interwoven throughout it and within her long, dark brown braid. She was looking down at Jaxon over a slim, upturned nose.

The men of Twelve Pools often whispered about the queen's beauty, but all Jaxon saw was how young his sister seemed, and how the frame of her body glinted like the sharpened edge of a sword. If he were to touch her, he was sure he'd slice his hand open.

"Oh, that's right, you go by *Jaxon* now." Jasmine smiled sweetly, but there was a note of mockery that Jaxon was all too familiar with. "Our father's name wasn't good enough for you."

Jaxon ignored her comment, trying not to fall for her favorite trick. All the air had left the tiny room, making it hard to breathe.

"I'll fight as long as Lukas does," he said. "As long as his heart beats, I'll be here."

Jasmine didn't care if Lukas lived or died. His ailment had always been reduced to a security risk to her, something that could be used against Twelve Pools. Even before Lukas had Lux Pox, he'd been a threat to her that she kept hidden from the world.

"Unless you need to retreat to Viridis again, I suppose," Jasmine said. Before he could stop himself, Jaxon flinched. Jasmine's smug smile was a slap in the face. Why wouldn't she just leave him alone?

"Was there something you needed?" His voice was strained.

"Can't a sister visit her brothers?"

"As you wish," Jaxon managed through clenched teeth.

As she leered down at him, a fresh wave of frustration washed over him. He hated that he had let her get to him. He hated that she always knew what he was feeling. If he didn't have his emotions plastered on his face, he was sure her stones would be glowing now as she read his aura. The thought made him stiffen. A memory of Mae repeated itself in his head. *"Jax didn't glow at all, as though he had no aura," she had said to Annabel in her usual airy voice.*

He had spent his whole life believing Jasmine could read his aura. What if that wasn't true?

"You'll join me for dinner then, won't you?" Jasmine's smile lingered. Jaxon stared at her as her question hung, unanswered, in the air.

She snapped her fingers at his face. "Are you in there? All these hours you spend here seem to be making your mind go."

His sister turned to leave, and a rush of rage swept through Jaxon.

"Why didn't you tell me?"

Jasmine faced him again. Her eyes widened when she found him standing with his fists clenched. Though he hadn't called on its power, the green stone around his neck was glowing.

"What's come over you?" Jasmine looked him up and down. "Shall I call in Healer Kyra?"

"I don't have an aura. You knew that. You never told me."

Jasmine's smile was gone now. "You flatter yourself if you believe I've ever felt the need to read your aura, *Jaxon.*"

Her dress swept the floor as it disappeared beyond the doorframe.

"Theo!" Jaxon heard her call. "Escort my delusional brother to dinner, won't you?"

A large man appeared in the doorway Jasmine had vacated. His broad shoulders reached from one side of the doorframe to the other. A permanent grimace was plastered on a face framed by scraggly dark hair. A bright ring of red stones wrapped his waist three times over. Theo blinked at Jaxon with eyes that were too small for his large, round face.

"I'll follow you," Jaxon said.

Theo hadn't left his side since the night Jaxon had returned from Viridis. Jaxon didn't want to look at the man, no less smell him, anymore.

He followed Theo from the room and shut the door softly behind him. Healer Kyra would be back soon to check on his brother's vitals, but Jaxon's feet still felt like they were drudging through mud as he walked away from the door. He couldn't shake the fear that Jasmine would finally let Lukas die. She seemed more on edge than usual.

Had she always known he didn't have an aura? Her face had remained stoic, but if it were true that she'd never tried to read him, wouldn't she have been more confused by the accusation? His stomach churned as he followed Theo up the stairs. How many lies had Jasmine told him over the years?

Theo pushed open the large dining hall doors, and the noise from inside slammed into Jaxon. Three long tables lined the hall, crowded by chatting soldiers clad in deep royal purple tunics. Each of their sleeves was marked by a small round leather patch that was divided by black lines into twelve slivers. The top sliver was colored in, marking them as a soldier of Hyacinth Pool. Here and there, Jaxon could see groups of soldiers with different slivers colored in, signifying to him that they had visitors from other pools joining them for dinner. Jaxon couldn't remember the last time he'd seen this many soldiers from across the pools all in one room together.

Hyacinth was a central point for much of Twelve Pools, but each of the pools had their own leadership, soldiers, and resources, prioritizing independence over most anything else. They came together only when called by the queen.

A few men watched him, noses wrinkled in disgust. One of them swiped a thumb across his cheek. Jaxon pretended not to see the flippant gesture. He didn't blame them. Viridis wasn't a place that anyone in Twelve Pools thought fondly of, and their prince had spent the last few months there, mingling peacefully with the people. While he was gone, he was sure that Jasmine had spread many lies about him.

As Jaxon moved through the room, he spotted a small group of men in uniforms he didn't recognize. They were wearing dark cloaks with intricate yellow markings decorating the hem line. Their heads turned as he passed, and the hairs on the nape of Jaxon's neck stood up.

At the back of the room, a shorter table overlooked the rest. It was framed by a backdrop of stained-glass windows that reached from floor to ceiling. In front of him, Theo moved to the side to find a seat, leaving Jaxon with a full view of the head table. Jasmine sat at its center, watching him in disapproval as he approached. A servant stepped into her line of sight to fill her chalice with wine. Jaxon's shoulders relaxed, free of her stare.

On the other side of the table, the servant's door opened. A man in all black slid through the opening. His skin was the typical sun-soaked color of the Twelve Pools people, but his neatly combed hair was unusually light, speckled with gray. Although the long, thin sword at his waist was the only weapon visible on his body, Jaxon knew if he pulled back his cloak, it would reveal a strap that stretched from shoulder to waist, decorated with sharpened daggers and a satchel filled with bottles of lethal liquids.

Jaxon remembered waking up after he'd been taken from Viridis to find the assassin's dark eyes staring down at him. The same eyes were watching him now, wrinkled in amusement. The left side of his face drooped where it was marked by a gruesome set of scars that traveled all the way down his neck. While Kiernan had said little to him in the weeks they'd spent traveling to Twelve Pools, the man's open disdain for him had never wavered.

Kiernan had been part of the Twelve Pool council since before Jaxon was born. He was known for collecting information from reluctant sources. Jasmine often hinted that Kiernan was responsible for the death of the Viridis queen during the war. Jaxon wasn't sure he believed this. If King Edward knew who was responsible for her death, Jaxon was confident he would never have let the assassin live.

After the deaths of Jaxon's parents, King Alexander and Queen Sophia, Kiernan held his position in the Twelve Pools court, now at Jasmine's side. The queen trusted few, and Jaxon guessed it was the magic of her purple stones that made sure of that. When she was younger, she often banished men to the Wastelands after her readings. But Kiernan's intentions must have always been true, because he was allowed to remain at her side.

The door Kiernan had slipped through creaked opened again, and an enormous, scaley creature followed Kiernan into the dining hall. Its long, muscular body seemed to take forever to fully emerge, though Jaxon knew it could move fast—faster even than a human could run. A tail nearly the same length as its body slid through last. The creature was longer than Theo was tall.

As it moved in front of the stained-glass window, its gray scales camouflaged themselves to match the dark blues and purple behind it so effectively that even Jaxon momentarily lost sight of it. A long, forked tongue darted from its mouth, reaching at the air around it. While the tongue touched nothing, Jaxon knew its purpose was to smell, not lick. The creature jerked his head and seemed to look right at Jaxon. Its eyelids closed by moving sideways, flickering at him hungrily.

Jaxon was all too familiar with Divoff, who never left his master's side. Kiernan had no stones, but Divoff made up for that. The creature tracked people with his powerful sense of smell and used his poisonous bite on his victims. At least, that's what Kiernan would tell Jasmine. The bodies Kiernan and Divoff hunted were rarely found. It was rumored that the enormous lizard swallowed his victims whole.

Jasmine motioned for Kiernan to join him in the seat to her right, and Jaxon reluctantly took the one to her left. Divoff settled down behind Kiernan.

"Look at us. One big, happy family." Jasmine strummed her fingers on the stem of her chalice.

Kiernan watched her, eyebrows raised. "It's past time you finally find a king to share the table with." His deep, quiet voice grated Jaxon's ears.

Jasmine laughed. "Now, now, Kier. You know I don't like to share."

Jaxon, who'd just swallowed a gulp of branberry juice, nearly choked on it as he tried to hide a snort.

Jasmine stared as Jaxon coughed into a piece of linen. "Why would I need a man to join me at the table, when I have the company of a *boy* who can't even drink properly?" she asked Kiernan, who grinned. "There are far more important items for us to discuss. What information do you have for me today?"

"No word from Windsor since your last correspondence with the prince," Kiernan said.

Jaxon caught a glimpse of a smile flickering across Jasmine's face. "And from the north?"

Kiernan shook his head. "Conditions are the same. The source of the green stone is being watched, but it's unclear if they truly plan to mine it and deliver it to Windsor in exchange for the princess. Their army hasn't left the city yet."

Jasmine's mouth was a tight, thin line. She took another sip of her wine. "There's still time then."

"Time for what?" Jaxon blurted.

"It's nice to see you take an interest in politics, Prince Alexander," Kiernan said. There was a sparkle in his eye as though he knew exactly why Jaxon was asking. Jaxon tried not to let his face give him away as he swallowed back a retort. Out of the corner of his eye, he saw Divoff's tongue search the air as though sniffing out Jaxon's weakness.

A woman in a soot-smeared dress had stationed herself in front of their table. She curtsied elegantly as a row of servants carrying full plates lined up behind her. Jaxon's stomach growled as the smell of fresh food wafted toward them.

"Dinner is served, Your Majesty," the woman said, addressing Jasmine directly. The row of servants moved forward one at a time to place the dishes on the table. "The lamb was gifted by the soldiers who arrived from Heather Pool today. The potatoes are Windsor-grown, from our western visitors."

One of the servants moved behind the table and placed a comically large slab of meat in front of Divoff. They hadn't bothered to cook it fully, and large bones were sticking out of it. Before the servant could pull her hand away, the lizard had opened its mouth wide, revealing rows of sharp, tiny teeth, and lurched forward. His mouth enveloped the meat and narrowly missed the servant's fingers in the process. His large flabby throat expanded as he swallowed the entire slab. Blood-stained saliva dripped out of his mouth and gathered in a pool beneath him.

The servant still standing in front of their table was now staring hard at the floor as though doing everything she could not to look at the lizard. The other servants fell back beside her, and she curtsied again before scampering back through the side door. They gave a wide berth to Divoff.

Jaxon looked down at a heaping plate of food, grateful that the kitchen staff hadn't turned on him like the Twelve Pools soldiers had. He shoved the chunks of salted potato into his mouth, burning his tongue.

He had learned to force himself to eat as much as he could whenever he was given the opportunity, as the food Jasmine had sent to his room was sometimes inedible. She only wanted him in the dining hall when his presence doubled as an opportunity to put his weaknesses on display. Overall, he preferred the moments when she ignored him, like she used to. In those days, he always knew what she was up to because she didn't care enough to try to hide it from him. He took another sip of branberry juice and tried not to think about what his sister was planning.

Next to him, Jasmine lowered her fork and sat back in her seat, her full plate of food still sitting in front of her. The stones on her head were emitting a gentle, calming purple light in sharp contrast to her frigid nature. Jaxon tensed and saw Kiernan shift on Jasmine's other side, as he followed suit and lowered his own fork. Her mood had shifted. Jaxon stared down at his plate, not hungry anymore. He braced himself for whatever was about to happen.

Jasmine leaned closer to Kiernan and whispered something in his ear. He nodded curtly, stood, and sauntered toward one of the tables with his hands clasped loosely behind his back. Jaxon watched what he thought was Kiernan's shadow before he realized it was a camouflaged Divoff, who had slithered undetected after him.

The assassin stopped behind two men, whose faces drained of color. He leaned between them and said something loud enough for the others at the table to hear. Silence spread throughout the dining hall like a wave making landfall.

The two men stood and followed Kiernan back to the table, each trying to fall back behind the other. Jaxon glanced at Jasmine, whose piercing gaze had locked onto them. There was hunger there, and he knew, despite the lack of a smile, that she was filled with joy thinking about the meal of minds she was about to consume.

As the men approached, Jaxon noticed that their Twelve Pools patches were colored in at the third sliver, marking their allegiance to Verbena Pool. They both dropped to their knees in front of the table.

"That won't be necessary," Jasmine said. "Kneeling is a sign of respect, and neither of you respect me much, do you?" Her head tilted ever so slightly to one side.

One of the men looked up, opening his mouth to protest, but as he did, Divoff dropped his camouflage. Startled by the large, gray, scaley beast appearing out of nowhere, the man let out a shout of fear. His hand jumped to cover his mouth, as if it would stuff the scream back inside. Both men rushed to their feet and moved away from the creature.

"Sir Kiernan, give them a little space. We wouldn't want to scare them, would we?"

Kiernan bowed his head to hide a smirk and let out a low, eerie whistle. Both him and the lizard took half a step closer to the men. Jasmine smiled at the soldiers from over the top of the elevated table.

"This is your first time in Hyacinth?" she asked.

The soldier who had screamed still had his hand pressed over his mouth. The other man swallowed. "Yes, my lady—Your Majesty," he said.

Jasmine's crown of glowing purple was brightening. Jaxon felt sick to his stomach. He wanted to look away. The two men were trying to concentrate on the queen, but Jaxon could practically see the internal struggle they were under as she manipulated their emotions. He was sure she was using one of her favorite tricks, clouding their brains with dark memories—most likely pulled from not just their brains but her own, too.

"If you don't learn our ways, Divoff will teach you them." She indicated the lizard. "And he's not a very good teacher, most don't make it through the lesson."

The man with his hand over his mouth removed it to clutch the sides of his head instead. He fell to his knees, his eyes now screwed shut.

"Please, Your Majesty!" he cried.

The other man was still standing, but Jaxon suspected it was because he was frozen in place. The soldiers at surrounding tables began pointing to the man's legs. It took Jaxon a moment to see the discoloration spreading below the soldier's waist and downward. He had emptied his bladder.

"You both seemed so concerned with my head you forgot to monitor your own," Jasmine said, watching them with unblinking eyes. "What was it you called me? Paranoid?"

"We're sorry, Your Majesty," the man on the ground whimpered. "We only thought it must be difficult to trust others because of your connection to the stones. We didn't mean to insult you."

Jasmine folded her hands in her lap and leaned forward, though her back stayed perfectly straight. As she moved, her dress shimmered violet, enhanced by the light of her stones.

"As you can see, I don't need help knowing who to trust." She paused, surveying them. One of the soldiers was clawing at his own head, as though trying to rip into his brain and pull her out. "That's enough. You may retire to your chambers." She glanced at the standing man's wet pants. "Though, I suggest a rinse in Lake Hyacinth first."

Color returned to their cheeks as Jasmine's purple stones dimmed. They backed away, nearly colliding with Kiernan, bowing over and over until they disappeared beyond the dining hall doors.

Kiernan returned to the seat beside Jasmine, Divoff following closely behind.

Jasmine scanned the room. "My favorite color." She grinned. Jaxon knew she was inspecting the aura of the soldiers in the room and that they were probably tinted in the deep black of fear. Seeming satisfied, her stones stopped glowing and she picked up her fork to continue eating as though nothing had happened. Jaxon, however, couldn't bring himself to finish his meal. Thankfully, Jasmine soon grew bored of him and called Theo over to escort him back to his room.

Grateful to be able to escape her company, Jaxon followed Theo from the dining hall and down the stairs. As he passed the infirmary, he stared hard at the door to Lukas's room, wishing that he could sleep in a bed beside his brother to keep a constant eye on him. A surge of rage burned in the pit of his stomach. Jasmine knew what she was doing, giving him just enough time with his brother not to get restless, holding him just an arm's length away. She controlled him like she controlled the others—with fear.

He climbed the steps of his tower up to his room, wishing he had the strength to fight her. He hoped the Verbena Pool soldiers were somewhere safe, recovering from their first night in Hyacinth Pool.

Theo stopped in front of Jaxon's door and grunted at him before shoving him inside. The sight of his barren room, empty but for a lone bed against the far wall made him want to turn and run. While he was in Viridis, Jasmine had removed everything from his room. It now resembled a dungeon cell. Theo had even used his magic to close up the windows, so Jaxon was forced to keep all of the candles in the room lit so he didn't sit in the pitch black.

The door slammed shut behind him and a brief shuffling sound near the keyhole indicated that he was now locked inside, his chance to run as fleeting as the thought.

Jaxon walked across the large, empty room and knelt beside his bed. He wiggled a loose stone beneath it and pulled, revealing a small hole in the floor where Jaxon's satchel was stashed. Kiernan had searched the contents of it when he kidnapped Jaxon but had determined there was no worth to the few items inside, so he hadn't confiscated it. Jaxon kept it hidden anyway, just in case. He suspected Jasmine would not feel the same.

He removed the satchel from the hole and peered at the handful of glittering red stones inside it. He had tried again and again to create more green stones. Each time he called on the same energy he had used to make the one around his neck, but nothing ever happened. Red stones, on the other hand, came easy to him. The drain he felt after creating them had lessened, and eventually he was able to make one without losing consciousness.

He had decided to make as many fusion stones as he could. He might not be able to grow his own power, but he could help Quinn grow hers—assuming he'd ever see her again. He hoped the stones could serve as a peace offering, an apology for the truth he had kept from her.

He shoved the stones back into their hiding place and pulled out Annabel's copy of *The Book of Stones* from beside it. The bed creaked as he flopped back on it, opened the book to the page he had folded over, and began to read.

# CHAPTER 3

# The Winged Visitor

Q uinn would rather fight a thousand soldiers than willingly walk another step. She itched to use her sword or to speak to anyone but Mae. It had been a week since their encounter with the soldiers on Brazen Way. They'd stayed off the main road since then, successfully avoiding human contact. Instead, they'd traveled west of Aster Pool and would soon travel south of Clematis Pool, which would once again double their travel time. The grassland area that had preceded the barrier lakes had been replaced by rolling green hills.

"We could go back to the road and find soldiers traveling by horse," she said to Mae. "It would be nice to move a little faster."

"We need to avoid drawing attention to ourselves." It was a line Mae had said repeatedly over the last few days, and Quinn mumbled it in unison with her. The siren ignored her and dropped down to put a comforting hand on Pima, who was growling softly.

"She's hungry," Quinn said, stopping beside her. She glanced at the darkening sky. The edges of the flat expanse were closing in on them. "We should set up camp for the night." As if offering his agreement, Kit poked his head out over Quinn's shoulder and squeaked.

Mae pulled her pack off her shoulders and unhooked a large cloth tied to the bottom of it, laying it over a patch of dirt. Kit jumped from Quinn's shoulder and curled up on Pima, who had plopped down to rest beside the blanket. Quinn pulled the assortment of cheeses, nuts, and fruits from her bag and sat. Mae dug into the nuts and Quinn watched her, not interested in any of it. She longed instead for one of her mother's fresh, buttery scones.

"We're running out of food again." Quinn absentmindedly tugged on the metal strand around her neck, running a finger over the engraved shield symbol that hung from it. Riley's necklace was useless all this way from the tunnels beneath Viridis, but it gave Quinn hope she'd return one day.

Mae chewed slower, not meeting her gaze.

"We're going to have to visit one of the Twelve Pool villages," Quinn said into the silence.

"We can hunt tomorrow," Mae said. "You enjoyed that rabbit—"

"I enjoy having a full stomach."

Mae smiled as she rolled her eyes. "You sound like Sir Greg!"

"Greg wouldn't have lasted this long." Quinn leaned back on her hands. "He'd be at the closest tavern in Aster Pool's city center right now." She imagined that even as they spoke, he was three deep at the Greedy Griffin. Across from her, Mae looked solemn.

"Did he know you were going to free me?" she asked. "And what about Gwen? Did they know what you'd planned?"

The knot of guilt that had made a permanent home in Quinn's stomach tightened. She avoided Mae's gaze.

"No," Quinn said quietly. "There was so much chaos in the days after Anna was taken." Her memories of that week were blurry. She wanted to visit the castle to see Gwen, to confess, but she was too afraid that Gwen would successfully talk her out of her plans. Gwen would tell her to be patient. To wait. To think of all the options. To slow down. To be more like Jaxon. To do anything, as long as it wasn't *that*.

Quinn swallowed her regret. "They were busy," she continued. "King Edward was causing mass panic. He was furious, blaming half his council for not knowing it was . . ." Quinn swallowed. She didn't want to say the Windsor prince's name. She didn't want to think about how he was responsible for Cassandra's body, drained of blood and life, lying helpless on her bed. ". . . For allowing the bloodsucker to live at the castle undetected. I still don't understand how it happened either. How did the bloodsucker fool everyone? How did he fool *you*?" She'd already made Mae answer this question more than once, but it kept popping up in her head.

Mae abandoned the handful of nuts she'd been eating. She didn't seem bothered by Quinn's repeated questioning. Instead, she stared off in the distance, deep in thought. "Maybe Prince Jonathan is really, really good at shielding his mind," she said, slowly. "Or maybe, he isn't the bloodsucker."

"What do you mean?" Quinn stiffened. She had doubted it herself, at first, but every time she replayed that night in her head, she came back to him. It was clear to her that a red stone bearer had murdered Cassandra, and Quinn had seen Jonathan slinking around the castle hallways not too long before the princess was murdered. *Slinking and kissing.*

"When I read Jonathan, his aura was gentle. His intentions seemed pure to me. He was set on being kind to Annabel."

Rage bubbled up inside Quinn. She sat up straight, her fists clenched. "You read him wrong then. There was nothing kind about the way he kidnapped her and murdered her sister."

Mae was silent for a moment. "What about his brother then?" she asked. "I read Prince Liam too, and it was the same. He seemed more interested in getting to know everyone. Jonathan wouldn't have hidden the truth from him, would he? If his brother was the bloodsucker, wouldn't Liam have known?"

"They're not brothers by blood." Quinn's face scrunched up in concentration, remembering a conversation she'd had with Prince Liam in the castle kitchen. "He came to Windsor with his mother when he was six. Maybe Jonathan is protecting his right to the throne by hiding the truth from him. He wants the throne just like he wants the green stones—all for himself. Maybe he'll banish the servants too, so he can live there alone with his mountain of green stones, his kingdom of one—" Quinn stopped midsentence as she realized she was ranting aimlessly.

"There's something you're not telling me." The siren's stones shimmered.

"Stop that," Quinn snapped, her anger turning to panic. "I thought you didn't read people without their permission."

"If someone is up to no good, I rethink my rules." The siren scanned her, and Quinn swatted her hand up and down in front of her face as if she could somehow wave the magic away.

"You should talk about it." Mae's stones had returned to their normal color, but she was still watching Quinn.

"Talk about what?" Quinn narrowed her eyes.

"Whatever is discoloring your aura."

Quinn's scowl deepened. She fought against her own memories, trying not to think them in case Mae tried to probe her brain again.

"I saw your aura last week . . . when we attacked those soldiers." Mae's words were slow and deliberate. "It's normally a vibrant crimson, but it was broken, with blue bleeding into it. Usually, the color indicates sadness. But when it cuts into pieces of your aura like that, it's because your heart is . . . fractured."

"My friend was kidnapped—of course my heart is hurting." Quinn took a large bite of an apple and stared at the white flesh. *Don't think about him,* she told herself. *Don't think about the kiss.*

"It's not that kind of heartbreak," Mae said. "I can ease it, you know? Whoever made you feel that way, I can push them back a little. Those kinds of feelings are powerful, so I can't fix it, but I can at least dull it."

Quinn was suddenly very calm. "No," she said.

"You still care for this person?"

"No," Quinn repeated. Her eyes met Mae's. "I want to feel all of my rage, all of my hatred when I squeeze the life from him." She tossed the rest of the apple to Pima, who ate it in one gulp.

Mae's hand twitched like she was about to reach out to comfort Quinn but then thought better of it. "Are you sure that's what you want?"

"I've never been more sure of anything." Quinn paused but kept her chin up. "I never want to fall for someone ever again. I never want to feel this weak again."

"The feelings don't have to be a weakness," Mae said. "They can be very useful when you know how to use them. I can help—"

Quinn's laugh interrupted her. "Easy for a siren to say. You love using people's emotions and breaking their hearts." She was grateful for the chance to steer the conversation from herself.

Mae's sympathetic gaze was replaced with a scowl. "If that's how you see me, I feel sorry for you."

"It's true, isn't it? You love getting whatever you want from men. You love when they swoon over you."

"That's a foolish way to look at it, and you know it." Mae stood, brushing off her skirt. The purple stones woven in her dark hair shimmered under the light of the full moon. She seemed to hover there, graceful, even in her anger. "Attraction can be a powerful weapon. Not using my own would be as foolish as you carrying that bow on your back and never firing an arrow from it. Mock me all you want, but you're the one who puts your beauty to waste, Quinn of the red stone."

Mae turned away and began to set up her bedding. She didn't say a word to Quinn the rest of the evening. Quinn didn't miss her constant positivity and her endless probing. Still, when she lay down sometime later, she found herself staring wide eyed into the night, unable to quiet her inner dialogue. Mae's soft snores sounded like thunder in her ears.

The night sky was freckled in the dull glow of thousands of stars, dimmed by the light of the moon. She wondered if Annabel too was looking up at the stars that night. Was she safe? She wished the princess was lying beside her, telling Quinn all about the local shrubs, animals, and fruits. Quinn knew she'd be in awe of everything around them, appreciating even the smallest of differences in nature between the mountain terrain of Viridis and the grasslands of Twelve Pools.

She rolled onto her side, and a pair of bright, violet eyes stared back at her. For a second, she thought she was looking at Mae, and then her stomach dropped. She leapt to her feet, sword in hand. The owl in front of her simply turned its head sideways at an almost comical angle.

Quinn didn't move, her sword still pointed at the owl. It was perched, unbothered on a rock jutting from the earth. Mae's snores continued. Why hadn't she woken? The siren's connection to her stones made it nearly impossible for her to sleep when danger was present. She was supposed to be their guard. Perhaps the owl presented no danger to them. Quinn lowered her sword.

The owl blinked at her, its head returning to an upright position. It shuffled its wings and then stretched them to take flight. They seemed to spread as wide as Quinn's own arm span. The dark black of its feathers revealed hints of shimmering purple as they extended outward.

The owl gave her one last look and then took off into the night sky. Quinn blinked and the creature vanished, leaving her to wonder if she'd imagined it.

# CHAPTER 4

# The Healer's Gift

Jaxon lay on his side, his eyes wide open. The room around him was quiet, but something had woken him from a deep sleep. Without moving, he glanced around the dark room, searching for the source of the noise. When everything remained still and silent, Jaxon decided it must have been part of his dream.

He rolled onto his back, and a hand pressed hard on his mouth. Jaxon flailed, grabbing for something, anything, that he could use to fight back.

"*Shush*," the girl with her hand over his mouth hissed. His panic faded as he recognized the scared eyes looking down at him. They belonged to his brother's healer.

"Kyra?" His voice was muffled from behind her hand.

"Shush," she repeated, eyes darting to the door. "I'm going to remove my hand. Please be quiet." Jaxon nodded, and she pulled away from him. He sat up in the bed, taking in the sight of her small figure and the two long chestnut brown braids that framed her face and fell to her waist. Her green stones were woven into the fabric around her neck, but sat dull and unassuming.

"What are you doing here?" he whispered.

"I came to warn you."

Jaxon called on his stone so he could see better, casting Kyra's skin in green light. Her usual calm features were twisted in fear as her gaze darted from the door to Jaxon's face and back again.

"Your sister is moving forward with her plans—" She shook her head when Jaxon tried to interrupt to ask what she was planning. "She can see everything; she knows everything."

Jaxon frowned. He recognized the fear in her voice. Jasmine had made him feel that way countless times.

When he didn't press her, Kyra's shoulders relaxed. "I'm not the only one, Jaxon," she continued. "There are many of us that hope you'll challenge her right to the throne one day." She held out a small pouch. "But that day is not today."

Jaxon stared at the pouch for a moment before he took it from her. She pressed her hands over his, and there was a long pause before she let go.

"You need to leave." She stumbled over her words as though she were trying to get them out before she lost her courage. "She knows Lukas is her only bargaining chip with you. Few of us even know he exists. She could've abandoned him long ago, but she knows how much you care for him. That's the only reason she let me keep him alive all these years. But she doesn't need him anymore. She doesn't need *you* anymore, Jaxon. She's got new plans for you."

Her mouth tightened, and she moved away from his bed, her face glimmering in green as she stared at the light of his stone. "When you first created it, I was afraid of you." Jaxon had to lean forward to hear her. "Boys don't have the power of the nurture stone. But you're no ordinary boy, are you, Jaxon?"

Jaxon didn't answer, and Kyra backed away, out of the light of the green stone and into the shadow of the night. He heard his chamber door open and then close behind her. He wondered briefly how she'd gotten past the guard, but he had bigger things to think about. The face of the banished seer had appeared in his head at Kyra's words. *Creator of the stones.* He'd tried to forget about that day and Okya's words, but they came back to him in nearly every one of his dreams.

A pounding in his hand, like a heart beating, interrupted his thoughts. He opened the satchel Kyra had given him and peered down at a small white seed surrounded by dirt. The seed continued to pulse in his hand, begging to burst from its case and spread its roots. Jaxon smiled down at it.

"Soon," he promised the seed. He needed a plan first; he needed to figure out how to get his brother out. He knew every entrance and exit in the castle; it was just a matter of choosing which one—and when. Then, he'd have the lake to worry about. All while carrying his brother. He found himself wishing for Greg and Gwen, who would both know exactly what to do, and who would both easily sling Lukas over their shoulder as though he were the size of Kit.

Morning light seeped through the holes in the poorly patched window. Knowing he'd be unable to sleep, Jaxon climbed out of his bed to work on his morning drills. First, the sword work Quinn had taught him. As sloppy as he still was, he could now maneuver with relative ease. His strength had improved since she'd started bossing him around. Lifting the sword had once been the most difficult thing he did during their training sessions.

Once he'd exhausted the last of his physical energy, he sat in the middle of the room and closed his eyes, ready to exhaust his mental energy too. His breathing slowed and deepened. He didn't have to look to know his stone was now brightening and dimming to the cadence of his inhales and exhales. The drills always made him feel like Gwen was back in the room with him again, teaching him the ways of the green stone while scolding Quinn for not paying attention. Where was Gwen now? Was she helping Quinn get Annabel back? Wherever she was, he hoped Quinn had the patience to at least ask for Gwen's advice before she ran off to save Annabel on her own.

As he moved through his exercises, the small seed, tucked safely under his floorboard, screamed for his attention. It was the only lifeform he could reach from his stone-enclosed room. Jasmine had made sure there was a wide, lifeless perimeter around his room. Gwen might be able to call on some distant life force, but it was still beyond his own capabilities.

He focused instead on moving the energy inside him, noticing how it flowed freely and effortlessly. So different, he thought, from how it had flowed when he'd tried to move it through Lukas. In Lukas, his magic had gotten stuck, like he'd run into a closed door.

Jaxon's eyes shot open, remembering the first time he had traveled through the Red Forest. He was kneeling over Healer Shay after she'd collapsed. His magic hadn't been able to flow through her too, caught in the same way. For her, it had been the Hirudo beetles, which had fastened themselves to her back. Was it possible there were Hirudo beetles somewhere on Lukas? No, Jaxon thought. He had never seen them in Twelve Pools. He had never even heard of them before his trip through the Red Forest. Besides, those still didn't explain the light patches on his brother's skin.

Annabel's note also didn't match this theory. If she had thought it was a Hirudo beetle, wouldn't she have just told him instead of drawing him a cryptic map?

He hadn't considered that there might be something that was actively blocking Lukas's magic. Were there ailments that could halt a healer's magic? If there were, they would be documented in healing books. They might give him a clue as to how he could heal Lukas.

As quick as his excitement had come, it was snuffed out. After Jaxon made his green stone, his sister had hidden all the books on healing in the library of her war room. If he wanted to search those books, he'd have to break into the room. Was it worth the risk? He thought about the seed under his bed. If he used it now, he might not be able to escape later. Kyra had given it to him to help him run from his sister, but it would be for nothing if he couldn't save Lukas.

Distant voices came from down the hall, and—with what seemed like an enormous amount of effort—Jaxon pushed his thoughts aside and refocused on his surroundings. It felt as though he had traveled to Viridis and back in the last few minutes. He made his way over to the door and leaned against the wood to listen.

"You better hope she never finds out."

Jaxon recognized the muffled voice of Zachary, who brought Jaxon his meals. Visits from Zachary were his least favorite part of the day. The first few times the servant entered the room, he had handed the tray to Jaxon, and then rapid-fired a dozen questions. At the same time, he studied the room so hard Jaxon wondered if he planned to go home and paint it. After a while though, Zachary seemed to lose interest in Jaxon, who gave vague answers to his questions.

"I don't feel right." A man grunted in reply. One of the night guards, Jaxon assumed. "Someone slipped me something."

"Won't make a difference if they did," Zachary said. "All she's gonna know is you was sleepin' on the job. Valoo and I'll keep quiet about it?"

The guard grunted again in response and Jaxon heard the clinking of coins.

He moved away from the door just in time. The deadbolt clicked as the guard unlocked the door and Zachary entered the room. The scrawny servant boy's jet-black hair was slicked back with grease. His pointed nose was framed by lines of freckles that spread like whiskers across his cheeks. Beady eyes searched the room and then Jaxon, before he handed him a tray of food.

"You missed dinner again last night," he said bluntly.

Jaxon put the tray on his bed. "I was invited to dine with my sister." Though, he thought 'dine' was a generous word for her torture sessions. When he turned back to face Zachary, he froze. Kiernan was in the doorway, standing over the boy's shoulder. He was blocking the hall light from entering the room, casting a shadow on Zachary.

"What did the queen say?" Zachary asked, unaware of the man looming behind him. "I heard she's sending men north."

Jaxon tried to speak, but his throat had locked up.

Zachary waved a hand in front of his face. "You still in there?"

"Don't—" Jaxon managed to say to Kiernan. The assassin smirked as Zachary whirled around to see who he was talking to. The servant boy took a step backward before bowing quickly.

"Kiernan," he mumbled. "*Sir* Kiernan, apologies for getting in your way." He moved to step around the man, but Kiernan held a hand up to stop him.

"Selling gossip about castle activity is treason," Kiernan said in his low, grating voice. "You've made a habit of it. Jasmine sent me to collect the cost." Jaxon knew what was about to happen and that there was nothing he could do to stop it. He closed his eyes. The thud that followed made him wince.

When he looked again, Kiernan was walking from the room, and Zachary was laying on the ground, a puddle of blood already forming under his neck.

"C'mon, Divoff," Kiernan said over his shoulder.

Jaxon's heart skipped a beat as the enormous lizard materialized beside him as if from thin air, its scales transitioning back to their normal ashen gray. The creature's mouth opened as it moved forward, wrapping around Zachary's legs. In three large gulps, Divoff swallowed Zachary whole.

The guard outside Jaxon's door had poked his head into the room. He saw the lizard's bulging stomach and let out an exasperated sigh.

"Waste of a valoo," he huffed.

Bogged down by the weight of Zachary, Divoff teetered from the room, moving slower than usual. The guard locked the door behind him, and Jaxon was left to stare at the blood now staining the floor.

# CHAPTER 5

# The Bigger Brother

Quinn watched the long grass, checkered by splotches of purple flowers, sway in the breeze. The slope was evening out beneath her feet as they neared the top of yet another hill. They had traveled past Clematis Pool, and at each new hilltop they ascended, Quinn would hope to finally look below and see Hyacinth Pool, home of Queen Jasmine. Quinn grimaced. Home of Queen Jasmine and *Prince Alexander*, she corrected herself.

Kit, who'd been resting on her shoulder, pressed his nose against her cheek. Quinn leaned into it and put a comforting hand on his fur. She wanted to assure him that she was okay, but Mae was in earshot, so she said nothing. She didn't want further questioning.

As they got closer to the castle, she became more and more unsure of the choices she'd made. What if she'd been wrong—what if Jaxon didn't want to help them? What if they had wasted precious weeks traveling to Twelve Pools when they could have been finding a way to save Annabel?

Pima emerged from the other side of the hill and barreled toward them, taking her usual lap around them. Instead of heading back the way she'd come, she slowed to a walk to match their pace.

Mae tossed the cub a strip of dried meat. "We're close then," she said. "If Pima doesn't want to go farther without us."

She turned to Quinn. "The Hyacinth clan is a savage bunch, and they don't like outsiders. We need to draw as little attention to ourselves as we can."

Quinn watched the ground as she walked, aware of Mae's eyes on her.

"Don't make any sudden movements. Don't attack anyone."

Quinn frowned harder at the ground.

"Quinn—"

"I get it," she snapped. "I'll play nice."

"No, look!"

The valley had opened before them. An enormous lake at the bottom sparkled in the sunlight, reflecting the valley around it. Small houses and docks crowded the lakeshore. A long, thin, stone road extended out from the shore to the lake's center, where the towering Twelve Pools castle was an island of rock in the water. A single tower in the castle's center rose higher than the rest.

Quinn's awe faded to dread. The castle looked untouchable, impossible to reach.

"How are we going to get to it?"

Mae scanned the area. She shook her head. "Swim?" she suggested feebly.

"It looks like there are boats on the water close to the castle," Quinn said. "Maybe we can wait until dark and cross the lake that way."

"I expect they're monitoring the water at all times," Mae said.

"Maybe a siren's song will keep guards distracted."

Quinn looked at Pima. Mae seemed to have the same thought, kneeling close to the bear.

"We need you to wait for us here, Pima." Her stones illuminated the bear's face in purple. "Do you think you can come find us when we leave the lake?"

Pima's growl echoed through the valley, and Quinn glanced around, hoping it wasn't as loud as it had sounded to her. Kit climbed onto Quinn's head, sat between her two red buns, and squeaked before darting back to her shoulder. His beady eyes were fixated on Pima. Mae tried to put a comforting hand on the bear, but Pima shrugged her off and moved to sit at Quinn's feet instead. The cub pawed at her leg, tearing four small holes in the fabric of her pants.

Quinn frowned and knelt beside the bear so that both her and Kit were eye level with her. "I'm sorry, Pima. You'll be safer here. The Twelve Pool people won't respond kindly to you."

The bear roared again, standing on her hindlegs so she towered over Quinn. Pima watched them for a moment, and then collapsed back on all fours. Quinn swore she saw pain in the bear's eyes as she gave one last feeble growl, turned, and fled. She didn't look back and soon vanished over the side of the hill.

"What if we can't find her after?"

"She'll find us," Mae said. "I promise."

But Quinn couldn't help but think about how Pima had only recently lost her mother, and how the cub was now far away from the only home she had ever known. A wave of guilt flooded Quinn, remembering the moment she'd thrust her sword deep into the belly of Pima's mother. Pima had grown since then, but she was still so young. Would she be alright out there on her own?

Mae put a comforting hand on Quinn's shoulder. "It had to be done."

Quinn tore her gaze from the spot where the bear had vanished. "We don't need to talk about it." She pried herself loose from Mae's grasp and began to walk in the other direction, down the slope. Unfazed by Quinn, Mae sang as she followed. Despite her best efforts to keep Mae's voice from calming her, Quinn's shoulders dropped and her frown lines softened.

As the pair descended the hill, more signs of village life appeared. A few goats eyed them as they passed but otherwise paid them no attention. A woman hanging clothes on a line behind a small house glanced at them as they went by but otherwise gave them no more attention than the goats.

The slope beneath their feet leveled. Mae wrapped her purple scarf around her head, hiding her stones. Quinn did the same with her red stones, tying a long, dark cloth around her waist. There would be stone bearers wearing their stones proudly for all to see, but Quinn knew keeping them hidden would help them blend in.

The main road opened before them, wrapping along the lake. Smaller roads branched off from it, connecting to the docks that extended out over the water. Quinn and Mae were soon mingling with the bustling lakeside clan, who were busy with their afternoon chores. Quinn watched one man struggle to pull a full net of fish from his small wooden boat, hollering at a young boy to help him.

In the distance, Quinn could just make out the well-guarded stone walkway that stretched out to the castle over Hyacinth Pool. As she scanned the water, looking for another way to cross, she spotted smoke billowing from a nearby building perched over the lake. A wooden sign out front read *The Lazy Leech*. Her stomach grumbled, reminding her that it'd been weeks since they'd had a proper meal.

"Food first?" Without waiting for Mae's response, she hurried toward the tavern. Kit squeaked from inside his bag. "I'll get something for you, Kit," she promised him.

As Quinn pushed open the door, she was met by a chorus of loud chattering and the overwhelming smell of roasted fish. Early drinkers, who had most likely just returned from a long day on the lake, crowded the tables.

"Take any seat, hun." A dark-haired woman in an apron winked at Quinn as she glided by, plates of food perched precariously across her outstretched arms.

"There's a spot there." Mae had materialized at her side, pointing at one of the only empty tables. They pushed through the packed room and collapsed onto the two seats on either side of the table.

"We made it." Mae let out a long sigh. If Quinn hadn't spent weeks with her, she might not have noticed how tired the siren was. She looked perfectly composed. Her dark hair was as neat as ever, and there were no bags under those large, violet eyes. Quinn, on the other hand, had seen her reflection in the tavern window and could not say the same for her worn, freckled face or the two messy auburn buns sagging on top of her head.

"Freshwater prawn? Eel? Bass?" The dark-haired maiden had returned.

"Prawn, please," Quinn said over the sound of her stomach growling.

"Do you have anything . . . without eyes?" Mae asked.

The maiden raised her brows in unison with Quinn. "Not from around here, are you? Egg cake then? The chef's doing a bake of three types of cheese, parsley, and onion."

"Thank you, yes," Mae said, gratefully.

"Branberry tea is the house specialty, if that'll interest you northerners."

"Yes, for us both," Mae said. The maiden huffed in reply and rushed back toward the kitchen.

"Nothing with eyes?" Quinn stared at Mae.

"If you could read animal emotions like me, you might feel the same."

Quinn studied the siren's face. "I've never met a purple stone bearer who had any qualms eating meat."

Mae shrugged. Quinn searched her memories from the last few weeks. She had hunted and roasted rabbits on a few occasions, but she couldn't remember Mae actually eating any of them. How hadn't Quinn noticed? What else didn't she know about Mae? She suddenly felt as though she were sitting across from a stranger. Mae had said she had nowhere to go after Quinn had freed her from the castle dungeons. Quinn had needed to believe it at the time, but now her blind trust seemed foolish.

"Why are you here?" Quinn's voice was soft and even.

Mae smiled sweetly. "For the chipper company, of course."

"No," Quinn said. "Why did you come here, with me, to Twelve Pools?"

Mae's face scrunched in confusion. "You freed me from my cell—"

"You could have left at any point."

"Annabel took me in, she fought for me when the king wanted me locked up. She's the first person who ever believed I was more than a siren, more than—" Mae stopped short, looking guilty.

"Than what?" Quinn demanded.

"It doesn't matter. When I read her—when I looked into her future—I also saw her aura. I've never seen one so golden—the soft gold of infallible kindness. All my life, I've only ever done what I've wanted to do. And right now, I want to help the princess."

Quinn was silent for a moment before she nodded. She stared toward the far end of the tavern where a wall of windows opened to the lake outside. There was no one she cared for or believed in more than Annabel, and as long as Mae was driven by similar feelings, the rest didn't matter.

"Here we are."

The maiden had returned with two cups of tea. She plopped them down and disappeared again. Quinn watched the steam rise from her cup, her eyelids growing heavy.

The doors of the tavern flew open, jerking her out of her trance. A man wider than the doorway slid through it sideways. His large scraggly beard hung low beneath a large smile. He looked familiar, though she was sure she'd never seen him before.

"Marrrriaaaa," the man bellowed. "The usual, and two for my friends here!" Two smaller men had followed him inside. They were greeted heartily by others as they passed Quinn and Mae and sat at a nearby table. Quinn couldn't help but watch the man, unable to shake the feeling that she knew him. The tavern maiden was already placing their beers on the table in front of them.

A soft whistle brought Quinn's attention back to their own table. She searched for the whistler but didn't see him. It happened again, and Quinn realized it was coming from the table next to them.

"Hi there, beautiful," said one of the men, holding up his jug of beer in a salute as he struggled to sit up straight. His large eyes were glued on Mae, like he had an empty stomach and she was his dinner. The other men at his table stopped chatting to watch the exchange. Quinn tensed, a small knot of anger clenching her stomach. Mae leaned back in her chair and crossed her arms, looking unbothered.

The man slid from his seat and staggered closer. Quinn increased her estimate of how many beers deep he was. Mae tugged at the scarf on her head, and Quinn guessed she was fighting the urge to use her stones.

"What's a pretty young thing like yourself doing in here with all these ratty boys?" The man leaned closer, spilling some of his beer before he set it down precariously on the edge of their table. Quinn's hand rested on the hilt of her sword, though she had no memory of putting it there.

"You might want to take a step back, sweetie," Mae said. She tilted her head at him, one corner of her mouth curled up.

The man wasn't deterred. "I like a girl who's mean to me," he said. He reached his hand out to cup Mae's face, and before Quinn could think, she was standing with the point of her sword pressed against the man's chest. He yelped in alarm.

"Touch her and you die," Quinn said. A dim red glow was seeping from the cloth wrapped around Quinn's belt. She glanced at Mae, expecting disapproval, but the siren was still leaning back in her chair, and her grin had widened. Emboldened, Quinn pushed her blade harder into the man's chest, tearing a small hole in the cloth.

"Oy!" he jumped back in alarm. "Get off me, wench!" Two of the men at his table jumped to his defense, fumbling to retrieve their weapons. The tavern chatter halted, all eyes on their group.

"Leave her be," Quinn said between clenched teeth.

"Lower your sword," countered one of his friends, offering up the point of his small knife. "Albert ain't mean no harm."

The friend on Albert's other side was staring at Mae. He raised a hand, pointing at Mae's head. With his other arm, he shook Albert, accidentally pushing him harder against Quinn's sword. The drunk man yelped, but his friend ignored him.

"That's made from Gnomish hand," he hissed, referring to the scarf tied around Mae's head. "I'd recognize it anywhere. My wife makes me pick up that silk fabric from Viridis traders when they pass through town."

Albert's eyes widened. "Viridis scum." Speckles of his spit landed on Quinn's sword. "Should have known you were northerners."

His friend moved forward with his knife. Quinn grabbed hold of his wrist, twisted his arm back, spun him around, and kicked his legs out from under him. Her sword never left Albert's chest.

"What's going on here?" The large man who had burst through the tavern doors moments ago had pushed his way to them. He reached over and picked up the drunken man with one hand, his beer still in the other. Quinn lowered her sword, watching in fascination as Albert was lifted off his feet. The other two men bolted back to their table.

"Won't Joan be waiting for ye, Al?" The man's voice was playful, but his firm grip on Albert suggested otherwise. "Run along to her now, won't ye? Before ye get yourself into trouble." He dropped Albert to the ground. The drunk man scrambled to his feet and stumbled toward the door and out of the tavern. Chatter returned to the room, and the bar maiden hurried through it again, with a fresh set of dishes on her arms.

"Thank you, Kraig," she shouted at the large man as she passed. "Darius says next one's on him!"

"I was managing it," Quinn said, sheathing her sword and slumping back into her seat.

"Almost peed myself when ye pulled that sword on 'em," the large man grinned through the slit in his large bushy beard. "Figured I'd save you the trouble of beating the stones out of that one. Not that I wouldn't have enjoyed watching, but Albert ain't worth the trouble, even if he does deserve it."

"We appreciate the help," Mae said, lingering on the "we" and shooting Quinn a look.

"Yes, thanks," Quinn muttered.

"Northerners aren't very loved here, are they?" Mae said.

"These Twelve Pools folks got a lot of feelings," Kraig said. "Many of their people died in the war of Isabela."

Quinn sat up straighter. "You're from the north too, then?"

"Grew up just north of the Trade Bridge," he said. "Still head up that way once a year. Papa makes us all come home for the Day of the Stones festival. If you frequent any of the taverns near the Viridis castle, you may've seen one of my brothers in passing. He's a knight under King Edward. Spends more time with a beer in his hand than I do. Though, I could still drink him under the table."

"You're Greg's brother," Quinn said. It wasn't a question. How hadn't she made the connection before? His boisterous laughter, large frame, and full beard were almost an exact copy of Greg's. Not to mention the way his voice filled an entire room. She suddenly felt warm and safe. She got up and pulled over a chair from one of the neighboring tables. Kraig plopped into it without question and took a couple of large gulps from his beer.

"Ye know my big brother then, do ye?" Kraig asked. "Well, big, but not bigger, if ye know what I mean. How's that scoundrel doing?"

"He's making preparations to journey to Windsor and bring Princess Annabel home," Quinn said quietly. She thought if there was anyone in Twelve Pools she could trust, it was Greg's brother. Maybe he'd be able to help them. Mae seemed to have the same thought; she sat straighter in her chair and exchanged a look with Quinn.

Kraig frowned. "That's true, then? Heard they took her, didn't want to believe it. Greg'll get the girl back, or he'll die trying. After Queen Isabela was killed, he went and blamed himself. Never seemed the same again—lost a bit of his joy. He won't let that happen again."

Quinn raised her eyebrows. If the Greg they knew was the less joyful version, Quinn couldn't imagine how boisterous he had been before.

"All Greg ever wanted to do was be a knight and protect the kingdom. Used to chase us all around with a wooden sword when we were young, yellin' about honor. But me, I just wanted peace and fish. Met a nice lady along the way, that's been nice too."

Mae leaned across the table and placed a hand on Kraig's.

"We're trying to save the princess, too," she said. "Will you help us with something?"

Kraig didn't hesitate. "For friends of my brother, how could I say no?"

Mae leaned in even closer. "We need to get into the castle," she spoke so quietly that even Quinn had to strain to hear her. "We're trying to speak with Prince Alexander, but we think the queen will turn us away. We know she's got him closely guarded. Do you know another way inside? Maybe a way across the water that isn't watched?"

Kraig searched her, glanced at Quinn, and then back at Mae. He grunted. "Meet me tonight at sunset on Pewter Dock. I'll get ye there."

"*Tonight*?" Mae's voice was loud this time, and she put a hand over her mouth, glancing around to make sure no one was listening.

"There's a storm rolling through, and the two of ye need the cover it'll bring." Kraig drained the last of his beer, and the belch that followed made patrons at neighboring tables turn their heads. "The lake isn't as calm at night. Bring that sword, Red."

Kraig sauntered back to his table. "Nice locks, good sir," Quinn heard him say to a man with long curly hair as he shook his own head of hair. "I'm tryna catch up."

Quinn watched him absentmindedly as she gripped the handle of her sword. *Hope you're ready for us, Jax,* she thought.

# CHAPTER 6

# The Queen's Tower

Jaxon pressed his face against the stone where his bedroom window used to be. Through a small hole, he could see the dimly lit sky. Clouds blocked out most of the moon, casting the courtyard below in darkness. Jasmine would be in her tower, preparing for bed. If he wanted to visit the library, now was the time.

He secured his sword around his waist and placed a hand over the satchel at his side, assuring himself that Quinn's red stones, Gwen's Guide, and Annabel's note were in there. *Just in case*, he thought. Not wanting to dwell on the what-ifs, he opened his satchel and pulled out the small cloth bag Kyra had given him. He scooped the seed from inside, and carefully pushed it into the hole, packing the dirt in with it.

He took a deep breath. As he exhaled, green light glistened from his stone. The energy of his magic surged from him and roots erupted from the seed, clinging to the dirt pile. He placed his hand against the gap in the wall, feeling a vine stretch from the roots, reach through the other side of the wall, and then twist downward.

*Come on*, Jaxon thought. *You can do it, little one.* He weaved and twisted with the vine, asking it to keep reaching and reaching. Finally, it touched the ground, feeding on the nutrients of the soil. His magic coursed through him, thickening the vine and binding it to the castle wall.

Jaxon focused on the piece of vine that was still stuck in the small hole and expanded it until it pushed against the walls it was encased in. A small crack extended down from the window to the floor of his room. Moments later, the stone wall burst under the pressure. Rocks spewed at his feet, leaving behind a Jaxon-sized opening. He paused to catch his breath and allow his magic to replenish before he squeezed through.

Clutching the side of the castle wall and trying not to look down, Jaxon wrapped the vine around his waist. He knew if Quinn were here, she'd already be scaling the wall, yelling directions back up at him. He tried to channel her fearless nature, but his shaking hands betrayed him.

Instead, he concentrated on his stone's power. The vine listened to him and grew, moving him toward the castle's central tower. All the while, he was very conscious of the fact that his feet were no longer touching solid ground. His jaw was clenched so tightly he thought his teeth might crack. He couldn't force himself to look down, so instead, he hoped the guards below were busy keeping watch, not looking upward. He tucked his glowing stone under his tunic to hide the green light, just in case.

Of the five spires, the one in the center was the tallest. In his parent's days, it was known as the Watchtower, but Jasmine spent so much time there, the castle staff now referred to it as the Queen's Tower. More importantly to Jaxon, this was the tower where they kept the family's collection of books.

The vines climbed up the side of it. He'd almost reached the top, where it began to narrow to a point. Here, the castle wall was wrapped in glass windows but for one lone wooden shutter used by archers and raven messengers. He pushed it open and paused to listen. When he was sure there were no sounds coming from the room, he nudged the vines once more and pulled himself onto the ledge and through the window. He fought the urge to sigh in relief as his feet touched solid ground.

A large, round, oak table took up most of the room, a map covering its surface. What little light there was outside trickled through the large windows circling the room. Each stretch of glass was twice the height of Jaxon and stained purple at the top.

On one side of the room, a wooden panel in the floor led to a staircase below. On the other side, a set of stairs climbed upward and connected with a ledge that circled around to the top of the tower. Shelving lined the ledge and hundreds upon hundreds of books were propped up on it.

Jaxon climbed, pulling out books as he went. At the top, where the ledge ended, there was a small opening in the ceiling. He pushed the books through it and then hoisted himself up after them.

He emerged in a small, pointed room. The singular wood-covered window surrounded by glass windows mirrored the ones in the war room below. In the center of the room, a small, golden tube sat on a metal stand, pointing toward one of the glass windows. The spyglass was a prized possession of Jasmine's, and for good reason. He'd never seen anything like it before. It came from Woodpine Hallows, near where his mother was born. She used to tell Jaxon that it was one of the few items she brought with her when she moved to Twelve Pools.

Intricate carvings of woodland creatures and a symbol that looked to Jaxon like a shield decorated the golden spyglass. With a pang, he remembered how much his mother had loved climbing up here and using it to get a closer look at passing birds and the busy market across the water. Her soft nature had always been a stark contrast to the abrasive temperament common among the people of Twelve Pools.

The wood shutter on the window rattled as a gust of wind slammed into it, jolting Jaxon from his thoughts. He had to focus. He had no idea how much time he had until someone entered the war room, or Theo noticed the gaping hole in Jaxon's bedroom.

Jaxon tore his attention away from the spyglass, sat down on the floor near his small pile of books, and began to read by the light of his stone. He started with a newer-looking book first, skimming through the chapters and stopping when something caught his eye.

By the time he got to the last book, the clouds had fully covered the moon and darkened the sky to black. The faint rumble of thunder snapped him out of his trance. He had no idea how much time had passed. He leafed through the last book, losing hope. It was worn and tattered, with loose pages and a cover doing its best to detach itself from the spine. There was an entire section outlining uncommon ailments, but nothing that sounded similar to Lux Pox. *What would Annabel do? Where would she look?* He wished she was here. He flipped back through the book, and a page fell to the ground. It looked well worn, frayed on the edges. Jaxon scooped it up and returned it to the center of the book. His eyes lingered for a moment on the page and excitement rushed through him. He had seen the section on stone christenings, but he'd skimmed it before.

Now, the words were jumping off the page . . . *stone christenings are believed to have originated sometime after the Great Convene. Older texts site the belief that the stone gods punished those who did not claim their stones . . .*

He flipped the page over, drinking in the words . . . *their punishment was a pox that covered the skin and shut down the insides . . . the stone christenings were enacted, and most cases of the pox vanished . . .*

His breath caught in his chest. He stared at the words, reading them again and again. He fumbled for Annabel's note in his satchel. The four stars stared up at him. The answer was there somewhere, just out of reach.

If the stone christening ceremony had almost eradicated Lux Pox, that must mean that people with the ability to use the stones were getting sick if they didn't have access to one.

But that couldn't be it. Jaxon could remember Lukas's stone christening; it stood out vividly because it took place shortly after his mother had died giving birth. The small ceremony was held behind closed doors. Jasmine was terrified to reveal that Lukas had survived the birth. Jaxon remembered feeling small and scared as she told him that the other kingdoms would come for them if they knew how weak and vulnerable Twelve Pools was—ruled by an eleven-year-old queen and her two very small brothers. When he looked back now, the truth seemed obvious. She had never been worried about Lukas's life. He could still hear her words in his head. *Let's keep him a secret, just for a little while.* The stones had not glowed for Lukas, and Jasmine had smiled in relief.

Had he somehow misremembered the ceremony? It was worth trying to give Lukas a stone to see how he'd react. As Jaxon gathered the books, his eyes lingered on the spyglass. It was one of the few remaining relics of his mother. He longed to take it, but that would be reckless. Jasmine would know he had defied her. That was something Quinn would do, not him. He grabbed the pile of books and descended the spire, returning them to the shelves as he went.

Voices carried through the tower, and Jaxon froze. They grew louder, and he abandoned the last book and raced back up through the hole in the ceiling.

The creak of the latch opening below echoed up the spire. He strained his ears, trying to hear what was happening below over the sound of his heart thudding loudly in his chest.

"It was in the letter, Theo, won't you pay attention?" His sister sounded irritated.

Theo's reply was a grunted apology.

"General Townsend, please explain it to Theo *again*." Jasmine's drawl was dismissive. She often lost patience with Theo, who was much slower and sloppier than the other members of her inner circle. As much as Jaxon despised Theo, he couldn't help but sometimes feel sorry for him. The man wanted so badly to please Jasmine, who probably wouldn't hesitate to feed him to Divoff.

"We already have a unit of red stone soldiers at the Trade Bridge." General Townsend's voice was loud and clear, bringing a picture of his grizzled, apathetic face to Jaxon's mind. "More are en route, and we're sending additional forces tomorrow, now that all the men from Heather Pool have arrived. When Viridis moves west, we'll be waiting south of the Trade Bridge. Once they reach the Way of Light, our men will cross the bridge and ambush the Viridis army from behind."

Jaxon felt like he couldn't breathe. He tried to process what he had just heard, but the words just bounced around in his head. His sister was still talking, and he forced himself to push his thoughts aside to focus on what she was saying.

"Captain Maxwell won't be expecting it. He has a thick, stubborn head and an undeserved arrogance. Who's the knight—the one that gave you trouble during the War of Isabela? The Lady Gwen?"

"Indeed."

Jaxon stiffened. He'd recognize that deep, scratchy voice anywhere. It was Kiernan.

"She wouldn't leave Queen Isabela's side," Kiernan said. "When she was finally called away, it was to help a child, one of the queen's daughters, I believe. Had Lady Gwen stayed, she would have laid her life down trying to protect the queen. The rumors and tales about her are still widely told across Viridis. Many believe that it was her that saved King Edward—that she raised him from the dead."

"You think she'll be with the Viridis army?" Jasmine's voice was stiff. "Is she someone we should be concerned with?"

"It's been a decade, and she wasn't young, even then," said Kiernan. "If her body hasn't gone, her mind surely has. If s he *is* with them, I'll see to it she gets what she so desperately seemed to want last time: to die protecting the scum of Viridis."

Jasmine snickered, and Jaxon's nerves turned to anger. There was something in Kiernan's voice that Jaxon couldn't quite place. He sounded eager, almost hungry, as though he were licking his lips as he talked of murdering Lady Gwen.

It was all true then, Jaxon thought. Kiernan *had* killed Queen Isabela. And now he stood there disrespecting Gwen, the greatest knight Jaxon had ever met, silver hair and all. The woman who had shared the great depth of her knowledge with him, a boy she didn't even know. His blood boiled, and he fought the sudden urge to reveal himself and attack Kiernan.

"What do you wish of me, my queen?" Theo asked. Jaxon guessed he hadn't followed much of the conversation.

"We're sending my brother out with the others tomorrow," Jasmine said. "I need you at his side until the end. I need you to make sure they reach the Trade Bridge. Don't protect him. If he's killed in the scuffle . . . Well, that's no one's fault but his own."

"The Windsor prince won't like that," Kiernan protested.

"That's not of my concern," Jasmine said. "This is the Twelve Pools way. You're strong or you die, there's no in-between. His death will make things easier for us, Kiernan. We can call on soldiers from all of the twelve pools to fight in the name of their dead prince. Our attack on Viridis will only be all the more justified."

The silence after her words clung to Jaxon, weighing him down. He couldn't move. He couldn't think.

"Apologies, my queen, the letter . . ." It was the assassin speaking again. There was a moment of silence before he charged on. "You've promised the Windsor prince you'll deliver Jaxon to them. Would his death not break that agreement?"

Jasmine's scoff was so loud, it sounded to Jaxon like she was crouched next to him.

"I have no interest in his obsession with my brother," she said. "Should he survive the battle at the Trade Bridge, he's all theirs. But it certainly doesn't nullify our agreement if one of their men accidentally kill him. We'll send his head on a stick then, if we must complete a delivery."

"If he falls into Viridis hands . . ." The assassin trailed off.

"Theo will make sure that doesn't happen. Won't you, Theo?"

The large man grunted in reply. Jasmine didn't explain what she meant, but Jaxon didn't need help guessing. This was a death sentence. As if on cue, a gentle patter of raindrops began striking the spire and sliding down the glass panes of the windows.

The conversation below sounded muffled to Jaxon now. He vaguely registered Jasmine dismissing Theo from the room. Heavy footsteps preceded the slam of the latch door. Jaxon knew Theo would probably head back to the southern tower, where he'd find a hole in the wall and a missing prince.

The room was spinning. All these years he had cowered in his sister's shadow, and now, he would finally pay the price for his fear. He'd never felt more alone, and more hopeless.

"Healer Kyra will need to be taken care of too." Jasmine's voice was barely audible over the rain. "If the spineless wench wants to run her mouth, she's no longer of use to me. I'll send her—and that black aura of hers—out to the battlefield with Jaxon."

The rain picked up, and Jaxon could no longer hear what was being said below. All other sounds had been swallowed by the relentless pounding of the rain. He stared at the golden spyglass in the middle of the room. He thought of Annabel, trapped in the Windsor castle, alone. He thought of Quinn, who would do anything for her friend. He thought of Lukas, who had been his guiding light, the little boy he'd helped to raise, and he was now failing to keep alive. He had to try—for them.

He snatched the spyglass from its stand, pushed it closed, and shoved it into his satchel. Before he could change his mind, he squeezed through the small window.

# CHAPTER 7

# The Lake Guardian

Quinn glanced up at the darkening sky. The stars were disappearing as a wall of thick clouds crept in their direction. A sliver of the moon still peeked through, providing enough light for Quinn to make out the rotting wooden dock beneath her feet. She stepped over a large gap, where a board was missing. The next piece she put pressure on groaned loud under her weight, threatening to snap in half. Kit's squeak of alarm was muffled from inside his satchel.

"He's there." Mae pointed toward the end of the dock. A large, dark figure was hunched over the edge. As they got closer, Quinn could make out Kraig's distinctive bushy beard and cheerful demeanor. He tossed a fishing spear into the small boat he was leaning over.

"Will you be fishing while we're in the castle?" Quinn raised her eyebrows. He turned to face them, grinning.

"There's more in the lake than fish, Red," he said. The wind ruffled his dark head of curls, and he glanced up at the sky. "It's gonna be rough out there. Are the two of ye ready?"

Quinn lowered herself into the boat in response, and Kraig grinned.

"A red stone bearer if I ever met one," he said.

Mae climbed in next. Kraig untied the knotted rope holding the boat to the dock before he jumped in after them. The boat wobbled, threatening to capsize them into the murky water below.

"Greg'd still be standing up there." Kraig pointed one of his paddles at the dock. "Doesn't like the water very much, does he?"

Quinn couldn't help but smile as she remembered Jaxon mentioning that on their trip across the Viridis River months ago. Greg wouldn't have let that stop him though. He was one of the bravest people she knew.

"I don't think he'd miss the chance to use his axe," she said. "There might be some soldiers to kick around at the castle."

Kraig chuckled. "Ye ain't wrong. Pretty sure he takes that axe to bed with him."

Mae was humming as she watched the cloudy sky. "The storm is almost here," she said, mid-hum. Quinn felt it too—the heavy humid air was cut by a cool breeze that smelled like rain. Kraig paddled harder as he pushed farther away from the store.

Seconds later, the rain came down.

"Here we go," Quinn grumbled. She was grateful the storm would provide cover, but it would also slow them down.

"Rain is a sign of life." Mae closed her eyes and tilted her face upward so that the rain raced down her cheeks and into the purple scarf wrapped around her head. "You should embrace it, Quinn!"

As if responding to Mae's words, the rain picked up pace and hammered down on them.

Quinn glared at Mae through the water now streaming down her face. Mae smiled sweetly in return, blinking rapidly as rain collected on her long eyelashes.

Quinn removed her knapsack from her back, stashing it under the seat. Kit peeked his shivering head out from under it. His dark red fur was soaked, clinging to his body.

"Sorry, Kit," she said, using her stones to pull some of the water from him. "Stay down there! I'm going to try giving us some relief."

Their boat was shrouded in red light as Quinn activated her stones, pushing the wind upwards and outwards to keep the rain from falling on them. Red light glittered across the surface of the lake.

"Thanks for that," Kraig said. "Ye may wanna cover up those stones. This path should be safe—not many brave it at night—but better not to draw attention . . . from the castle or from the water."

Not wanting to know what that could mean, Quinn focused instead on wrapping a cloth around her waist to cover up her stones. Holding off the water was taking up most of her concentration. The next time she was able to look forward, they'd moved considerably closer to the castle.

"We're almost there," Kraig said.

The boat jolted, almost throwing a standing Quinn overboard. She glanced at Mae; the siren's face was drained of color. Kit had darted out from under the seat, his squeaks echoing over the rain. She gently pushed him back under the seat, his little body shaking against her fingers.

"Kraig," Quinn said slowly. "What was that?"

Kraig's strokes quickened. "Might want to help move us faster, if you can," he said. The water beside them rippled, and Quinn swore something broke the surface of the water.

"Kraig." Quinn's voice was less calm this time. "What in the name of the stones was that?"

"Well, ye see, there's a reason this part of the lake isn't traveled at night."

Quinn groaned. "You're just like your brother."

"Thank ye." Kraig beamed at her.

Trying not to roll her eyes, Quinn let the rain fall on them again and instead, focused on moving them through the water.

A rush of water erupted in front of them, and what looked like a giant fin emerged before sliding back down below.

"Was that . . ." Quinn choked. "Was that a tail?"

"No," Kraig said. Fear finally seemed to have caught up to him. He stopped paddling and picked up the enormous fishing spear he had brought with him. "That'd be the top of its head."

Mae's head was glowing enough to shine through her scarf. She said something, but Quinn couldn't hear her over the rain.

"What?" she yelled.

"It's an Abaia," Mae shouted. "She thinks we're a threat to the lake! She's protecting the creatures in it."

"Tell it that's not true—tell it we're just passing through!"

"Not helpful, Quinn! And stop tapping into your stones, the red glow isn't helping either."

Quinn tried to quiet her magic and resist the urge to draw her sword. Kraig was spinning around, rocking the boat with him, as he tried to follow the movement below.

"What do you usually do when this happens?" Quinn strained to be heard over the rain.

Kraig swallowed. "Run away."

"Brace yourselves!" Mae yelled.

Something below them slammed into the boat, and Quinn flew through the air. The last thing she saw was Kraig's hand reaching for her before the lake engulfed her. Water flooded her lungs as she sunk downward. Ripping the cloth from her waist, she called on her stones, displacing the water around her over and over again to propel her to the surface. Her head burst above the lake. She coughed and spat water from her mouth, drinking in the air.

A purple glow in front of her indicated that the boat was close.

"Quinn!" Mae screamed.

"Grab hold!" Kraig had tossed a rope to her, and Quinn reached to grasp hold of it.

Her heart in her throat, Quinn scanned the boat for Kit, hoping he hadn't been thrown overboard too. "Kit?" she called to the others as they pulled her toward the boat. "Is Kit safe?"

"He's okay. He's here," Mae said, as Kit squeaked in unison with her.

Kraig was watching the water behind her. "Look out!"

Quinn was ready. She managed to hold her breath this time as she was yanked beneath the water. The Abaia dragged her down, deeper into the lake. She struggled for her sword, but the creature had wrapped one end of itself around her. She opened her eyes, and the length of the Abaia's long body extended outward in the red glow of Quinn's stones. It was as thick as ten of her put together, covered in white scales with trails of purple running across them like veins.

Quinn fought against the creature's grasp, using her magic to push water between herself and the scaly body wrapped around her waist. It worked; she was able to wiggle free.

The creature's tail vanished, and Quinn kicked out, trying to float away from the deep abyss of the lake, toward the periwinkle glow above.

Two large, electric purple eyes sprang into view in front of her. Quinn's whole body lurched, and she almost swallowed water as she fought back a scream. A certainty that she was about to die washed over her.

A large fin protruded out the top of the creature's head and ran the entire length of its body as far as Quinn could see in the murky haze. Its enormous mouth opened wide, and a chilling sound erupted from it.

Quinn grasped for her sword, then paused. She was close enough that she could stab the creature in its open, unsuspecting mouth, but a voice in her head told her not to. It felt as though both Jaxon and Gwen were there with her, pushing down on her hand so that she couldn't draw her blade.

The creature moved closer to Quinn, its nose nearly touching her. Blazing purple eyes blinked, and lines of brighter purple moved outwards from the pupil like little shocks of electricity. Quinn let the light of her red stones go out. In the darkness, the scales of the Abaia shimmered, illuminating the water around them in purple.

Quinn's lungs ached for air. She couldn't hold her breath much longer. She struggled to stay still, allowing the creature to look her over in the haze of the light. She stared back into the Abaia's eyes, watching the electric purple strands wiggle and dance as they escaped the iris and disappeared into the corners.

The creature blinked once and then moved, circling Quinn as it dropped deeper into the lake. Quinn spun as best as she could in the water and watched the creature dip below her before it tilted its head up and opened its mouth as if to swallow Quinn. Instead, the Abaia screeched and the shock waves propelled Quinn upwards through the water where she burst above the surface, heaving as she drank in air. The world blurred around her, and she blinked to steady it. She felt two sets of arms haul her up and into the boat, where she lay, gasping for breath. Kit had emerged from under the seat. He licked her cheek and buried his wet head into her neck.

"It left," she heard Mae exclaim. The siren wrapped her arms around Quinn and squeezed, her wet black hair sticking to Quinn's face. "You did it. You passed her test!"

Quinn tried to push Mae off, spitting the siren's wet hair out of her mouth. "What was the test?" She coughed again, expelling more water from her lungs.

"I don't know," Mae exclaimed gleefully. "But you passed!"

Kraig, who'd already started paddling towards the shore again, stood up, squinting through the rain. He let out a shout of joy loud enough to drown out the sound of the rain.

"We made it," he said.

# CHAPTER 8

## The Four Stars

Jaxon's clothes clung to him as the rain continued to pelt him. In his haste to get out of Jasmine's tower, he hadn't had time to worry about the slippery conditions, but it quickly became apparent that the vines weren't holding him quite as well as they had on the way up.

With great effort, he focused on the vine, using the path he'd created earlier to move back down the stone the way he'd come. He held his breath as he moved past the wooden window that opened to the war room. If Jasmine or one of the others heard him, they'd be able to open the window, reach out, and pull him through. He let out a sigh of relief as the vines lowered him below the war room, but the feeling didn't last long.

With every slight movement, Jaxon was slipping through the vines. They slowly slid up his waist to his chest. He tightened their grip around him. The sick ward was on the first level of the tower. *All I have to do is get to the bottom of the tower*, he reminded himself. This didn't seem to work. If he wasn't already thoroughly soaked, he knew his hands would be sweating right now.

Jaxon batted his eyelashes, trying to clear them, but it was no use. He strained to remember Gwen's lessons and use the vines as his eyes instead. His stone blazed as he reached deeper into them, feeling the walls of the castle as they lowered him to the bottom of the spire. He nearly fell to his knees when he finally touched down. The ground beneath him felt welcome, solid, and stable. *You can't linger here*, he reminded himself.

Swallowing his fear, Jaxon righted himself and hurried around the side of the tower's base. He could only hope the rain disguised him from any guards on patrol. He slipped through the wooden door and came face to face with a sword.

The soldier behind the blade lowered it. "Prince Alexander?"

Jaxon froze, water dripping from his wet clothes and forming puddles on the ground, grappling for an excuse as to why he was there. As he stalled, he couldn't help but notice that the soldier's features looked familiar. A scruffy beard was attempting to disguise his boyish features but was betrayed by a pair of wide, youthful eyes.

"Page Flynn?"

The young man huffed out his chest. "It's Squire Flynn now," he said.

Despite the adrenaline still rushing through him, Jaxon felt a rush of joy for his friend. He smiled and clasped a hand on the boy's shoulder. "Well done, Squire Flynn. I knew you'd do well!" Water from his sleeve was dripping onto Flynn's armored shoulder. He withdrew his hand, but Flynn hadn't noticed.

"It's been too long," Flynn said, still smiling. "I've got so much to tell you! I saw Henry last week; he told me you spent some time in Viridis and Queen Jasmine was punishing you for it. I was hoping the three of us could get together, like old times. When the queen allows you to wander again."

"I'd like nothing more." Jaxon didn't have the heart to tell his friend that he'd be lucky to make it through the night.

"Where are you off to anyway?" Flynn asked, seeming to remember that Jaxon was sopping wet.

"I was hoping to visit Lukas," Jaxon admitted.

"Yes." The squire frowned. "My deepest condolences, friend. When I returned from my apprenticeship in Wisteria Pool, I heard whispers that the Lux Pox had worsened." His eyes shifted as he searched the hall for others. "I saw nothing," he said. "I'll be staring at the wall in that direction until the door closes behind you."

"Thank you, Flynn." Jaxon moved toward the door and then stopped. "You'll make a fine knight one day," he told his friend.

The squire grinned. "If the general doesn't kill me before then. Now, *go*, before someone comes."

Jaxon slipped past Flynn, down the hall, and into Lukas's room.

Kyra yelped as Jaxon opened the door. She had been deep in concentration, her hands hovering over his brother as the stones around her neck glowed.

"Kyra, go home," Jaxon said firmly.

She stared at him with flushed cheeks. "Home?"

"Back to your pool. Now. You're no longer safe here. Tell the men at the gate that you need to tend to a sick family member."

"Prince Alexander—"

"Thank you for your service to my family." Jaxon's voice was steady. "Lukas would not be alive without you."

Kyra wrung her hands but nodded. She glanced one more time at Lukas and then back at Jaxon. "Don't give up on him," she said. "He's still in there, I can feel it." She crossed the room, stopping only to curtsy in Jaxon's direction before disappearing behind the door.

Jaxon stood over Lukas and stared down at his pale, still face.

"Lukas," he whispered. "If you're in there, I need you to come out. We have to get far away from this place. Remember how you used to love to hide? I need you to find us a place to hide—somewhere Jasmine can never find us."

Lukas didn't budge. Jaxon squeezed his eyes shut, fighting off the sadness threatening to wash over him. He called on his magic, moving his hands over Lukas's body. The energy of the green stone was searching through Lukas, following the length of his bones and the flow of the blood in his veins. There. He felt it again. The slight catching of his magic, like fabric caught on a thorn.

He thought of the stone christenings again. The text claimed they'd been formed to prevent an illness just like Lux Pox. Was he sensing channels of magic in Lukas that were clogged because they had nowhere to go?

He pulled one of the red stones from his satchel and placed it on Lukas's chest. He tried again to search him, but nothing had changed. He returned the red stone to its place in his bag and instead reached for his own. Green light seeped between his fingers. No, Lukas wasn't a green stone bearer. Although his brother was kind to everyone, the Goddess of Nurture would not have chosen him; he was too quick to take action. But then again, he was too logical for the Goddess of Fusion and too emotional for the Goddess of Clarity. None of the stones would have chosen him.

Jaxon stared at the light patch on Lukas's face and felt his stomach drop. The four stars on Annabel's map burned an imprint into his brain. Blood pounded in his ears as realization flooded him. What if those stars marked the location of the source of the stones? But there weren't three stars, signifying the purple, red, and green stones. There were four stars, four stars that marked the location of *four stones*. What Annabel had uncovered wasn't a cure at all—it was the existence of a fourth stone.

On her map, there was a star in Viridis indicating the location of the nurture stone that Annabel had taken them to. In the Red Forest, there was a star exactly where he and Quinn had found the fusion stone, where it was protected by the gnomes and sirens of the forest. One of the remaining two stars must be where the source of the clarity stone was. And the fourth star . . . The fourth star marked the source of an unknown stone.

Jaxon knew exactly what he had to do.

He reached into his satchel and pulled out one of the rocks he'd not yet given the energy of the red stone, and placed it on Lukas's chest. He didn't know what color the fourth stone might be or what magic it contained, but he did know his brother. If Lukas had the magic of this stone, that meant that it would contain some of the attributes that made Lukas who he was.

With his hands on either side of the stone, he thought of everything Lukas was: a guiding light, thoughtful, driven, incapable of allowing injustice. Jaxon called on all of the light in the room, pulling it from every corner. The light of the lantern on the table snuffed out. For a second, Jaxon was in darkness as he pulled everything he could into the stone on Lukas's chest.

A loud boom reverberated throughout the room. Jaxon stumbled backward. He tried to steady his feet as his legs wobbled. Heart racing, he looked down at the rock still resting on Lukas's chest.

A yellow stone stared up at him, glittering and fresh. Quickly, he put his hands back over the stone, preparing to try to push the magic through Lukas. Before he could call on his magic, the yellow stone ignited, illuminating Lukas's chest. His brother's head twitched, his eyes fluttered, and a small gurgle escaped his mouth.

Relief like he had never felt before flooded through Jaxon.

Outside the room, a loud crash shook the castle. Jaxon's joy was replaced with fear. He had to get Lukas out of here. He shoved the stone into the pocket of Lukas's pants and hoisted him up out of the bed, straining to lift him. Lukas's body was light, but Jaxon was drained from creating the stone.

Another crash, louder and closer than the last.

The door flew open.

# CHAPTER 9

# The Giant Man

Quinn leaned back to search the tall bed of rock propping up the Twelve Pools castle. Where the rock met the castle wall, there was a small ledge that wrapped around the sides for as long as the eye could see. Quinn swallowed. If it weren't raining, she wouldn't think twice about the climb. But the glistening, wet rock, promised a slippery ascent.

Kraig was maneuvering with just one paddle in the water now. He held it still, forcing the boat to drag and then slow to a stop, getting as close to the rock wall as he could.

"Now what?" Mae asked over the pounding rain.

Kraig pointed a finger along the ledge. "Once you're up there, you'll want to follow the ledge for about fifty paces," he said. "There you'll find a door recessed in the stone—it opens to the courtyard. Jaxon's room is at the top of this one—" He indicated the tower extending up over them. "I don't know how many guards will be in the courtyard, but the rain should keep numbers in your favor."

Quinn looked in the direction Kraig had pointed, but they were so close she couldn't see the top of the spire. They had a lot of ground to cover, and they needed to stay undetected for as long as they could.

"Do you think the guards will hear your voice over the rain?" Quinn looked at Mae, who'd also been straining her neck looking up at the tower.

Mae beamed. "Only if you'll amplify it for me."

"Gladly," Quinn said.

Kraig's eyebrows were furrowed in confusion. He opened his mouth to say something but seemed to think better of it, closed it, and shrugged his shoulders.

Quinn placed a hand on the red stones around her waist, conscious of how exposed she was. The cloth she'd used to disguise them was now at the bottom of the lake, so she'd have to be extra careful not to light them inside the castle walls.

She knelt in the boat and motioned to Kit. At once, the fox climbed to her shoulder and disappeared into her bag. The boat rocked beneath her feet as she stood and scanned the wall for handholds. She carefully reached over the edge of the boat and held onto the piece of rock closest to her. The sharp red light from her waist penetrated the stormy darkness of the night and cut through the drops of rain.

The stone wall shifted beneath her hand and she managed to move some of the rock downward, forming a hole in the wall and a small ledge below it. Pushing off from the boat with one foot, Quinn stuck the other into the newly formed hole and hoisted herself up, hand latched onto a protruding rock just above her head. She reached up just a little farther and grabbed hold of the ledge, using her magic to siphon off enough of the water to get a firm grip. She grunted as she propelled herself up over the top of the wall.

Down below, Mae was staring up at her hopelessly. Kraig kneeled at the edge of the boat and cupped his hands. After a moment's hesitation, the siren put her foot into them and pushed off, grabbing hold of the same rock Quinn had moments before. Kraig steadied the boat as her weight left it.

Quinn lay on her stomach and dangled one arm over the side of the wall. Her hand connected with Mae's, but she couldn't get a firm grip on her wet fingers. Quinn scooted further out on the ledge and strained to reach down, grasping onto Mae's wrist this time. In one yank, she lifted Mae up. The siren seized the ledge with her other hand, hoisting herself over the side as Quinn supported her weight.

Still breathing quicker than usual, Mae looked back over the ledge at Kraig, who was waving cheerfully up at them.

"How will we—"

Quinn was already on her feet. "A problem for future Mae and Quinn," she called over her shoulder as she headed in the direction of the door. They'd have to move fast if they were going to find Jaxon. She had no time for Mae's dallying.

The door was where Kraig promised it would be. Quinn took a moment under the shelter of the archway to shake water free from her sleeves. She cracked the door open with one hand, the other on the hilt of her sword. She could barely make out anything in the dimly lit grounds. A light in the distance emerged from the central tower but was moving in another direction.

Mae pushed her head between Quinn and the door so she could look through the opening herself.

"You ready?" she asked Quinn, opening it farther so there was enough space for them to stand side to side.

"Always."

Mae began to sing. So softly at first that Quinn hardly heard her over the pounding of rain, and then louder, filling their small corner of the courtyard. Quinn closed her eyes and focused on the siren's voice, pushing it out farther and faster. The sound echoed around them, bounding off the walls and coating the air. In the distance, the man with the light swayed. He set his lantern on the ground and sat next to it. The rain fell on him faster than ever, but he remained seated and unbothered.

Still using her magic to push the sound outwards, Quinn grabbed Mae's wrist and raced through the courtyard. Though the rain was weighing down their hair and clothes and Quinn was sure that she personally looked like an ogre who had just emerged from the lake, Mae was a beacon of beauty. Each bolt of lightning illuminated her as she glided alongside Quinn effortlessly, like a flower petal in the wind.

They reached Jaxon's tower and slipped through the wooden door. The large room was empty but for a stone statue in front of a large spiral staircase. On both sides of the large round room, two tunnels reached outward. Quinn used her magic to siphon some of the water off herself and Mae, who was standing very still.

"Quinn," she said.

Still focused on drying them both off, Quinn ignored her.

"Quinn," Mae repeated. Her tone made Quinn look up. The large figure in the room that Quinn had mistaken for a stone statue was looming over them. His features—which were too small for his face—were screwed up in confusion as though he were still trying to register that two girls had fallen through the tower door. The many stones around his waist glowed a fierce red. He was staring at the ceiling above her as his magic worked.

"Get back!" Quinn shoved Mae out of the way and threw up her arms, blocking her head as she forced air between her and the stone ceiling now collapsing on her head.

"Kit, get to Mae!" she shouted. When she felt the fox kick off from her back, she threw her arms outward and the ceiling pieces scattered to either side of her.

The giant growled in rage and drew his sword. She jumped to the side, scrambling to grasp for her own sword as he swung at her. He lunged in her direction, and Quinn launched herself forward, ducking and rolling between his legs at the last second. She stood back up, her sword in front of her ready to block his next swing. As he spun around to meet her, he brought his sword around with him. The speed and size of the sword crashing into Quinn's sent her flying backward.

Pain seared through her as she collided with the hard floor and rolled into the wall. She struggled to stand, but her body felt heavier than usual. She collapsed to her knees, panting as she searched the room for Mae. *Stand up*, she told herself. She put her hands on the ground, and they shook beneath her. It took her a moment to realize it was not from her own weakness, but from the giant's footsteps as he sauntered closer.

She scrambled for her sword, lifting it up to block him. He stopped, leering down at her.

"Who are you?" His voice was unexpectedly soft. It sounded almost like he was about to fall asleep. Was he getting closer? Were his eyes shutting? She jumped to her feet and backed into the wall as his body crashed to the ground in front of her, revealing a purple-shrouded Mae.

"I was handling it," Quinn huffed.

"It took a lot of magic to bring him down," Mae said, ignoring her. "We don't have long. I'm going to read him, see if he knows where Jaxon's chambers are."

Quinn nodded and stepped away from the giant, allowing Mae to come closer and kneel beside his head. She put her hands over his temples and closed her eyes. Her nose crinkled.

"What is it?" Quinn asked, her hand tightening around the hilt of her sword.

"He smells," she said.

"*Mae.*"

"Sorry, focusing!" A purple glow was seeping out the sides of her scarf. There was silence for a moment, and then she looked up at Quinn.

"He's the one who guards Jaxon. He was sent to bring Jaxon to the queen . . . but Jaxon wasn't there. I can't really read clearly what he's thinking. His brain is so messy, feels like a bunch of strings all twisted and knotted up. He was headed toward the sick ward. Seems like he thought Jaxon might be there."

"Where's that?"

"The central tower."

"Quinn, wait—"

Quinn was already at the tower door.

"We can't just leave him here," Mae said.

"Can't we?"

"I mean, shouldn't we hide him?"

"You've surprised me many times before, Mae, but something tells me you don't have the strength to lift a giant."

Mae laughed, jumped over the man's head, and followed Quinn out the door.

# CHAPTER 10

# The Grumpy Gnome

Jaxon froze as the door flew open. A fierce looking redhead, with a shivering fox on her shoulder and a sword extended out in front of her, burst into the room. She was followed closely by a tall, strikingly beautiful young woman with a silk scarf tied around her head. Both the girls and the fox were drenched in water.

Jaxon stared. He must be hallucinating. His feet had become impossibly heavy, rooting him in place as he struggled to understand what he was seeing. How were Quinn and Mae standing in front of him right now? Confusion turned to relief and then to worry. Why were they here? Were they in trouble?

Mae crossed the room in two strides and reached over Lukas, who was still in his arms, to embrace Jaxon and plant a kiss on his cheek. The pressure of her lips on his skin lingered after she had pulled away, confirming to Jaxon that she wasn't an illusion. She looked down at Lukas and then back up at Jaxon before she placed a comforting hand on Lukas's head, her eyes creased in joy.

"Can we do that later?" asked Quinn, half-heartedly. Her gaze was moving back and forth between them and the doorway.

Jaxon still hadn't moved. "How—" he managed to splutter.

"We'll explain later, traitor," Quinn said, this time with an impatient edge to her voice. "We're a little busy right now!" *Traitor.* So she hadn't forgotten—or forgiven—him. Even in Jaxon's confusion, the word stung. Quinn jabbed her hand toward the door. "What are you two waiting for? We need to get out of here!"

She caught sight of where Mae's hand was resting and seemed to realize that Jaxon was holding a human.

"Is that—"

Jaxon nodded, and without asking any more questions, Quinn crossed the room and lifted Lukas, tossing him over her shoulder like he was an empty knapsack. Kit sniffed Lukas and then proceeded to shower him with licks.

"Now will you come?" But Quinn was already halfway out the door. Jaxon shook his head to clear it and hurried after her. He'd worry about the how's and why's later. Right now, he needed to get Lukas to safety.

In the hallway, Squire Flynn was crumpled on the ground. Jaxon ducked down to check on him as he passed, just to make sure his heart was still beating.

"Mae!" Quinn yelled as they reached the courtyard door.

"I'll do what I can," she said, pushing in front of them. "We're going to have a bit more trouble getting out of here than we did coming in. They'll be less susceptible to me now. We haven't exactly been quiet, and I'm sure someone's spotted the giant by now."

"The what?" Jaxon asked, alarmed.

"That big bloke who guards your room," Quinn said. "We left him passed out on the floor of your tower. Might be awake by now, come to think of it."

Jaxon's eyebrows shot up. "You knocked out Theo?"

Quinn scowled. "Mae did," she said begrudgingly.

"Quinn helped. She distracted him while I worked on his mind."

"Don't take pity on me," Quinn snapped at Mae. "Are you going to sing, or what?" She held the door open and the siren's eerie, wordless tune filled the air around them. Jaxon's eyelids grew heavy as his body relaxed. He felt an incredible urge to lie down and sleep . . .

"Ow!"

Quinn had pinched him.

The sharp pang startled Jaxon from his trance. He glared at Quinn, but she had already turned her attention forward, her stones glowing as they worked to amplify Mae's voice. Quinn poked her head out the door, balancing Lukas on her shoulder as she leaned forward and then motioned to Jaxon to follow. They hurried toward the outer wall. Jaxon tried not to slide on the wet stones beneath his feet.

*Ding. Ding. Ding.*

The ring of the bell cut through the sound of the rain and made the hairs on Jaxon's arms stand up.

"Run!" he shouted at the others.

They took off at full speed now. Jaxon didn't dare look around. An arrow slipped by him, narrowly missing his right shoulder. The group reached the door, and one after the other they threw themselves behind it as more arrows slammed into the wood. Quinn paused for a moment, and a cascade of rocks fell in front of the door. Even with the temporary barricade, Jaxon knew they wouldn't be safe here, but Quinn and Mae were already moving.

"Do you have a plan?" Jaxon yelled as he ran after them.

"Something like that," Quinn shouted over her Lukas-free shoulder. She came to an abrupt halt at the ledge.

"Incoming!" she shouted. And then she heaved his brother over the ledge. Jaxon cried out in alarm. Mae jumped gracefully after Lukas, and Quinn swung over the side of the wall and began to climb down.

His breath still caught in his throat, Jaxon peered over the side of the wall. Below them, a large hairy man stood in a small boat, cradling Lukas in his arms. Mae's head poked out of the water, and the large man set Lukas down before he yanked her out of the lake and placed her in the boat beside him.

"Come on, traitor!" Quinn yelled, pushing herself off the wall and into the boat, which teetered dangerously. Jaxon pulled his satchel from his waist and dropped it down to Mae, who caught it. Not giving himself the time to think, he jumped over the edge after it. The cold water swallowed him, and he struggled to propel himself to the surface. An arm pulled him up, and Jaxon spat out a mouthful of water as he was dropped into the boat.

Quinn's waist lit up red, and she propelled the boat away from the castle. Jaxon knelt over Lukas, shielding him from the rain. His green stone glowed as he searched his brother's vitals. Although Lukas's energy cells were still depleted, everything else was normal. The yellow stone had survived the fall into Kraig's arms and was still safe in his brother's pocket.

Jaxon's heart leapt as something brushed his hand. It was Lukas's fingers, reaching for him. Jaxon grabbed hold of them and squeezed tight in response. Lukas's lips moved, but Jaxon heard nothing over the sound of the rain. His eyes flickered before his body went limp again.

"I can help." Mae's hand was on Jaxon's shoulder. "I'll check his mind when we're safely on land." Her purple light was the same color as Jasmine's, but it felt gentler, comforting and warm. Her violet eyes crinkled at him, and he nodded his thanks. Gratitude washed over him. She was actually here—both Mae and Quinn were actually here. A small black nose emerged from beneath the seat, sniffing at Lukas. Warmth flooded Jaxon's chest, and he put a hand on Kit, who immediately licked him.

As quickly as the warmth had come, it turned to ice. Something in the lake had caught his eye. He squinted at the water, wondering if he'd imagined it. And then a long, thin object pierced the calm surface before vanishing back beneath it.

He scrambled to his feet, pointing, but Mae and Quinn seemed unconcerned.

"An Abaia." The large man sitting across from him grinned as the boat rocked from Jaxon's sudden movement. "Doesn't seem to want anything to do with us, Prince Alexander." He bowed his head. "Kraig, at your service," he added, sticking his hand out for Jaxon to shake it.

Jaxon's whole body shook up and down in Kraig's clasp.

"Call me Jaxon," he said as he surveyed the man's jubilant expression, his bushy beard, and the locks of dark curls on his head. Something about him looked familiar. "Have we met?"

"He knows Greg, too," Quinn said to Kraig, not looking up from the water.

"My brother really gets around, doesn't he?"

"Incoming," Mae interrupted.

From around the other side of the castle, a line of narrow boats emerged, moving at a steady pace. Jaxon scanned them. He should've known Jasmine would waste no time sending her men.

In the back of the boats, archers were perched on raised seats. Even from their distance, Jaxon could see their bows nocked with arrows.

Quinn shouted again and stopped moving the boat forward. She stood and drew her sword, slashing it through the air to block an incoming arrow. Kraig took over for her, paddling with broad, rapid strokes.

"What can I do?" Jaxon shouted at Quinn.

"Duck!" she shouted back, pushing the air sideways. More arrows dropped into the water as she knocked them from the air. Mae pulled the purple scarf from around her head and wrapped it around Quinn's waist.

"What are you doing?" Quinn staggered as Mae caused her to lose her balance.

"You're a glowing target with those stones," Mae said. "I'm trying to hide you."

"Let them aim at me then." Quinn waved one of her hands in dismissal. "At least I know where they'll land."

Jaxon was half-listening to them argue as he stared at the boats. Something didn't look right to him. "Is the water rising?"

Beside him, Kraig stopped paddling and stood, turning around to survey the situation.

"Ah!" There was excitement in his voice. "They should know better than to follow that way."

Water exploded upward and outward as a large creature erupted from the lake, sending two of the boats flying. Men soared through the air. Jaxon stared in disbelief. He had heard legends of the lake guardian, but he'd never seen it before. The long sleek body of the creature, marked by veins of purple, glittered as it stretched out in an arch over the other boats. The soldiers jumped into the water just before the Abaia crashed down on their boats, splitting the wood in half. Seconds later, the creature had vanished back below the water, leaving behind a sizable trail of destruction. Weighed down by armor, the soldiers scrambled for the only boats still floating.

Kraig nearly capsized their own boat as he whooped, jumping in the air. Jaxon grabbed the sides to steady himself.

"That's right, ya Hyacinth cowards! Unfit to tread the waters of the mighty Abaia!"

Looking amused, Quinn handed Mae her purple scarf.

"Don't think I'll be needing this anymore," she said. Mae fastened it back around her head, and Quinn returned to her seat, stones glowing as she pushed them forward.

"There'll be more on the shore," Jaxon said as the castle shrunk into the distance behind them. Soldiers were still lifting the others into the remaining boats. "She has men everywhere."

He turned to survey the shore, but Kraig was already scouting a route. He tapped Quinn on the shoulder and pointed left. "Last dock that way," he said. "There'll be plenty of drunken men to keep them distracted. I'll stir up some ruckus while you kids make a run for it. Pull right up to the shore; I'll worry about the boat tomorrow."

"How can we repay you?" Mae asked.

"Next time ye see my brother, remind 'em I'm bigger than 'em," Kraig said. "And that he still owes me that beer."

As they pulled closer to the shore, Kraig's words proved to be true. Lights flickered from several buildings hugged up against the lake. A tavern was perched over the water, its open windows emitting a constant buzz of noise punctured only by loud cheers and laughter. Jaxon scanned the shore, but if there was a soldier there, he couldn't see them.

"There, under the tavern." Kraig pointed. Quinn steered into the side of the lake and jumped into the ankle-deep water to help Kraig pull the boat ashore. The tavern above their heads hung out over the lake, shielding them from view of those who might be on the road above.

Jaxon hoisted Lukas into his arms and passed him to Quinn. She tossed him again over her shoulder, and Kit poked his head out as if to keep watch on their new companion. The group crouched near one of the wood posts supporting the tavern and listened.

"Don't move," hissed Kraig. Above them, the tavern noise had quieted. They could hear one voice, louder than the others, but the words were muffled. "I'll go first," whispered Kraig. "When you hear me enter the tavern, start moving."

He climbed up the side of the lake that wasn't facing the road. Jaxon heard him make his way around to the other side of the building and burst through the door.

"Good evening, gents! The wait is over, I'm here!"

The door slammed behind him, and the group wasted no time hurrying toward the blackness in the opposite direction of the bustling village, castle, and main road back to Viridis. The rain was coming down harder than ever, and a bolt of lightning flashed across the dark sky, casting them in fleeting light. They put a good amount of distance between themselves and the outskirts of town, but Jaxon knew it wasn't enough.

Ahead of him, Quinn turned around and began walking backward. "Your brother is the heaviest light person I've ever carried." She was out of breath. Jaxon motioned that he'd take Lukas, and she obliged, helping to hoist his frail, waterlogged body over Jaxon's shoulder. Lightning flashed again overhead, and a loud rumble of thunder followed. The red stones decorating Quinn's belt glowed as she pushed the water away from them, creating a pocket of calm that gave them a momentary break from the rain.

"We're going the wrong way—we need to start moving toward Windsor," she said, looking up at the sloping green that would take them away from the lake. "If we travel out of the valley from here, we can take the long way around the southern lakes and avoid the queen's men."

"No." Jaxon's voice was firm. She whirled around to glare at him through the droplets in her eyelashes, but Jaxon didn't budge, refusing to shy away from her scowl. He knew what Quinn didn't—Jasmine wouldn't stop until she found him. "We need to find shelter; we need to find a place to hide."

"We've wasted weeks on the road. What we need is to stop moving in the wrong direction!"

"We won't make it there if we get caught," Jaxon countered. "And she *will* catch us."

"Quinn, Jax is right—"

The redhead turned to glower at Mae.

"—the storm is getting worse," Mae continued. "We can't travel in this!"

"It hides us," Quinn protested.

Jaxon understood the reason for her urgency, but every second they spent out in the open was dangerous. He looked back the way they'd come, toward the flickering light of the Hyacinth city center. Were those dark figures moving toward them or was he imagining it? His heart, still pounding in his chest from the escape, beat even faster.

He focused his attention on Quinn, trying to remain calm. "I promise we will move north as soon as we can. But we can't go that way with Jasmine after us and Lukas unable to walk. For now, we have to hide."

"What are your promises worth to me, traitor?" Quinn's fists were clenched, her stones casting her face in red light. Jaxon flinched at the insult. There was a time when he was sure Quinn would've listened to him—would've at least considered what he was saying. He knew he didn't deserve her trust, but did she have to pick *now* to question him? They didn't have time for this. His cheeks burned as anger boiled inside him. All that effort to get away from Jasmine, and they were going to be caught because of Quinn's stubbornness.

"Why'd you even come here if you don't trust me?" he lashed at her.

Quinn's stones lit even brighter. "I thought you'd have better ideas than *hide*!" she yelled over the sound of the rain. "I thought you'd create more green stones, so we could trade them for Annabel. I thought you'd help us negotiate for her return. I didn't know you couldn't even negotiate a place at the table in your own castle, *Prince* Alexander!"

Jaxon knew the words should sting, but his mind had frozen at the mention of creating green stones. That's why Quinn and Mae had come back for him. They thought he could make more. He opened his mouth, trying to force the truth out that he couldn't—that the only green stone he had managed to make was his own. Before he could say anything, glowing purple light escaped from the edges of Mae's scarf, infiltrating Quinn's red light. Quinn jerked away from the siren as though another step would be enough distance to prevent Mae from using her magic on her.

But Mae wasn't looking at her; she pointed at the sky. Jaxon followed her finger and saw something move. More lightning flashed around them, revealing a winged creature flying overhead. As bands of light bolted across the sky, the owl's wings shimmered in violet before it vanished up ahead.

"I know that owl," Quinn's voice was soft, a sharp contrast to her anger from moments before. She watched the creature fly east with an eerily calm expression on her face. Her desperation to leave Twelve Pools seemed to have vanished. "I think he wants us to follow him."

Without another word, she moved after the winged creature. The bubble of air she'd created disappeared, leaving them in the soaking rain once again. Mae and Jaxon exchanged a look and silently agreed not to question this stroke of luck before they followed after Quinn. Jaxon felt relief wash over him. He knew Quinn might change her mind, but for now they were moving farther from the city, away from Jasmine's men, and that's all that mattered.

As they followed along the lake, it became more and more difficult to navigate the terrain. Jaxon wasn't sure if it had been minutes or hours since they'd begun to follow the owl. It kept circling back to meet them before continuing on, forcing them to climb over and between large, slippery rocks. Closer to the castle, the slope had been covered in green grass, but here it was a sea of rock, overgrown with splotches of reed as tall as Jaxon. He kept glancing over his shoulder, expecting the Twelve Pool soldiers to already be advancing on them, but buried between rocks now, he could no longer see the city lights. He swore he heard the shouts of men over the pounding of the rain, but he ignored the sounds and concentrated on moving forward.

Quinn and Jaxon took turns carrying Lukas as they moved. Each time Jaxon held his brother, he felt heavier than the last time.

The owl screeched and then swooped downward. It circled the area, perching itself on a small boulder. Beside it, a wall of rock was shrouded in a thick layer of reeds, blocking them from moving forward. They'd reached the side of the canyon, where the steep hill made it impossible to follow alongside the lake.

"Does it expect us to climb to the top?" Quinn asked, searching the rocks the owl had come to rest at.

Jaxon followed her line of sight up the rocks to the top of the canyon.

"This isn't a safe place to leave Hyacinth," he said. "The slope is steep, and the rain will make it worse." The air around him felt heavier, accompanied by a soft, deep humming, barely audible over the rain. Something told him he should be worried about the sound, but instead it was calming him.

Were the others hearing it too? As he turned to ask Quinn, a hand emerged from the thick of the reeds and latched to Quinn's arm, pulling her through the wall.

"*Quinn*!" Mae screamed.

Jaxon lurched forward to where he thought he'd seen her vanish, desperately pushing against the reeds, the rock wall on the other side unyielding. He moved further and pushed again, this time meeting no resistance. He stumbled forward through the hidden gap, straining to keep Lukas balanced on his shoulder. The sound of the rain vanished almost instantly in the enclosed space behind the wall of reeds.

Quinn was kneeling on what appeared to be a child. Her stones were glowing, and she was pressing her sword against the back of his neck. Her other hand was pushing the person's face into the dirt of the cave, muffling his protests.

"Give me one reason not to slit your throat right now!" she shouted.

Mae, who followed Jaxon through the reeds, relaxed as she took in the scene. The purple light around her head dimmed.

"Quinn, stop!" Jaxon said, feeling far less confident than Mae's body language suggested he should be. "Let him talk."

He lowered Lukas to the ground and approached Quinn and her victim.

Quinn stood, keeping her sword pointed as the child scrambled to his feet, brushing off his bushy beard. Jaxon stared. Not a child then, but not a human either. His head was level with Quinn's stomach. *A gnome.*

Jaxon thought gnomes rarely ventured outside Woodpine Hallows or the Red Forest, although this one didn't look like any of the gnomes Jaxon had ever encountered before. His face was chiseled and sharp with dark eyes and even darker hair. The deep lines at the corner of his mouth that dropped down to his jaw seemed to be an active protest to the rest of his smooth, unmarked face.

"You—" Mae stopped, searching his face. "You're—"

The gnome spat at the ground. "Do you really need to say it out loud?" he grumbled, his voice shockingly deep for his short stature. "Everyone in this room has eyes."

"A siren," Mae finished.

"Oh," the man said, "that. I prefer to go by Ollie, but call me whatever you'd like." He pushed the tip of Quinn's sword aside with one finger and then picked up the lantern resting on the ground beside him.

"I've never met a gnome siren . . . a siren gnome?" Mae seemed unsure what to call him.

"I could say the same to you, stone bearer." He indicated the stones poking out of the soaked scarf that had begun to slide down her hair. "Siren or stone bearer—pick one, won't you?"

Mae adjusted her scarf, and Ollie continued talking.

"As much as I love this . . . *warm* . . . appreciation for rescuing you, feel free to find your way back into the storm."

When none of them moved, his frown deepened. Jaxon hadn't thought that was possible.

"Why do I get the sense I'm about to regret pulling you in here?" He started walking toward the long tunnel extending in the other direction. "Curse that owl," he muttered.

Jaxon hurried to lift Lukas onto his shoulder again and follow the gnome. "Uh . . . Ollie, sir," he called after him. "Do you know a safe space we could shelter for a day or two? I need some time to get my brother back on his feet."

Ollie stopped. "I can't say I'm thrilled to host the prince of Twelve Pools, but at least you're not your sister. Come along—bring the others if you must."

Jaxon glanced back at the girls. How did Ollie know who he was? It made him uneasy. Both Mae and Quinn looked less concerned. Jaxon directed his attention back to the gnome. The light from his lantern bobbed up and down as he continued down the long, dark tunnel. The choice to follow him or to go back out into the storm didn't seem to be much of a choice at all.

Jaxon wondered if Quinn would fight him. Instead, she glanced at Lukas on his shoulder and then at Mae, who was clutching her arms around her body and shivering. She sheathed her sword and gave him a curt, reluctant nod. They hurried to catch up to Ollie.

As they moved through the tunnel, Jaxon hiked his brother up again. He had lost feeling in his shoulder. His consistent morning exercises had strengthened him, but not enough for this. Just when Jaxon was sure the right side of his body was going to give out under the weight of Lukas, the tunnel widened.

Disguised on the side of the wall was an archway over a small door. They ducked under the frame to follow Ollie inside.

Jaxon marveled at the size of the room. Lanterns rested on every available surface, including on a table in the middle of the room that was piled high with trinkets, parchment, books, and dust. A long wooden bench along one wall was draped in a soft, white material that reminded Jaxon's tired brain of fluffy clouds. Along another wall were shelves that reached almost to the ceiling, lined with small glass jars of different colored liquids. A ladder was attached at the edge of the shelves.

The high ceilings above them were bare but for a large, rusted circular plate in the center. A piece of metal extended outward from the plate and down the side of the wall, connecting to a large wheel.

Ollie caught Jaxon staring at it. "Those Red Forest gnomes may be comfortable living underground with no sunlight, but I certainly am not. If you turn that handle, we'd suddenly be very wet. It opens to the skies above. A life of luxury I live, don't I, prince?"

Jaxon wasn't sure how to respond, but the gnome didn't seem to need a response to anything he was saying. If Jaxon hadn't seen the tunnels under the Red Forest for himself, he'd have no clue what the gnome was even talking about.

"Tea?" Ollie asked them, before disappearing into another room.

"Did you get a read on him?" Quinn asked Mae under her breath.

"A quick one. Seems harmless. I didn't feel any negative energy, and his aura is pure."

Jaxon moved away from the girls, toward the cloud-covered bench. He lowered Lukas from his shoulder, using his other arm to protect his brother's head as he laid him gently on the bench. His arm was tingling, but he ignored it.

His stone glowed as he reached into Lukas and used his magic to nourish his cells. He massaged the muscles using a technique Gwen had taught him, wakening them as much as he could. It was difficult for his magic to flow through them. Normally his healing moved through the body like water, but this was like moving through mud instead. Kyra had done what she could to keep Lukas's muscles healthy, but Jaxon could feel the weakness that had taken hold in the months he had been in the coma. It would likely take more healing sessions before Lukas would return to normal—if he woke up.

A hand on his shoulder pulled Jaxon from his thoughts. Quinn stood over him, offering a mug. Swirls of steam floated off the top of the dark liquid. He took it from her, and she moved closer to his brother. She held one hand over Lukas, and the stones around her waist glowed. Jaxon noticed Lukas's clothes lighten as Quinn siphoned water from them.

Kit emerged from her knapsack to watch. He leapt from Quinn's shoulder to the bench and then curled up in a ball in the center of Lukas's chest, where he promptly fell asleep.

Quinn motioned at the space beside Mae, who was already cozied up on the bench, her hands cupping the mug for warmth as she drank. Jaxon collapsed next to her, elbows on his knees as he hunched forward over the tea in his hands, staring at the liquid.

"He's going to be alright." Mae's voice was soft, but there was something in it that sounded almost like uneasiness. On his other side, Quinn shifted as though she wanted to say something. He glanced up to see Mae and Quinn exchange a quick look, before settling into the silence.

Guilt and worry tugged Jaxon. The air between him and the girls felt heavy. He knew Quinn hadn't forgiven him yet for lying to her. Why had she even come? Why was Mae here too? Quinn had never seemed to like or even trust the siren. He had a thousand questions to ask them both, but the adrenaline from the escape was wearing off. For now, they had successfully hidden themselves from Jasmine's men, and the tension gripping his body had eased. The questions could wait.

The smell of the tea overwhelmed his nose as he took another large gulp. It was fragrant like flowers but tasted earthy, as though Ollie hadn't properly strained the herbs and added some dirt. He found himself not caring either way. There was something about the tea that was spreading outward from his stomach. He leaned against the wall, feeling less in control of his body. The liquid had done more than warm his insides; it had washed a calmness over his body and brain. He sipped from the mug again.

"What kind of tea is this?" Quinn asked, crinkling her nose as she forced herself to swallow another mouthful of it. "My tongue feels numb."

Ollie had left to return the kettle to the kitchen and was now standing on top of the crowded table, digging through the items and cursing under his breath.

"Huh?" he asked, his dark hair poking out over a pile of books. "Oh. It has that effect sometimes. Don't fret, it wears off."

"What kind of tea is this?" Quinn repeated, this time less kindly. Jaxon was trying to pay attention, but his eyelids were growing heavy. In fact, all of his muscles seemed to be melting into the bench beneath him.

"Root of Twilight Prulane."

Jaxon fought his sleepiness to look up at the gnome. "You mean *Midnight* Prulane?" he asked.

"Kid, did I say midnight or did I say twilight?"

Jaxon returned to drinking his tea. He'd never heard of Twilight Prulane, but he vowed to search Gwen's guide later, rather than argue with the very confident gnome. Quinn, however, was undeterred.

"And what does root of Twilight Prulane tea do to your body?" she asked. But Jaxon couldn't help but notice she was leaning into Mae as she said it, her eyes half closed.

"It relaxes your muscles and calms the mind," Ollie said. He finally looked up at the three of them. "No, no, no." He waved his hands frantically. "I said—you're supposed to sip it *slowly!*" But Jaxon wasn't listening anymore. He fell sideways onto the bench of clouds as sleep claimed him.

# CHAPTER II

# The Guiding Light

Quinn's body was heavy when she woke, like someone was pushing her down. She cracked her eyes open. Through a haze of blurriness and eye boogers, she saw the outline of a face inches from her own. She lurched back, hand grasping for her sword.

"I like your fox." Lukas's voice was a hoarse whisper. He was leaning over her, giving her a wide smile that took up his entire, gaunt face. Fierce eyes, the color of gold, crinkled at her from under a mop of white hair.

Quinn let go of the sword hilt and rubbed her eyes to clear them. Lukas was swaddling Kit like a baby. She fought the urge to laugh. She glanced from one to the other, feeling a little uneasy. The white patch around the fox's eye mirrored the white one around Lukas's eye. The young boy was unsteady on his feet, and it reminded her that he hadn't stood in months.

"Sit down." She got up to make space for him on the bench beside her and a still-sleeping Mae. Lukas wobbled closer to the bench and collapsed on it. As she watched him, an overwhelming need to protect the boy swept through her like wildfire. She glanced around the room; Jaxon and Mae were sound asleep beside her, and Ollie was nowhere to be seen.

"Does he have a name?" Lukas whispered. Kit had curled up in his lap, his head resting on Lukas's hand.

"His name is Kit." Quinn watched the fox lick Lukas's hand affectionately. "Thank you for keeping him company. He's been a bit lonely lately—we had to leave one of his friends behind. Will you look after him for me? Just for a while?" Lukas's golden eyes widened, and he nodded eagerly. Quinn put her hand on Kit, stroking his snout with her thumb. "Did you hear me, Kit? Lukas is going to look after you for a few days." The fox lifted his chin and gave her a soft squeak. Quinn suspected Kit wasn't fooled by her request and knew that he was being tasked with keeping an eye on Lukas.

Their conversation had woken the others. Mae sat and stretched her arms, her flawless complexion and straight hair looked undisturbed by sleep. Jaxon bolted upright. When he spotted Lukas, relief washed over his face.

"Lukas," he breathed. "You're awake."

He ran to his brother and wrapped his arms around him so tightly Quinn was afraid he'd break the kid's frail bones. He put his hands on either one of Lukas's cheeks and drank in the sight of his face. Quinn could see similarities in their thin noses and the light smattering of freckles on their cheeks, but the contrast in their hair, brown versus white, countered the rest. For a moment, she forgot her anger at Jaxon as she watched them. In all the time she'd known him, she'd never seen Jaxon so happy.

"Your eyes," Jaxon said to Lukas as he continued to study his face.

Lukas's nose scrunched in confusion. Quinn guessed that Lukas had shown signs of Lux Pox long before his coma but that his face must've changed quite a bit since then. She wondered how alarmed he'd be when he finally saw his reflection.

"They're different?" he asked.

"They're gold." Jaxon's voice was gentle. He tugged lightly at his brother's hair. "And your hair is white." He paused, and Quinn guessed he was trying to figure out if he should mention the patches of white skin on his face. He seemed to decide against it. "But you're still *you*."

"You look different, too," Lukas said, studying his brother's features. "You look old. How long have I been asleep for?"

"Almost six months."

"Jax." Mae's voice was quieter than usual. Quinn thought there was a trace of fear in it. "How did you cure him? No one has ever woken from a Lux Pox coma."

A knot formed in the pit of Quinn's stomach. Mae was right. How was it even possible? Had he somehow lied about this too? As far as she knew, Gwen's lessons had never led him to any answers about Lux Pox. Jaxon's hands had dropped from his brother's face. Quinn resisted the urge to shake him and demand answers, but it was Lukas who responded. He reached into his pocket and removed a small, yellow stone.

"With this," he said.

Quinn stared at it, not really sure what she was looking at.

"Ah, curses."

Ollie had returned to the room. His pitch-black hair was sticking up in random places. Despite the fact that it looked like he'd just rolled out of his bed, he seemed alert. He was fixated on the stone in Lukas's hand.

"He told me there'd be one of each of you." Ollie sighed, pulling a small book off his table of things. "Didn't mention you'd be annoying children though." He held up the tattered book, as though this explained everything. When the four of them continued to stare blankly at him, he sighed and tossed the book over his shoulder, where it landed haphazardly on the table.

"The book doesn't matter. I used to record everything that happened each day, but my notes have gotten . . . sloppier over the years. The days really blend together, and five cups of Root of Prulane later . . . anyway, I remembered. I knew it was strange when the owl led you all here. The last time that happened was over a decade ago, when that batty seer visited me. I checked the book, and it was all there, just as I remembered it."

Ollie paced back and forth. "Of course, I was hoping I was wrong. I didn't see a fourth stone on the kid and thought I was safe from the seer and his blurry visions. Well, not totally safe. Few of my things definitely went missing the week he was here. A collector of things that don't belong to him, that one. Then he took my stash of Twilight Prulane after I refused to take him to the source of the plant."

Quinn tried to process what she was hearing. "A seer told you that we would come?" she asked. Hundreds of other questions chased one another around in her head, but she pushed them back.

"*Guessed* you would come," Ollie corrected her. "He mentioned it in passing, after he read me. Then told me about the yellow stone hidden in the cliffs of Windsor. He knew Queen Sophia . . . your mother—" He motioned to Jaxon. "They both were born in Woodpine Hallows. He was here to warn her not to get involved in northern affairs."

"How—" Quinn paused for a moment, still trying to wrap her mind around the fact that there was a stone that no one knew existed sitting in front of them. "There's a yellow stone? What does it do? Why doesn't anyone know about it?"

"Where has it been all this time?" Mae piled on. "Are there more stones out there?"

"You're asking the right questions," Ollie said. "I know this because they were my questions too. You try understanding descriptions of the past and the future from someone who sees scatterings of it but never the whole picture." He motioned vaguely at Mae. "Well, you would know, wouldn't you, Mae of the Purple Stone."

"I think the stone helps you hide," Jaxon said. Quinn and Mae both turned their heads sharply toward him. "Lukas was always really good at hiding." Lukas grinned at him. He seemed far less interested in the conversation than the others were and had laid down on the bench, his eyes half closed. Kit was more alert. He was curled up next to him, resting his head on Lukas's shoulder as his eyes followed Ollie around the room.

"In a matter of speaking, yes," Ollie said. "The yellow stone gives you the ability to manipulate light, to create illusions. Just as the God of Fusion brought the elements, the God of Nurture brought life, and the God of Clarity brought connection, this fourth stone was brought to our world by the God of Light. It brought brightness to a once dark place."

Jaxon looked down at the green stone resting on his chest and touched his fingertips to it. "The stones are the outlets to our magic. When I was traveling through the Red Forest, Healer Shay fainted because some hirudo beetles were latched to her back. I tried to heal her, but the beetles were creating pockets in her where the magic wasn't able to flow properly. I think the same happened to Lukas—to all those with Lux Pox. Without his stone, the magic was trapped in him and it was slowly killing him. I needed to—I created the yellow stone to heal him."

Quinn leaned in closer, taking in his every word. He paused before he locked eyes with her, as though only speaking this next sentence to her. "Annabel knew it. She figured out there was a fourth stone. She was trying to tell me the night of the Suitor's Championship."

Quinn's heart skipped a beat. *Of course Annabel knew,* she thought. *Annabel knew everything.*

"If that's true, she's one of the few who knows," Ollie said. "The seer told me the knowledge has been lost—buried after a thousand years of being hidden. He suspects that if any still remember, it's kept secret among the High Council. Our people don't exactly trust human's ability to use the stones without greed." He looked around at them all, seeming to remember that there were humans standing in front of him. "Oh, um, not all humans, of course."

Quinn ignored him. "What did the seer tell you about us?"

"That you would come here and disturb my peace."

Jaxon, who'd begun working his magic again on a now-sleeping Lukas, turned to Ollie with raised eyebrows.

"That's all?"

Mae was also staring at the gnome, her head cocked sideways.

"Yes," said the gnome, not meeting any of their eyes. "Now, you must all be hungry. Shall I whip us up some breakfast?"

Quinn forced herself to ignore the way his words made her stomach growl in hunger. "What else did he say?" she asked.

Ollie's exaggerated sigh was loud and long. "I'll tell you what, he didn't mention how . . . inquisitive . . . you all would be." He moved across the room to the large circular wheel and turned it. The metal plate above screeched before it began to move. Sunlight streamed through followed by a deluge of water. Ollie ignored the newly formed puddle in the center of the room.

Quinn was losing her patience. "Are you going to tell us or not?" she demanded.

Ollie finished opening the window above. The sunlight beamed down, casting them all in a soft glow.

"He told me to take you to the cave," Ollie finally admitted. "And to the cave, I'll take you. So you can forget about using that." He was pointing at the sword on Quinn's waist, which she hadn't realized she was gripping tightly. "For extra measure, I'll make sure you get all the way to Verbena Pool after. I admit, that's more of a favor to me. There are only so many days I'm willing to host children in my home."

He crossed the room and climbed the ladder up to the shelves filled with glass jars, muttering to himself.

"What's in the cave?" Quinn asked.

"The source of the purple stone." But the answer hadn't come from Ollie. Mae was watching the gnome sort through bottles, a smile on her face. "You're one of the guardians of the purple stone."

"Keep your voice down," Ollie snapped at her, as though someone might hear.

"I knew it was in Twelve Pools, but I didn't know where."

Ollie pocketed a few jars filled with purple liquid and descended the ladder.

"I've heard about you," Mae continued. "You deter any who wander near the stone. You grew up here. Your father was the warden before you."

Ollie moved closer to Mae, his head tilted up as he scanned her face with narrowed eyes.

"And *your* father is Councilor Mori, isn't he, Maelyn *Mori*? I've heard about you too. Always speaking out of turn and causing trouble. They sent you to live with the gnomes and put you to work at the Crow's Nest, but you wouldn't stop flirting with the soldiers who passed through. Your mother was trouble too."

To Quinn's surprise, Mae gave him her sweetest smile.

"The Council always think they're right," she said. "That lack of trust in humans you are so excited about will destroy us, while you all bicker about formality and keep your silly secrets."

"There will always be rules and secrets," Ollie said. "The sooner you learn to live by them, the sooner you'll find ease in this world."

"I don't want an easy world," Mae said. "I want a good world."

Quinn couldn't help but smile. She wondered less and less every day if she'd done the right thing by freeing Mae from her cell in Viridis.

"Good is relative," Ollie grumbled. "You'll learn. When you're older, you'll learn." But the gnome seemed to recognize that the conversation was a lost cause. He handed each of them a glass vial of purple liquid. "We'll let the young one rest today, but tomorrow, before we leave for the cave, the four of you should take a sip of this. The purple stone has many invisible defenses. The Twilight Prulane that grows near it produces a pollen that gives you a false sense of calmness. This will combat its effects."

Ollie clapped his hands together. "Now," he said. "Can I make us all some breakfast, or does someone else want to argue with me some more?" When Quinn and Jaxon didn't respond, Ollie huffed and left in the direction of the kitchen.

Quinn waited until he disappeared before she turned her attention to Jaxon, who hadn't stopped working his magic on Lukas. There were bags under his eyes. She couldn't help feeling a twinge of worry for him. It reminded her of how gentle his nature was and some of her frustration faded. She moved closer to him and put a hand on his shoulder.

"Jax," she said. "Take a break."

He pulled his hand away from Lukas and shook his head as if clearing it from a trance.

"He's safe now," she promised. "He's going to be okay. *You're* going to be okay."

Jaxon's shoulders relaxed. He took a seat on the bench next to Lukas and slumped against the wall.

"What now?" He rubbed his eyes. Kit, whose head had been resting on Lukas's shoulder, relocated himself to the young boy's feet, squeezing into the small space between the brothers. Jaxon scratched the fox's head.

Quinn took a seat on his other side. "We save Annabel," she said firmly.

Mae dropped to the ground and crossed her legs, leaning back on her elbows so that her hair hovered inches from the ground. "We can't leave yet," she said. "We have to go to the purple stone."

"Why?" Quinn crossed her arms. "Because some seer said we should ten years ago? I don't buy it."

"We don't know what we're walking into when we arrive in Windsor," Mae said. "Jax said his power was stronger when he was close to the source of the green stone; maybe my power will be stronger too. I could see something in the future that helps us better prepare."

"I don't want to waste any more time. We don't know when the Viridis army will reach Windsor. They could already be on their way."

"We have a bigger problem," Jaxon said. Quinn was surprised to see absolute certainty on his face. "I believe my sister has formed an alliance with the Windsor princes. She kept mentioning letters that had been exchanged between them. As the Viridis army moves west, from Prasine Road to the Way of Light, they'll pass just north of the Trade Bridge. That's where the Twelve Pool army will be waiting for them. They're under orders to wait until the Viridis army passes before they move north over the bridge to ambush them from behind. They'll weaken the Viridis army before they even arrive in Windsor."

Quinn fought the sudden urge to empty the contents of her stomach. People she loved dearly would be among those soldiers. Gwen and Greg would both be on the front lines. And, she thought begrudgingly, her father too. Most importantly, Annabel would be waiting for them—expecting those soldiers to arrive prepared to win her back.

"We have to leave." Quinn jumped to her feet. "We have to warn them!"

"No," Jaxon said quietly. "You don't know my sister. She's cunning. We can't just charge at the problem; we need to be strategic about this. If there's even a small chance that the purple stone will increase our odds, we need to go there first."

"Won't she still be tracking you too?" Mae appeared re-laxed as though they were discussing the weather. Quinn wanted to shake the siren, whose calm was a striking contrast to the anger flooding Quinn's insides.

"There'll be soldiers out now, searching for me." Jaxon was speaking slowly, as if contemplating each word he was saying. "She'll call them back eventually . . . but I don't think she'll stop looking for me. When I left Twelve Pools to find Gwen, she sent her assassin to find me and bring me home. If she sends him, it will only be a matter of time before he finds us." Something gave Jaxon pause; he rubbed his temples with his palms. "She wants me dead. But the Windsor princes asked her to deliver me to them, and she was going to do it."

"Such a charming sister," Quinn scoffed. She had always thought Cassandra's endless grumbling at Annabel made her a bad sister, but now she seemed harmless in comparison. A soft pang squeezed at her heart as she imagined Annabel trapped in Windsor, having to carry the burden of her sister's death alone. Annabel had always loved Cassandra, despite her faults.

Quinn clenched her fists, digging her nails into her skin as she thought about the reason Annabel was alone right now, without support. She couldn't wait to cross paths with Jonathan again. She glanced at the others, but neither had noticed that her cheeks were now flushed with heat.

Across from her, Mae was studying Jaxon's face. "What could the Windsor princes want with you?"

Jaxon shrugged. "I don't think she asked. Or if she did, she didn't share that with her council."

Mae touched the stones on her head absentmindedly. "The men of your kingdom respect her, but it's driven by fear," she said. "Every soldier's aura darkened when I read their memories of her. I can give you some relief from whatever she's done to you. Just say the word."

Jaxon shook his head. "I don't want my defenses down around her."

Lukas let out a soft snore, and the three of them watched his small, frail figure rise and fall. Quinn felt a quiet rage bubble inside her for this queen she had never met, who had caused pain to her friends and was colluding with the people responsible for Annabel's imprisonment. Her rows of red stones glittered on her waist. Beside her, Jaxon sat straight up and dug into the satchel on his waist. He pulled out a small pile of red stones and held them out in front of her.

"Thought you might want these."

Quinn stared at his hand in disbelief. She held out her own hand and let Jaxon drop the stones into it. For the first time in a while, Quinn felt a glimmer of hope. The anger she harbored for Jaxon's lies felt distant.

"I guess I need to stop calling you traitor." She whistled as she examined them. "How about Alexander?"

Jaxon flinched. "That's my father's name."

This was something that Quinn understood. "Just Jaxon then." She unstrapped her belt, laid it across the bench, and fastened the new stones to it.

"Can you make clarity stones too?" Mae's smile was playful, but Jaxon gave her a serious answer.

"I'll see what I can do," he said. "I haven't tried yet, but if I can make red and yellow, I don't see why I couldn't make purple too."

"If you start making the green stones now, we might have enough to trade them with the Windsor princes," Quinn said, refusing once again to say Jonathan's name out loud.

Jaxon nodded, though Quinn couldn't help but notice that he did not seem particularly enthusiastic about this plan.

"So, is it settled?" Mae asked tentatively. "We go to the cave first?"

"Yes," Jaxon said. "And then we travel north to warn Gwen and Greg that Twelve Pool men are waiting to ambush the Viridis army."

They both looked at Quinn, waiting for her to protest. She wanted to reach Annabel as soon as possible. She wanted to do something with her anger, to act. But she had come here for Jaxon's help. She had come here because she still trusted him even after he'd lied to her. If Gwen were here, Quinn knew she'd tell her to listen to Jaxon. So instead of arguing, she nodded at the other two and sat back down on the bench.

"How did you find me, anyway?" Jaxon asked, after a long pause. "How did you know that Jasmine had me?"

Quinn and Mae exchanged a look.

"It was Pima that led us most of the way," Mae admitted.

Jaxon raised his eyebrows. "The dire bear?"

"*Your* dire bear," Mae smiled. "She's still convinced you're her mother."

Jaxon put a hand in his hair and tugged in distress. "Where's Pima now? Is she safe?"

"Close by," Mae said. "She'll find us when she can."

"Children!" Ollie was screaming at them from the other room. "I'm not your servant. Come plate your breakfast."

Quinn grinned and followed the others to the kitchen.

# CHAPTER 12

# The Hidden Cave

Jaxon struggled to yank his sword up in time to block Quinn's next swing. She had backed him into Ollie's table, and the pile of things on it wobbled precariously. He shoved one of the chairs between himself and Quinn in an effort to give himself time to recover from her volley of swings. Instead of being deterred, Quinn knocked it down, planted a foot on it, and launched herself up onto the table.

With her new height advantage, Quinn was able to bring her blade down harder. Jaxon managed to hold onto his sword as he blocked her and then aimed his counterattack at her ankles. She jumped backward, narrowly avoiding a large pile of parchment.

Jaxon heard Lukas cheer in support of him. The previous day of resting had a significant effect on his brother's spirits. He'd almost returned to his normal, jovial self.

"What are you waiting for?" Quinn jeered. He climbed up on the table after her with far less grace. She ducked behind a teetering pile of books, and as Jaxon turned the corner, she was launching herself over them, knocking his sword clean from his hand.

"What on earth are you children doing?" Ollie had emerged from the room. He scowled at Jaxon and Quinn, who stood frozen amidst the pile of things.

"Practicing?" Quinn said sheepishly, her sword still extended in front of her. "I wanted to see how Jaxon's training was coming along," she added, as though that explained why they were destroying his possessions.

"On my dining table?" he demanded.

Jaxon sat down and slid back to the ground. "Sorry." Though he did think the term *dining table* was a bit generous.

"Yes, sorry," Quinn added, sheathing her sword and jumping off the table after him.

Ollie covered one hand over his face, his fingers pressed against his closed eyes. "Can we please be normal for a moment longer? I'm going to grab my knapsack, then we can leave, and you all can go far away from my home. Forever."

He left the room, and Mae, who was sitting on the bench next to Lukas, erupted into giggles. She doubled over, clutching her stomach. Lukas watched her and began to laugh too.

Jaxon's guilt vanished as he watched his brother. Lukas was already looking healthier and less pale. The darker shade of skin highlighted the white patch on the right side of his face.

"Here, take this," Quinn said to Lukas when he stopped laughing. She tossed him the small bag that she carried Kit in. "Kit can go in there. If he gets too heavy, I can carry him."

Lukas threw the bag over his shoulder, and Kit immediately found his way inside it, his small head poking out.

Jaxon secured his sword belt and satchel around his dark purple tunic. Ollie had given him a small knapsack filled with supplies he might need, including a change of clothes for Lukas—who happened to be roughly the same size as the gnome—and two sets of animal skins to sleep on. As Jaxon secured the bag to his back, he found himself wishing he'd thought to bring a change of clothes for himself before he left the castle. The purple of his tunic would tie him to Twelve Pools. The brown dresses Quinn and Mae were wearing over their trousers were far more inconspicuous.

The two girls also had packs that Ollie had helped them restock. Mae was securing her silk scarf around her head while Quinn fastened her quiver on her back. The redhead then propped her leg up on the bench and wrapped a leather holster around her thigh. The crimson handle of a small blade poked out the top before Quinn threw her dress back over her leg, hiding it from view. How many other weapons did she have hidden on her that he hadn't seen? Jaxon smiled to himself, feeling just a little less worried about the road ahead.

Beside him, Lukas was feeding Kit bits of scone.

"Are you sure you're strong enough to walk?" Jaxon whispered. Lukas nodded eagerly and gave him a large, toothy smile. Jaxon could feel the energy radiating off him. "And you're alright carrying Kit?"

"I'm fine, *Jax*," Lukas teased. Jaxon reached over and tugged one of his brother's earlobes. Lukas swatted him away and stuck his tongue out.

"Are we ready?" Ollie had emerged from his chambers, a small knapsack over his shoulders and what appeared to be a handkerchief tied around his neck. "Don't forget to drink your Twilight Prulane antidote."

Jaxon tried to give Lukas another burst of healing while his head was turned away, but his brother wasn't fooled. He looked back at him with raised eyebrows. Jaxon reluctantly pulled away, the light of his green stone fading.

They each drank their antidote then followed Ollie out the front door and into the tunnel. It was a much shorter journey to the cave entrance than Jaxon remembered. But Ollie kept going, past the entrance they'd found him at, and down another tunnel leading past it.

As they walked, Jaxon kept a close eye on his brother. But, if anything, Lukas seemed to be thriving on the movement. He was soaking everything in, and he kept narrating what he was seeing to Kit, who was secured in the knapsack, where Jaxon guessed he was sleeping. Ollie kept turning around and scowling at Lukas's commentary, but his brother hadn't noticed the gnome's annoyance.

"Are we near the castle?" Lukas asked. "You didn't tell me there were tunnels here!"

"I didn't know," Jaxon admitted.

"You and your friend Henry never explored over here?"

"We did, but we never found these."

"You wouldn't have." Ollie glanced back at them, holding his lantern up so he could see their faces. "The tunnels are protected by more than just me."

Quinn eyed the lantern in his hand. "I can help with the light," she offered, reaching for her gloves. Jaxon remembered the last time he'd seen her hold flames in her hand. She'd been tossing balls of fire at Prince Jonathan's face.

"No, no," Ollie said, turning back around. "We won't need light here soon."

His words proved to be true moments later when they turned a corner and sunlight streamed in from the outside. The tunnel continued, but a space on their left opened to a view of the lake below them. Bushels of purple flowers crowded the side of the opening, reaching into the depth of the cave as far as the light would allow.

Jaxon rubbed his eyes as they adjusted to the brightness. The group moved to the opening of the cave and stared out over the great expanse of the lake. The castle rising from the water was now a distant blip on the horizon. The lake was still, reflecting the vast blue sky and the scattering of white clouds so well that it was hard to tell up from down. Ollie pushed past them.

"You've seen the lake before, no?" he grunted. "Keep moving." It looked like he was about to walk off the side into nothing, but instead his feet found a narrow ledge alongside the cave opening that had disguised itself in the stone wall. It was marked only by the long line of purple flowers growing from it, which Jaxon guessed was Twilight Prulane. Quinn and Mae followed without hesitation. Jaxon swallowed as he watched them; Quinn wasn't even looking at her feet as she moved. Lukas gave him a knowing look.

"Want me to walk with you?" he asked, as though Jaxon was the child.

"I'll be okay. You go ahead." Lukas smiled at him and joined the others on the ledge.

Jaxon tried to steady his feet as he followed. The path continued for what felt like miles. By the time he got the courage to glance up, the others were far ahead of him. He looked quickly back down, his hand glued to the wall. As he moved, a few rocks loosened on the side of the path, plummeting hundreds of feet down into the lake. He took a deep breath. He had no choice but to keep going.

Finally, the ledge sloped downward. Relief flooded him as the ground opened beneath his feet. He'd made it to a large patch of level rock that reached to meet the water's edge. The path narrowed up ahead, decorated again by purple flowers, but it appeared to stay level to the lake.

Mae was sitting closer to the wall, eating a slab of bread and cheese next to Ollie. They were deep in conversation. Lukas was on the other side of the rock, crouched over the lake and looking down at where the water touched his feet. Quinn was standing beside him, frowning. Concerned, Jaxon moved to join them. As he got closer, something told him to wait. Their backs were to him, and they hadn't realized he was there yet. He paused within earshot.

"Do you think it will always be there?" Lukas touched his face where the white mark of Lux Pox still lingered. Jaxon winced. He knew Lukas would see the changes to his face soon enough, but he hadn't been sure how he'd react. His brother had never once expressed interest in how he looked. But he was growing. Even in his coma, he had grown. And Jaxon knew those feelings were inevitable.

"I do," Quinn said. Lukas's head dropped, and though Jaxon couldn't see his face, he guessed there was sadness there.

To his surprise, Quinn sat down beside Lukas and hugged her knees to her chest.

"It's a mark of your strength, Lukas," she said. "A symbol of the battles you've already won."

Lukas was silent, and Jaxon suspected he was staring at his reflection again. Kit's head poked out from the pack still fastened to Lukas's back. The fox scurried up and over Lukas's shoulder and then onto the ground, where he licked the lake, causing ripples to erupt on its surface.

"Your scar ties you to Kit," Quinn said so softly that Jaxon had to strain to hear her. "I can't think of a greater honor."

Lukas placed a hand on the white patch of fur around Kit's eye.

"What do you feel when you look at him?" Quinn asked.

"Happy."

Quinn turned to Lukas, and Jaxon noticed a smile tugging at the corner of her mouth.

"The same way Jaxon feels when he looks at you," she said. "That's what matters. I won't lie to you—the world will try to judge you for what you look like. But you get to shape your own world and fill it with the people who don't look at you and *see* but look at you and *feel.*"

Lukas was silent for what felt like a long time. "Thank you, Lady Quinn," he said, finally.

"Go eat your lunch." Quinn waved him off with a flick of her hand. "You need energy." He jumped to his feet, spun around, and grinned at the sight of Jaxon. "You made it!" he said before he ran toward Ollie and Mae.

Kit climbed onto Quinn and perched himself on top of her knees as Jaxon moved to sit beside her.

"Thank you for that," he said. "I wouldn't have known what to say." Quinn was avoiding looking at him. Tears slid down her cheeks. Jaxon froze. He'd never seen her like this before; he wasn't sure whether to stay or give her space.

She took a deep breath. "I didn't know what to say either," she said fiercely. "Everything I said, Anna's said to me before. She was—she *is*—the best part of me."

Jaxon put a hand on her shoulder. "We're going to get her back."

"And what if we can't?"

Jaxon smiled. "*You*, Quinn of the red stone? Who would move mountains and time itself for Anna, *not* save her? I wouldn't make that bet."

Quinn's laugh was shaky. She wiped the sleeves of her brown dress forcefully against her cheeks. Something shifted in her eyes, and she tensed, lifting her head to meet Jaxon's gaze.

"After the Suitor's Championship, Prince Jonathan kissed me." The words rushed out of her, like she'd been waiting a long time to say them. Jaxon stared at her, mouth agape, trying to process what she'd said.

"What?" A gasp of surprise interrupted his shock. Mae had wandered over to them bearing loaves of bread and cheese. Her eyes looked like they were trying to pop right out of her head. It was the most rattled he'd seen her since they fought a dire bear together.

Quinn groaned and turned back to the lake. "You weren't supposed to hear that."

Mae dumped the food on the ground and began to pace back and forth.

"We traveled together, alone, for *weeks*," she said, pulling at her hair. "We walked in silence for entire days! And all that time you were keeping *that* from me? That's the most interesting thing I've heard since we left Viridis!"

Quinn was grinning now. "You just found out that another stone god exists, but a stupid kiss is what you think is interesting?"

"Not just a kiss," Mae said, swooping in to lean over Quinn's shoulder, inches from her face. "A *forbidden* kiss!"

Jaxon had stood and now took a step back, wishing he could vanish into thin air. This didn't feel like a conversation meant for his ears.

"A traitor's kiss," Quinn corrected, as Mae paced again. "And the traitor was me, because I let him do it."

"Did you kiss him back?"

Quinn looked away, and Mae threw her head back. "*And you kissed him back!*" she cried out. She fanned her face with both her hands. "Is anyone else feeling a little warm?"

"He was betrothed to Anna! If he hadn't turned out to be a liar and a murderer, they'd be married right now. What I did is unforgiveable."

"Oh, please," Mae waved her hand in dismissal. "We all know Anna was smitten with Jax anyway."

Jaxon's cheeks burn. Quinn was staring at him as if she was trying to burn through his skull to find the truth in his brain. He did everything he could not to look over at her. Even in his embarrassment, he couldn't help but feel a small spark of hope that what Mae said was true. He had thought they might kiss, the night of the Suitor's Championship, but Annabel had pulled away from him.

Mae's eyes ticked back and forth between them. "I guess that's not something we all knew."

"She would've told me," Quinn said.

"Maybe," Mae shrugged. "It wouldn't have been very honorable for her to court Jax while betrothed to another though. And our Anna is nothing if not honorable."

This seemed to cross a line for Quinn. She stood and pushed a finger into Mae's chest. "*My* Anna," she said. She started to walk away but doubled back, picked up a loaf of bread, and then continued to storm off.

Jaxon helped Mae grab the rest of the food.

"I don't need to use my stones to know how *you* feel," Mae said with a knowing smile. She swung her hair over her shoulder and followed Quinn.

Ollie led them back onto the path. The lake narrowed as they moved alongside it, and the rock walls that towered above them narrowed with it, closing in on them. A sliver of blue sky was still visible above them. It cast a soft glow on the rocks, dancing in the places where green had managed to grow.

"Is this a joke?" Quinn sounded angry.

She stood at the end of the path. They were at the edge of the lake, and the water was pooled there, stagnant beside the wall of rock. There was nowhere left to go. They had reached a dead end.

"I hope you're all really good at holding your breath," Ollie said, dropping his knapsack on the ground. Without another word, the gnome dove into the lake, disappearing beneath its surface.

The four of them stood frozen, staring at a few bubbles that had emerged in his wake. Jaxon wasn't sure what to do. Beside him, Quinn shifted as she dislodged her own backpack.

"Quinn, no—" But he was too late, she was in the water, sword and all. She disappeared beneath the surface, and the arrows that had been in her quiver floated to the top. Seconds later, red hair emerged again above the water. Quinn spluttered and grabbed some of the loose arrows, tossing them back up on the ledge.

"Can you all swim?" The red buns on the top of her head were drooping to the side under the weight of the water now soaking them. "There's a tunnel under the rock wall here. I don't think it's far. I could see some light coming through from the other side."

Jaxon removed his satchel from his waist and took his small pack off his back, resigning himself to what was about to happen.

Red light glimmered from beneath the water around Quinn. "I'll move you through," she said, looking at Mae. The siren nodded, stripped her own belongings, and gracefully lowered herself into the lake.

"Lukas, are you—" But Lukas's yell drowned Jaxon out. He'd taken a few steps backward and was running toward the lake. He leapt in, and the resulting splash dumped water on a laughing Mae and Quinn. Lukas's shock of white hair emerged from the water seconds later and Kit, who'd been on his shoulder when he'd jumped, scrambled to climb on top of Lukas's head.

Quinn swam over to him, and the fox clawed up on top of her instead, further disheveling her buns. "You need to stay here, Kit," she instructed him, moving closer to the ledge.

Jaxon lifted the fox's wet and shivering body from Quinn and placed him back onto solid ground. Quinn's stones glowed again as she dried his fur. He squeaked in appreciation and curled up on Mae's backpack, shivering.

"What are you waiting for, Jax?" Lukas called up to him.

Jaxon lowered himself into the water, clenching his teeth together at the shock of cold.

Quinn kicked off the ledge. "Come on," she shouted. There was no time to adjust to the temperature as Quinn vanished again. Mae and Lukas following behind her. Jaxon took a deep breath and dove after them, getting sucked into the current Quinn was creating for them.

He followed Lukas's feet as they kicked up and down in front of him. For a moment, it was almost too dark to see as rock surrounded them. And then, the light from the other side of the tunnel began to brighten. He squinted. Were the walls glittering purple?

Just when Jaxon was sure he could no longer hold his breath, Lukas floated upward. Jaxon followed. His head broke the surface and he drank in the air as the sound of rushing water bombarded his ears. He blinked to clear his eyes and then surveyed the water around him, making sure the others had made it. All three of their heads were bobbing in the center of the small pool, basked in a dim purple light. Lukas was staring wide-eyed at the cave walls around and overhead. Jaxon followed his gaze, scanning the glittering shards of purple scattered throughout the walls.

"Took you kids long enough." Ollie was sitting on the ledge, grinning. "Get up here, before the waterfall treats you to an unexpected dive." Jaxon swam to the ledge, hoisted himself up onto it, and then turned to help the others. From the new height, Jaxon was able to get a better view of the water they had emerged from.

Stalactites hung from the ceiling, reaching toward the small pool of water, like teeth protecting the cave entrance. The walls wrapped around the pool and then curved outward, leaving a large hole in the center of the cave.

Stone steps dropped downward, following the circular shape of the wall as they spiraled into the depths of the cave. Water spilled over the side of the pool, into the opening. Jaxon's eyes followed the flow of water, but he couldn't see where it stopped falling. A dark violet haze rose from the depths of the cave. The splotches of sparkling purple stone in the walls increased the farther down he looked.

Mae and Lukas were right behind Ollie as he began to climb down the spiral steps alongside the wall. Quinn and Jaxon exchanged a glance before following them. Jaxon tried again to focus on the solid ground beneath his feet and not the gaping hole to his left.

"They should rename the endless staircase in Viridis," Jaxon said after what felt like hours of descending.

"Only you ever call it that, Jaxon," Quinn said.

Mae laughed. "It was endless the day we saw the acrobats perform."

"When we were running from the bloodsucker's victim?" Quinn scoffed. "Every moment felt endless that night."

"Bloodsucker?" Lukas was intrigued. Jaxon listened as Mae told him the story of the man who could use his red stones to draw water from humans, sucking the life out of them, and how he'd threatened the kingdom for months before taking Princess Cassandra as his last victim.

"Did you catch him?" Lukas asked eagerly. "Who was it?"

Jaxon's mouth tightened. He didn't say anything. Quinn's shoulders stiffened in front of him.

"It was Prince Jonathan," Mae raised her voice so he could hear her over the sound of the crashing water.

"One of the Windsor princes?"

"Yes," Mae said.

"Did you say something, Lady Quinn?" Lukas looked back at Quinn.

"She said he's very handsome," Mae piped up.

"I won't hesitate to push you off this staircase, Mae*lyn*."

The siren didn't respond to Quinn, but Jaxon could practically hear her smile.

The purple haze thinned around them, and Mae let out an audible gasp. Jaxon descended a few more steps before he saw it. The mist had cleared, and in its place was an enormous purple stone emerging from a pool of dark water. Behind it, the waterfall finally met the end of its journey, spraying mist up around the stone. Dark purple shards jutted from the sides of the stone and the cave walls.

From where he stood, Jaxon could now see how the shards were creating paths from the central stone, almost like veins spreading outward from the center. A line of shards pierced through the waterfall as they zigzagged up and across it, disappearing behind the water as it climbed. In the middle of the cave, the stone's center pulsated light like the persistent beat of a heart.

They reached the end of the staircase. Mae appeared mesmerized as she walked—or, Jaxon thought, was pulled—toward the pool of water. He followed her, concerned she might fall in. Mae took another step, this time into the shallow water at the edge of the pool. Quinn moved behind Jaxon, seemingly just as concerned. Before either of them could react, Mae's head shot backward. Her hair flew outward as though being swept up in a gust of wind, the deep black of it shimmering violet.

Alarmed, Jaxon reached out to steady her as she swayed. His hand touched her shoulder, and magic jolted through him like an electric shock. His vision blurred, blackened, and then swam with vibrant color. Muffled voices grew louder and louder and then became clear.

*"Where is she now?" A gnome was standing in front of him, leaning over a map, a mug of liquid in one hand. There was*

*a quiet rage in his narrowed eyes. He tugged at his long beard with his free hand. Jaxon was standing opposite, looking down at him.*

*Where was he—and how did he get here? The colors around him were dull and washed out. A hand extended out from his body, one he didn't recognize, and shoved the map aside. It dawned on Jaxon then that he was in someone else's mind, watching from their eyes.*

*"You were supposed to look out for her, you should know where she is," the man said.*

*The gnome across from him slammed his drink on the table. "You asked the impossible. I could contain her no more than you can halt the rain."*

*"She's the least of your problems now. I hope you're ready."*

*The gnome clenched his teeth together. "Enough. I've never heard someone use so many words to say nothing."*

The man replied, but Jaxon couldn't hear him. The room was fading away. It became clear once again, and Jaxon recognized the mishap of items and the tall walking stick leaning beside the fireplace. Opposite of it, tucked in the corner, was a suit of armor with three gashes down the middle.

*"Where is she now?" This time, the voice coming from Jaxon was quiet, clenched with fear. He was in a woman's mind this time. She was sitting opposite the fireplace, her hands wrapped around a mug of tea. Jaxon could make out whisps of auburn hair along the sides of her face, punctured by patches of gray.*

*"I can only see glimpses." The man that answered said it almost gleefully, as though presenting a delightful mystery. Jaxon recognized Okya, the banished seer that they'd traveled to see so many weeks ago.*

*Another woman with silver hair emerged from the shadows. A deep frown stretched across her face.*

*"Is she safe?" Gwen asked.*

*"She's right where she needs to be," the banished seer said.*

*Gwen seemed to glide across the room. She clutched the seer's tunic, yanking it upward so he was lifted off the ground.*

*"Listen, you crazy kook—" Gwen hissed.*

*The door burst open, and a large man, hunched over, tried to enter the room. His axe got caught on the sides of the doorframe, and he had to turn and move sideways through it. Finally, he straightened and surveyed the scene in front of him, eyes flickering between the purple-glowing Okya and the green-glowing Gwen.*

*"Thought I heard trouble in here," Greg grinned. "Was tired of waiting out there, anyway. Smelled like something was cooking in here."*

*"I'm roasting some turnips." Okya, who was still hanging off the ground, motioned at the fire behind him.*

*"Ah," Greg said. "Disgusting." He rubbed his nose like it had deceived him. He scanned the rest of the room, and he caught sight of the armor in the corner. "Oy!" he cried. "That mine? Looks like my axe's work." He moved closer and touched the*

*three gashes in the center, examining the damage to the armor and the dried blood still splashed across the metal. "No," he said. "These are claw marks. I probably killed the dire bear that attacked him, though."*

*Okya still hung a few inches above the ground. "Will you set me down, Lady Gwen?"*

*Gwen's frown deepened, but she lowered him and let go of his tunic.*

*"Please." The woman whose mind Jaxon was in had stood. She took Okya's hand in her own. "I need to find my daughter."*

*Okya put his other hand over hers and squeezed.*

*"I can only see your future, Lady Rosa," his voice softened. "And there is no future for you that will lead you to her right now. I can't promise you her safety or tell you which path forward she will take. All I can promise you is that there are paths that lead her back to you, should she choose to take one of them. Which means that, for now, she is alive."*

*Silence followed.*

*"Comforting," Greg said, finally. The smallest of smiles flashed across Gwen's face.*

The room was fading again, replaced by dark stone walls and large beautiful windows that opened to striking views of the sky.

*"Where is he now?"*

*Uneasiness washed over Jaxon as his vision cleared. He'd recognize the large, round table in front of him anywhere. In the chairs around the table were some of Twelve Pools most prominent advisors. General Townsend and Theo were sitting on either side of the person's mind he was in now. Jasmine's war room was the last place Jaxon wanted to be, both physically and mentally.*

*Long, thin fingers decorated in silver jewels folded in the lap in front of him. He was in Jasmine's mind.*

*"They've been unable to locate him," she said. Though Jaxon couldn't see her face, he knew Jasmine well enough to know how uncomfortable she was admitting to uncertainty.*

*There was movement behind the table. From the shadows, a lizard-like man with a scarred face and speckled gray hair emerged. A few sitting at the table shifted uncomfortably, as if they hadn't known he was standing there.*

*"My Queen," Kiernan's gruff voice was quiet but confident as always. Beside him, the wall shifted as Divoff appeared out of nowhere, his shimmering gray scales the same color as the wall behind him. The creature's tongue darted around licking at the air, his tail sliding across the floor as he moved forward to join Kiernan. "If you'll allow it, Divoff can get a scent on him."*

*There was silence as Jasmine contemplated this.*

*She leaned forward in her chair. "Find him," she said. Jaxon felt his blood go cold, and he tried to step backward—*

He was yanked from the room. The cave appeared in front of him as his hand fell away from Mae's shoulder. He blinked rapidly, steadying himself as the rock walls spun around him.

Mae was beside him, her head obscured by purple. Her eyes were wide in excitement, but she was tight-lipped and looked as though standing upright was taking every ounce of her concentration. On his other side, Quinn was clutching the sides of her head and breathing deeply.

"What just happened?" she managed to say.

"Jaxon amplified my magic," Mae said as she stared at him. "I saw things I've never seen before."

Lukas and Ollie were still standing next to the water. His brother's head was tilted in concern, but Ollie merely looked on with a grim curiosity.

"What do you mean?" Jaxon asked.

"Truly powerful purple stone bearers can see others from afar, but I've never done that before. My stones only allow me to see into the minds of those within my magic's reach. Except I just saw into minds far beyond that."

"Because of the clarity stone's source, you mean," Jaxon corrected. He remembered how strong his magic had felt when they were in the mountains close to the source of the green stone. That must be what she was feeling now.

"No," Mae said. "I mean yes, but it's more than that. I was looking into my own future, searching to make sure we're safe from those who are after us. It was all muddled, unclear. But when you put your hand on my shoulder, I saw them all . . . Everyone who is looking for us right now."

"I saw it all too," Quinn said. She seemed to have recovered, the excitement in her face matching Mae's.

"Does this mean you can take us to Anna? Can you show us where she is? Can you show us if she's okay?"

Mae smiled, and before Jaxon could react, she reached both of her hands out, tethering herself to him and Quinn. Again, he felt the pull of his magic as Mae reached for it. The cave faded, and he was in a very small room, looking out a very small window.

*Endless blue water stretched before him. The person whose mind he was in now, extended their hand. Delicate brown fingers gripped the edge of the windowsill, tightening around the stone.*

*It was her. Annabel. She was muttering to herself. It sounded almost like a chant. It took a moment for him to understand what she said, but as soon as the words registered, he pulled back.*

The cave appeared around him, but he had eyes only for Mae and Quinn. They looked just as alarmed as he did. The words reverberated in his head, loud and on repeat.

*Don't come here.*

# CHAPTER 13

# The Turtle Tavern

Quinn was not thrilled to be spending her days walking again. Though she suspected her reluctance stemmed from an impatience to get to their destination faster, her dragging feet suggested otherwise. A strange, deep tiredness had taken over her body since they'd left the cave the day before.

Green stretched around them for miles, broken up by budding purple flowers, which Jaxon said would soon be snuffed out by the cold of the late autumn air. They were in the fields sandwiched between Wisteria and Hyacinth. Ollie had led them up and out of the valley, where they emerged north of Hyacinth Pool. They spent the night camped there before they began to move west across the grassland, back toward the Trade Bridge.

Ollie was sticking to his promise to take them as far as Verbena Pool, though none of them had asked for his company and had, in fact, repeatedly told him he was welcome to head home. *Encouraged to head home, really,* Quinn thought to herself as she eyed the grumpy gnome. He was making audible huffing noises every time they walked up even the slightest of inclines.

Up ahead, Mae bent over again to pluck one of the heather flowers from the ground, tying them together to form a long strand. Quinn envied the lightness with which the siren glided across the fields, humming to herself. Quinn's own feet felt unusually heavy. She was having a hard time breathing, as though there wasn't enough space in her lungs for the air she needed.

"Are you alright?" Jaxon had dropped back to walk beside her. Quinn hadn't realized how far she'd lagged behind. "You look pale, well, paler than usual." He reached out to touch her, his stone glowing, but she shrugged him off.

"I'm fine." She was afraid if she said anything else he'd hear her struggling to breathe.

He continued to watch her, and she looked determinedly forward. Kit, who had been napping in Lukas's knapsack, poked his head out from the bag. Even from this distance, she could tell he was watching her. *I'm fine,* she wanted to assure the fox.

Next to Lukas and Kit, Mae made one final knot in her flower string, tying the two ends together so that it formed a circle. She placed it on Lukas's head of white hair like a crown. He playfully mimicked a bow and Mae laughed, taking his hand and twirling him around and around and—

"*Quinn!*"

She was on the ground, looking up at the sky. The blue of it was now shrouded in green light. Jaxon's hands hovered over her. In her haze of confusion, she noticed he was frowning in concern.

"What's happening, what's wrong with her?" Mae's black hair dangled above her. Quinn wanted to tell her to back up, but words refused to come out of her mouth. Something wet touched her cheek. Kit had found her, and the worry that had taken hold of her diminished.

The green light vanished, Jaxon's face coming into view.

"Quinn, I'm going to roll up your pants."

*What? No*, Quinn thought fiercely. A gurgle of nonsense is what came out of her mouth instead.

"I'm taking that as consent," Jaxon said, and he disappeared.

Mae was looking at her with pity. "Here," she said. "Ollie, help me prop her up."

The world was upright again. Kit climbed up into her now available lap and made himself at home.

Jaxon had removed her boots and rolled back the dark trousers she was wearing beneath her worn brown dress. Her ankles were exposed, revealing the white of her skin and random patches of glowing, worm-like creatures that had fastened themselves to her. Something about the sight of them gave her strength. She sat up straighter.

Jaxon looked around. "Does anyone have something, anything we can—"

Quinn moved Kit gently aside and hiked her dress up farther to retrieve the small crimson-handle knife she kept strapped there. She pushed the tip of the blade into the edge of one of the glowing worms and flicked outwards. The worm-like creature flew up and plopped onto the ground, flailing around. Quinn ignored the trail of blood it'd left behind and moved on to the next one. One by one, she flicked each of the glowing worms off of her body. Jaxon's magic followed behind her, healing each of the wounds as she dislodged the creatures.

"What are these things?" Mae asked. Lukas was squatting beside one of them, flipping it over with a stick as he inspected it.

"Spilja leech," Ollie said grimly. "One of the creatures that protect the purple stone. That cave is infested with them. They feed on your magic."

"And you didn't think to warn us?" Quinn snapped as she removed the last one from her body.

Unfazed, Ollie shrugged. "I didn't expect all three of you to climb in like that. I actually forgot they lived in there, since I've never personally had the urge to take a swim in magic-infested waters."

Quinn opened her mouth to retort, but Jaxon gave her a look, and she reluctantly closed it.

"I need you to relax," he said to her. "I'm going to finish healing these wounds and try to return some of your strength to you."

Ollie, who seemed far less interested in the conversation now that they'd gotten rid of the leeches, stood and laid a small piece of animal skin on the ground some feet away from them.

"Wake me when you all are ready to start walking again." He fell backward onto the cloth and pulled the handkerchief that was around his neck up over his eyes. His arms were wrapped around his chest, and his legs were straight out in front of him, toes pointing to the sky. Quinn couldn't help but notice how uncomfortable the sleeping position looked, and yet, she thought, it was exactly how she would've imagined Ollie slept.

Mae sat down next to Quinn and leaned back on her hands, her head tilted at Jaxon in curiosity. "How did you know?"

"The hirudo beetles," Jaxon said as he worked. "And Lukas's blocked magic. I'm learning that magic requires its own type of healing. It moves differently through the body."

"What is a hirudo beetle, again?" Quinn asked.

"Small beetles that drain the magic from you like the leech did," Mae said. "The Red Forest is filled with them, but they linger most in the areas closest to the Red Stone. Gnomes and sirens never have to worry about them because they don't have magic that the beetles can steal from them—at least not that type of magic."

Quinn tried to stand, but Jaxon shot her a stern look again.

"I'm good enough," she insisted. Jaxon ignored this and continued to work on her. She found herself sitting up straighter as her strength returned. The cloudiness that had layered her thoughts had vanished.

"You're getting good at that," she admitted to Jaxon. She'd only ever seen combat healers replenish energy like he was doing now, and those types of healers had years of training at the School of Nurture.

"Look!" Lukas moved on from his inspection of the leech and was holding out his hand. On it, a butterfly perched, flapping its delicate yellow wings. Kit pushed his nose up over Lukas's hand and sniffed at the butterfly, which took off into the air, dancing in front of Quinn. She held out her own hand. It landed on her, but Quinn felt no pressure from its weight. She stared at Lukas. The boy's smile stretched across his entire face.

"Magic," he said, and the butterfly disappeared.

The others stared.

"That was incredible," said Mae. "Do it again!"

Lukas's smile vanished as he concentrated. Another butterfly appeared, and this time, it landed on Mae's knee. Quinn leaned in to look closer at it. This one was even more detailed than the last.

"Lukas, where did you learn that?" Jaxon asked in awe.

The boy shrugged. "You were talking about magic moving through your body, and I tried to move it through mine. It was really easy once I found it. I think I used it sometimes when I was hiding from Jasmine, but I didn't know what it was then."

Jaxon didn't look surprised to hear this. The butterfly moved to Kit's nose, and the fox pawed at it, trying to swat it off. Quinn remembered how exciting it used to be, when she was a kid, to explore her stone's power. Lukas sat next to Kit and continued to put on a show for the fox, who observed attentively, occasionally chasing after the butterfly.

Jaxon watched the light show with almost as much interest as Kit.

Quinn felt strong enough to walk again, but all the talk of magic had reminded her of Mae's new ability.

"I want to see Anna," she said. Mae spun around. Jaxon didn't take his eyes off Lukas but gave a small, curt nod, as though he'd been expecting the request.

"Do you think you can pull the magic from me again?" Jaxon asked Mae. "I don't know if it'll work when we're not near the source of the purple stone."

Mae smiled. "It'll work. I remember how it felt, and I'm sure I can do it again. Our connection to Annabel is strong. It would be difficult to reach someone we didn't know. But Annabel we can find." She sat across from them, forming a small circle. She held her hands out for both of them to take. As Mae's hand tightened around Quinn's, the field of green and the wide, blue sky faded to gray walls.

*Annabel was standing next to the window again, but she was facing the door. A blonde man with a handsome face was offering her a tray of food. He was wearing a thin gold crown and blue tunic. Annabel hugged her arms tightly around her body as she watched him.*

*"What do you want?" she demanded. Her voice was quiet, but there was a subtle rage in the stress she put on each syllable.*

*"If you're thinking of escaping through that window, I wouldn't advise it," Liam said. "It's a long way down."*

*Annabel stared at him. "Ha," she said, but there was no trace of amusement in her voice.*

*Liam set the tray on the bed, revealing an assortment of colorful fruit. "Princess," he begged. "I just want to help."*

*"I don't need your help."*

*"If you think Lady Quinn will come—"*

*Annabel cut him off. "Quinn would never fall for this trap."*

*The prince shook his head. "It is not a trap, princess, merely an exchange of valuable items. Don't you agree that Windsor should have access to the nurture stone?"*

*Annabel took a step back and shook her head. "I know what you're really after."*

*Did Annabel know something they didn't? Say it out loud, Quinn thought desperately. But Annabel didn't elaborate, and Liam's expression was unreadable as he searched her face. Without a word, he disappeared behind the door. Quinn thought he'd left, but it wasn't long before he reemerged. A petite woman had followed him, peering out from behind him with round eyes that took up an unusual amount of space on her face. A mess of dark hair was pinned back, away from her rosy cheeks, and her floor-length dress was a royal blue that matched her protuberant eyes. There was a nervousness about her that felt eager, curious even.*

*Liam swooped an arm around the girl, moving her in front of him. "This is Lorrella," he said. "She'll escort you to the library and make sure you get everything you need while this is your home."*

*A soft sound like a hiss escaped Annabel. "This will never be my home." There was a coldness to her voice that Quinn had never heard before.*

*Liam smiled. "Visit the library before you decide that," he said. "Oh, and don't try wearing out Lorrella with questions. She's deaf and won't hear a word you say."*

*This time, when Liam left he didn't return.*

*Lorrella gave Annabel an encouraging smile and took her hand, dragging her from the room. They moved through the halls in silence. Lorrella would occasionally look back at Annabel to smile again.*

*Quinn could faintly feel their own world tugging at them, but she held Mae's hand tighter, wanting to stay with Annabel as long as possible.*

*They arrived at a pair of large wooden doors. Lorrella opened them, trying to pull Annabel through. Quinn could just make out the rows of endless books beyond the door. Annabel didn't enter.*

*"I'm so sorry, Lorrella." She ripped her hand free of the girl and shoved her into the room. The servant stumbled and fell to her knees. Annabel pulled the wooden doors shut and wrapped the handles together with what looked like a ripped piece of fabric from her own dress. Quinn's breath caught in her throat. What was she doing? She'd never be able to escape—there would be guards everywhere.*

*Annabel raced through the hallway. She burst through the end of a corridor and emerged on a balcony that wrapped around the upper level of a great hall. Intricate carvings of crashing waves and sea creatures decorated the hall. Before Quinn had time to take in the sight, Annabel turned down another hall. Her labored breathing was loud in Quinn's ears. What she would do to be there, to help her!*

*Sunlight streamed in through large open windows. Beyond them, a courtyard appeared with a large, golden fountain in the center, glittering as water trickled down it. Archways spanned the length of the yard, enclosing it. Through the arches, Quinn could make out the great expanse of the Endless Sea. The edge of the world.*

*Two young men, one with dark curls and the other with smooth blonde hair, sat in one of the open windows that faced the courtyard. Annabel dropped to the ground, hiding beneath one of the window ledges.*

*"I thought he was getting better."*

*Quinn recognized Jonathan's voice, and her insides squirmed.*

*"When we returned from Viridis, he was in good spirits. Now, he's back to his old self. Not even able to walk around the castle." He sounded defeated. Who were they talking about? Quinn's face screwed up in concentration as she listened, trying to absorb every word.*

*"We're going to heal him, don't worry," Liam reassured his brother. "Will you be ready to leave tomorrow?"*

*"I'm ready," Jonathan said grimly. After some silence, he continued, "You still think we should take the princess with us? She won't be easy. The servants all say she's constantly asking questions. Wants to know everything about everything."*

*"We can't let her out of our sight. I'll handle her."*

*Annabel shifted and removed something from the front of her dress. It was a small glass vial swimming with black liquid. Quinn tried to take a closer look, but Mae's vision was becoming blurrier by the second. Hold on a little longer, Mae, she thought, squeezing her hand again.*

*Annabel stared at the vial, moving the cap back and forth as though contemplating whether or not to open it. Seeming to make a decision, she stuffed it back down her shirt.*

*"Did you hear that?" Liam's voice was tense.*

*A shadow fell over Annabel.*

*"Look what the sea washed in," Jonathan said. A hand reached down and grabbed Annabel roughly by the arm, yanking her to her feet.*

"Oy," a voice called out, pulling all three of them from the vision. Quinn blinked as the brightness of the sky blinded her. Ollie had woken from his nap. "I hate to break up whatever this—" he motioned at their circle "—is. But shouldn't we get moving? I'd like to go home and forget this ever happened, and I thought you three were in some big hurry."

His voice sounded almost muffled to Quinn. His words unimportant. She longed to return to Annabel, but she knew they'd stretched Mae to her limits. Quinn's heart was racing. She'd understood so little of the conversation between the princes. Where were they taking Annabel now? And why? She couldn't imagine how scared Annabel was, and how alone she must feel. *I'm coming, Anna, I promise.*

Quinn stood, not wanting to waste any more time. She reached down to grab a winded-looking Mae by the arm, pulling her upright. She could tell that the long-distance visions took a lot out of the siren, whose cheeriness had faded. When they began to move again, it was Mae now who was falling behind the rest.

As they walked, Quinn and Jaxon discussed Mae's visions in hushed tones, trying to guess what the princes were up to. A gloominess had fallen over the group, along with a new urgency to move faster. Only Lukas was unfazed by the change in mood and unbothered by this new topic of conversation. He continued to practice his manipulation of light, occasionally interrupting the conversation to ask Jaxon questions about magic and breathing techniques.

Quinn was only half-listening as Jaxon repeated lessons that Gwen had given him. She kept replaying Annabel's words in her head. *Quinn would never fall for this trick.* While Quinn had guessed that they wouldn't be walking into a peaceful exchange with Windsor, this certainly wasn't enough to stop her from going there anyway. There was nothing, Quinn thought, that would stop her from trying to rescue Annabel. And there was no one who would know this to be true more than Annabel. Was Annabel playing her own mind games with the Windsor princes?

Either way, Quinn knew they'd need to make a plan soon. The farther west they traveled, the more in danger they would be of crossing paths with the queen's men. From the sounds of it, Jasmine had also sent her assassin after Jaxon. She didn't know how much of a danger he posed, but didn't love the look of the large lizard that Jaxon darkly referred to as the assassin's "best friend." No matter which way they traveled, it seemed like they were moving closer to danger.

Just when Quinn decided she couldn't walk any farther that day, Ollie let out a cry of joy.

"There!"

Quinn squinted at the distant object. She'd thought it was an enormous boulder half-buried in the ground, but on closer inspection, she realized the mound was actually a mud structure shaped into a dome. Patches of light dotted the curved building, revealing round windows freckling the surface.

As they got closer to the tavern, the road split into multiple directions. At its center, stood a wooden post taller than their heads, with arrows sticking out from it in every direction. Each of the twelve pool's names was written across individual wooden arrows. *Red Passage* was scrawled on one arrow and *Brazen Way* on another. The final arrow pointed in the direction of the inn, down a smaller road that looked more like a worn path. Written on this arrow were the words *Turtle Tavern*.

The group followed the path down to the building. Quinn was breathing easier than she had all day, relieved that they'd finally have a proper meal to fill their stomachs and four walls to shield them from danger. She arrived at the tavern first and led the way inside, marveling at the high ceilings and intricate hexagon pattern decorating the walls. Past the front desk, two sets of stairs framed the large, circular building, wrapping upward in opposite directions. The stairs leveled out every once in a while to make ledges for the doors to each room. In the center of the dome a round counter space enclosed large barrels of mead and ale. Above it, a bulky storage area hung precariously from the ceiling, and a ladder extended from it to the ground. Quinn watched a bartender descend the ladder, clutching a box against his hip. Tables circled the bustling bar, and at least two maidens moved from table to table, delivering food.

"No children!" a raspy voice said.

A very old man was standing on his toes to see over the front desk. He glowered down at them through a pair of round spectacles.

"Sorry?" Quinn asked, confused.

"No children allowed!" the man barked at her, droplets of spit flying from his mouth.

"We don't have any children with us, my good sir," Ollie said.

The old man stood, leaning over the counter, searching their faces. Quinn too looked around, expecting to see proof of Ollie's lie, but Lukas was nowhere in sight. She exchanged an alarmed look with Jaxon, who seemed less concerned.

"Hmm," the old man shook his head. "Could have sworn. How many rooms, then?"

"Two will be just fine," Ollie said. He had to stand on his tippy toes to put a handful of valoo and kuwies on the counter.

"You'll need to wait," the old man grumbled as though they were inconveniencing him. "We'll need to clean them for you."

"Take your time, take your time," Ollie said cheerfully, looking out over the dining space. "Let's eat, shall we?" he said to the others.

They followed him to a table along one of the walls. People stared as they passed. Before Quinn could ask Jaxon where Lukas was, she realize that he was right there, walking with them. Kit squeaked at her from his knapsack.

"How?" she whispered to Lukas, unable to hide her awe.

"Just a little trick," Lukas grinned. "Sometimes people look too hard for something in front of their face."

Quinn was unsure what this meant but didn't question him. She sat on the bench across from Ollie, and Lukas sat beside her, keeping a gap between them for Kit. The fox climbed down from his shoulder to claim the space, resting his head against Lukas and his tail against Quinn. Lukas whispered something about sneaking him some food when it arrived, and Quinn smiled. She watched him scratch Kit's head, understanding more than ever why Jaxon had risked everything for his brother.

A bar maiden nearly collided with their table in her sprint to get to it. She straightened herself, looking flustered, and gawked at Ollie.

"What can I get for you, sir?" she asked breathlessly.

Before he could respond, another maiden pushed herself in front of the girl.

"This is my table, Allison," she said, tossing her blonde hair in the other maiden's face. Allison looked like she wanted to protest, but instead, she huffed and retreated. More than once, Quinn saw her glance back at Ollie.

She'd become very accustomed to people not being able to take their eyes off Mae, so she watched the interactions in fascination. A number of other women at nearby tables were staring at Ollie too. Quinn studied his face, trying to understand what they saw in him. His dark hair and sharp features were handsome enough, but his siren effect didn't work on her. At most, she was amused by his grumpiness and tolerated his facial features.

"Fish stew all around," said Ollie, who seemed not to notice any of the attention.

"Just vegetable stew for me, please," Mae interjected.

The bar maiden scowled at Mae as though she'd been asked to move a mountain, before she left the table in a hurry.

Ollie strummed his fingers together, searching the room around him.

"You're popular," Mae grinned.

He scowled. "A waste to be popular with the wrong crowd."

A sympathetic frown replaced Mae's smile.

Ollie stood. "I need a drink," he said before walking to the bar through a sea of staring women.

Jaxon, who clearly hadn't been paying attention to the conversation, leaned forward. "We can't follow Brazen Way any longer. It's too risky."

Quinn had known this was coming. "We can follow it well enough from a distance," she said. "Mae and I stayed off the main road for a ways too when we traveled to Hyacinth."

"And when we reach the Trade Bridge?" Jaxon asked. "Then what? All of her men will be stationed there. Waiting. They'll know to look for me, too."

"We can wait 'til dark and sneak past them," Quinn said. "We'll figure it out."

Mae cleared her throat. "There's another way. Neither of you will like it. *I* don't like it. It's risky."

They both watched her, waiting.

"We can travel north of Verbena Pool and cut through the Red Forest to the Viridis River. There's a lesser-known crossing south of the Red Forest Port. It's mostly used by gnomes and sirens trying to avoid attention."

"Before the waterfall?" Quinn asked.

"Yes," Mae said. "It's the last place to cross before the river drops into the valley. If we cross there, we'll be past the city walls, just a few hours walk from the Trade Bridge."

"Through the Red Forest?" Jaxon's eyebrows furrowed.

Mae's mouth was twisted in a half smile. She nodded.

"How long would we be in the forest for?"

"A few days, if we move quickly."

Quinn's eyes were on Mae, but she wasn't really looking at her. She was remembering every rumor she'd heard of the Red Forest and the dangers within it. She'd braved the forest with Jaxon not too long ago, but that had only been for a few hours, not overnight.

"And what if the forest works its magic on us?" she asked. "I've heard men sometimes enter it and wake up back where they started. Others enter and never return."

Mae waved her hand dismissively. "You don't have to worry about that," she said. "I know how to move us through the forest."

Quinn turned to Jaxon, who had stayed quiet. "Jax?"

He shrugged his shoulders. "Do we have a choice? It's that or walk past the army of Twelve Pools soldiers waiting near the Trade Bridge."

Quinn couldn't think of an argument for this. "I'm in," she said to Mae. "I'll take a forest trying to kill us over an army trying to kill us."

# CHAPTER 14

# The Market

Jaxon woke the next morning to find Lukas curled up in a ball next to him. His head was digging into Jaxon's armpit, forcing Jaxon to spread his arm across the length of the bed and over the edge of it.

Lukas was breathing lightly. Despite being uncomfortable, Jaxon laid there for a moment and listened. Part of him still couldn't believe his brother was here, safe, and healthy. Finally free of Lux Pox and—equally as important—free of Jasmine. The other part of him was painfully aware that Kiernan and Divoff were out there, searching for them both. Every second they weren't moving was one second that the assassin could be using to gain ground on them. Jaxon knew that if he caught up to them, they wouldn't stand a chance. An image of Divoff swallowing the servant in Jaxon's room flashed in his brain, and he fought a shudder.

In the bed next to them, Quinn snored once and then went quiet again. It looked like Mae had cuddled up against her, one arm draped over Quinn's stomach. Kit was resting on top of Quinn's head, between her red buns. His little black nose pressed against her forehead.

A sliver of sunlight cast a line of light across both beds as the sun rose. Jaxon guessed that Ollie had already left. The gnome had said his farewells the night before, promising to head home early to get away from them as fast as possible. Jaxon was both relieved and disappointed that they were on their own now. Though Ollie had complained a lot, he knew where to go and what was happening, two things that Jaxon hadn't felt sure of in a very long time. Deciding it was time to get up, Jaxon carefully moved his arm out from under Lukas and sat, rubbing his eyes.

"Would you stop trying to cuddle me?"

Quinn had woken and pushed Mae's arm off her. She was now standing and brushing off her dress as though Mae had dirtied it. Looking nearly as annoyed as Quinn, Kit retreated to the warmth of a still-sleeping Lukas, taking up the space that Jaxon had just vacated.

Mae sat up, stretched her arms wide, and yawned. "I thought we were finally becoming friends."

"I don't cuddle my friends," Quinn said.

Mae stood and twirled, her dress falling around her, wrinkle-free as though it hadn't been slept in every day for weeks. "That's silly," she said to Quinn, a twinkle in her eye.

Jaxon shook Lukas gently. As he stirred, Kit's beady eyes peered up at Jaxon as though he'd betrayed him. Lukas hid his face under his arm.

"Not yet," he pleaded.

"Guess you won't mind if we eat breakfast without you then," Jaxon said.

"I'm up, I'm up!" Lukas leapt out of bed amid Mae's musical laughter and joined the others in packing their belongings.

On their way out of Turtle Tavern, they stopped to ask the grumpy old man behind the desk about where they could replenish their supplies. The only food left in their bags was enough bread for a light breakfast and the Root of Twilight Prulane that Ollie had gifted them. However, at the front desk they found the old man fast asleep in his chair, his face pointing to the ceiling and his mouth agape. Jaxon had no desire to wake him.

They left the inn empty handed and made plans to take a quick detour to Verbena Pool's city center to restore their dwindling rations. The others seemed unconcerned, but Jaxon couldn't help worrying. Any interactions they had with people in Twelve Pools increased the likelihood that information on their whereabouts would be reported back to Kiernan or Jasmine. If he encountered any Hyacinth soldiers, they would most likely recognize him.

Verbena Pool was a half day walk from the inn. Lukas kept them entertained with his butterflies, which were getting bigger and more intricate. Jaxon was impressed, but not surprised, to see that his brother's connection to his magic was already growing. Jaxon and Quinn took turns teaching him the breathing techniques they'd learned from Gwen until Lukas's attention faded. Before long, the blue of the lake in the distance sparkled in the sun and they began the descent down to the pool. Just like in Hyacinth, sheep grazed along the hillside and purple flowers dotted the vibrant, tall grass.

Lukas ran in front of them. "Watch this!" he shouted before he fell to the ground and rolled down the hill, almost colliding with one of the sheep. Kit chased after him, diving between the legs of the sheep in an attempt to outrun the rolling boy.

Just like in Hyacinth, Verbena Pool was at the bottom of a valley, but the drop down wasn't nearly as steep as Hyacinth's was. As they approached the shimmering lake, Jaxon surveyed the bustling city wrapped around its edge. Houses lined the shore, and boats were scattered across the still water.

Jaxon tucked his green stone under his tunic as Mae tied her scarf around her head and Quinn wrapped a dark cloth around her waist.

It was midday, and the city was bustling with activity as people went stall to stall, shopping for fabrics, vegetables, and fresh fish. A blacksmith's sign hung crooked over one stall, smoke billowing out one side as a sweating man hammered a sword into shape.

Beside the blacksmith, there was a stand overflowing with traveler's cloaks. The man selling them was holding up a cloth and waving it aggressively, trying to dispel the persistent stream of smoke coming from the blacksmith's fire. He was glaring at the blacksmith, who was blissfully unaware of his disgruntled neighbor.

Mae pulled them over to this stall, and they each picked out a cloak. The autumn temperature had continued to drop, making it more difficult to stay warm at night. As Quinn paid for the cloaks, Jaxon tried not to think too much about their limited supply of valoo and kuwie. He wasn't sure how much she'd taken when she left Viridis, but he knew there couldn't be much left at this point. When he pulled on the cloak and soaked in the new warmth wrapping his body, his reluctance faded.

Lukas tugged on Jaxon's sleeve and pointed out one of the stalls they were passing. *Stone in a Bottle* was written on a large sign in front of it. A man was restocking glass bottles on a wooden wall lined with shelves. The bottles came in different sizes and shapes. Curious, Jaxon looked closer at the labels.

*Fire in a bottle. Healer in a bottle. Love in a bottle.* Each label was colored either red, purple, or green.

"How can I help you, good sir?" The man had noticed him and started pulling the bottles off the shelves. "We got the essence of the stones bottled-up and ready for use! You name it, I got it!" He pushed *Love in a bottle* into Jaxon's face. "You look like you could use this one!"

Jaxon felt his cheeks flush. "No, thanks," he muttered, before hurrying from the stall. Mae caught up and leaned in closer.

"Good choice," she whispered. "You don't need any help with Annabel." The image of Annabel leaning toward him as though to kiss him popped up in his head against his will. His cheeks burned as they flushed even more. He glanced back, hoping Mae hadn't noticed, but she had stopped walking. The others were lingering next to her as she leaned over a small table, admiring a collection of metal jewelry.

She motioned Lukas to come closer. "Where do you feel most connected to your stone?" she whispered to him. Lukas scrunched up his face as he thought.

"My hands, I think," he said. "It feels stronger when I'm holding it."

She touched a long strand of thin metal with small, empty cages lining it. Jaxon guessed the cages were used to hold green stones.

"How much?" she asked, pointing at it.

"Six kuwie for you, beautiful," the woman selling them smiled at her, revealing several missing teeth. Mae dropped the coins into her hand and picked up the necklace. She knelt next to Lukas and wrapped it three times around his wrist before fastening it.

Lukas tilted his head at her, but she held a finger up to her lips. "For later," she said. "For your stone." She touched the empty metal cages hanging from the chain. "Jaxon will have to make you more. Won't you, Jax?"

But Jaxon had stopped listening. He had locked eyes with a man in a black cloak standing at a stall a few feet from them. Intricate gold markings decorated the seams of his cloak, and when the man moved his arm, Jaxon saw that the underside of the cloak matched the golden stitches. There was something particularly unfriendly about the way the man was watching them. Jaxon tried to get Quinn's attention, but as soon as he turned away, the man was gone.

"What is it?" Quinn asked, her hand on her sword as Jaxon searched for the man.

Mae was staring at the exact spot the man had been standing. She put a hand on her stomach. "I felt it," she said. "A lot of negative energy."

Jaxon swore he heard a squeak of agreement from inside the bag on Lukas's back, where Kit was hidden.

Quinn frowned. "We should restock on food and then leave."

The others agreed, and they hurried to the nearest food stand to buy all the fruit, cheese, and bread they could fit into their knapsacks. Quinn led them back the way they'd come, toward the long winding road to the top of the valley.

"He's back," Mae hissed. "Whoever was here, I can feel him again."

Quinn sprinted ahead. Jaxon grabbed Lukas's hand, and they raced after her. She made a sharp turn down one of the roads branching from the main street and then cut down another, doubling back the way they had come. Jaxon struggled to follow her as she weaved down the side streets.

A woman yelped. In front of him, Quinn had taken another sharp turn and nearly collided with the bucket of soapy water the woman was washing a pile of clothes in. Jaxon grabbed Quinn's arm to steady her. Undeterred, Quinn kept moving. She led them down a narrow alley between two houses before she finally stopped.

Jaxon panted in unison with the others, scanning the alley for something, anything, he could use as a defense. The run-down house to their left had vines twisting and growing up the side of it.

"Mae?" Quinn asked as she tried to catch her breath.

But Mae shook her head.

"Everyone stay still," Lukas's little voice was surprisingly firm. "Don't move."

There was no time to question him. Three men in gold-lined cloaks had followed them into the alley. Jaxon froze, but they looked right past him as they searched, all three sets of eyebrows furrowed in confusion.

Lukas's face contorted in concentration. Jaxon reached out to touch him, to see if he could help the same way he'd helped to amplify Mae's visions, but it was too late. A small grunt escaped Lukas's lips, and the three men were no longer looking past them, but instead, straight at them.

Quinn was ready. She yelled as she charged forward with her sword. Jaxon called on his stone and reached for the vines, urging them to grow. They twisted up the ankle of one of the men, pulling him down so hard his face cracked against the stone ground. Jaxon moved the vine up and around the man's legs, wrapping them together so he couldn't move.

Next to him, Quinn was caught between the two men as she parried their swings.

"A little help here!" She jumped sideways as one of the men kicked at her legs. The other soldier took advantage of her moving feet, and his next swing forced her against the wall. She ducked, and his sword hit the stone where her head had been. A loud ringing echoed through the alley.

Jaxon unsheathed his own sword and stabbed wildly at the shorter man on her right. He got a few swings in before the man sent Jaxon's sword flying across the alley, where it hit a wall and clattered to the ground. Jaxon called on the vines again as the man advanced on him.

Mae was screaming, warning Quinn, who was still engaged in her own fight. Jaxon called on his stone and pulled at the vines he'd used to knock the other man to the ground, but he wasn't quick enough. The short man had raised his sword and Jaxon's breath caught in his throat as the blade nearly impaled him.

At the last second, the man hesitated, his sword inches from Jaxon. His wide eyes danced in the light of Jaxon's green stone. Quinn yelled, and the man in front of him was thrown sideways by her tug of air, knocking the sword away from Jaxon's chest.

Jaxon wrapped the vines around the man's waist, slamming his body against the wall. Gasping for air, the man lifted the sword he had managed to hold onto and sliced at the vines.

"It's him!" he was shouting at his friend. "It's him!" But the other man had been sent flying by Quinn. He was on all fours, looking up, blood dripping from a gash on his arm. He held a hand up and pointed past Jaxon, his face stretched in terror.

A loud roar thundered around them. Jaxon followed the sound. At the other end of the alley, a dark figure rose on its hind legs, its mouth open wide as it roared, exposing impossibly sharp teeth. Lukas rushed to Jaxon's side to help him.

"You're getting really good at your illusions," Jaxon breathed in amazement.

Lukas gulped. "That's not me!" he said, grabbing Jaxon's sleeve.

The dire bear fell back on all fours and charged forward. Quinn, on the other side of the alley, let out her own roar of rage as she ran toward the man still on the ground, undeterred by the bear. The two men didn't stick around to find out if they could take on a wild dire bear *and* a wild redhead. They stumbled away and bolted from the alley.

The bear circled back. Its next growl was much softer and showed far less teeth.

"Pima!" Quinn and Mae cried in unison.

"I didn't recognize her!" Jaxon said as a rush of warmth and relief swept him. Pima had grown at least a foot since he'd last seen her. She pushed her nose into Jaxon's hand. He rubbed her head affectionately. He was happy to see her, and not just because she had saved them.

Lukas, seeming to understand that the bear was an old friend, wrapped his arms around her neck. "Thank you for saving us!" he said.

"We can thank Pima later. We'll give her some apples—they're her favorite," Quinn said. "But right now, we should go. We have no idea if those men will come back or if they've got more friends."

Mae was leaning over the other cloaked man, purple light radiating out from beneath her scarf. "Can you give me another minute?"

"We can't stay here," Quinn said. Mae reluctantly pulled away from the man, leaving him unconscious, with half of his body still wrapped in vines.

They hurried the rest of the way between the houses and back up the side of the valley. Jaxon kept glancing over his shoulder, but no one was following them.

"Did you manage to read anything before we left?" Jaxon asked Mae when they emerged from the valley and the city was far behind them.

Mae shook her head. "A little, I'm not sure," she said.

"They weren't my sister's men?"

Mae shook her head again. "No, they were from Windsor. They were . . . they were here for a funeral, I think?"

"A funeral?" Quinn's eyebrows were furrowed in confusion.

"I don't really understand it either," Mae said. She looked at Jaxon. "It was definitely you they were after though. He heard me say your name."

A chill ran down Jaxon's spine. "What was he going to do with me?"

"Take you to Windsor."

Silence followed this. Jaxon wasn't sure what to think. Was it really the Windsor princes after him again? Jasmine had said they wanted him too. None of it made any sense to him.

"Bet they have horses." Quinn broke the silence. "We're going in that direction anyway. Maybe we should've let them give us a ride there."

Mae laughed, and Jaxon couldn't help but smile.

Quinn stopped short. The color had drained from her face. "I told those dumb princes that you could make the nurture stone. The night of the acrobats' show! The reason they were in Viridis was to get the green stone. What if they decided they don't need the stone anymore, they just need *you* to make the stones for them?"

Jaxon's blood ran cold. Quinn was now pacing back and forth, becoming increasingly more distressed.

"That's the reason we went to find you, to help us make more nurture stones so we could use them to bargain for Annabel. What if they had the same exact thought?" She stopped pacing, her hands on either side of her head now. "What if that's why they're after you? This is my fault!"

Jaxon couldn't meet her eyes. He had to tell her. Now. He couldn't hide it any longer. It felt as though his throat closed as he tried to speak. Quinn's only hope for getting Annabel back was to offer Windsor green stones that he made, and he was about to tell her that her plan was impossible. He was about to snuff out all of her hope.

"It doesn't matter." His words stumbled out of his mouth. Quinn stopped, the panic in her face momentarily frozen. Next to her, Mae and Lukas watched silently. In the distance, Pima continued in the direction of the Red Forest, clueless to the commotion behind her. Flashes of Kit's auburn fur appeared as he weaved between the bear's legs.

"What do you mean?" Quinn demanded.

"I can't create the green stone."

"*What do you mean*?" Quinn repeated. "There's proof you can create it around your neck right now. There's proof around my own waist that you can create the red stones. Are you telling me that you lied?"

"I didn't lie. I created those stones. I created more purple stones for Mae too. But I haven't been able to create another green stone."

Quinn shook her head. The light in her eyes dimmed, even as she continued to fight him. "No." Her voice cracked. "You just have to try again. You just have to keep trying."

"I've tried," Jaxon said firmly. "I've tried many times."

Quinn looked like she might continue to argue. Instead, she closed her mouth, and Jaxon watched as defeat washed over her face.

"I—" his words caught in his throat again. "I'm so sorry, Quinn."

"This can't be true," she said through gritted teeth. Her hands were balled up at her sides, and her stones were ablaze in light. "Why didn't you tell me? We came all this way for your green stones."

The words stung. Ever since he'd met Quinn, she had dragged him around using her stubborn insistence that she always knew what was best. Now, she'd put all of these expectations on him that he couldn't meet. Was she really just here for his ability to create stones? Did she even want him here? Were they even friends?

"I didn't want you to come to Twelve Pools," he shot back. "I didn't ask you to save me. And I never lied to you. You got an idea stuck in your head and never stopped to think—or ask—if you might be wrong."

Mae stepped between them, reaching for Quinn's shoulder as her stones ignited. "It's alright, we'll find another way!"

Quinn jerked away from her. She glared at Jaxon through the purple barrier of light that Mae's stones had created between them.

"There's no other way!" she yelled. "We have nothing! It's just the four of us. There's an assassin chasing us, an army waiting for us, a forest that'll make us disappear, and Annabel is far, far away. Farther than she's ever been! There's nothing we can do. I've failed her!"

Jaxon's chest tightened as tears trailed down Quinn's cheeks. It wasn't him she was angry at. It was herself. For not knowing what to do and how to save the person that meant the most to her. He recognized the fear in her voice because he had felt it when trying to help Lukas, when he had first realized he didn't know how to save his brother. His anger calmed as quickly as it had arrived.

Ignoring Quinn's protests, Mae reached forward and wrapped her arms around her friend. Quinn's body remained rigid, refusing to bend into Mae's hug, but her tears stopped, and her glare softened.

"I don't know how we're going to save Annabel," Jaxon said calmly. "But you haven't failed her. We're going to get her back. I won't stop trying. I'm with you, no matter what."

"*We're* with you," Mae corrected as she continued to hold Quinn. The redhead's shoulders sagged as she leaned just a little into the siren's embrace.

"We have to focus on getting to Gwen and Greg so they can warn the Viridis army," Jaxon said. "We have to keep moving forward."

A golden butterfly appeared between them, flapping elegantly as it circled them. Another appeared, and then another, until a hundred butterflies were flying around them, their golden light drowning out the faint purple glow of Mae's stones. Lukas took Quinn's dangling hand and squeezed. He was smiling so big at Quinn that she let out a shaky laugh.

Mae's stones stopped glowing and she pulled back from the embrace, her eyes dancing in the yellow light. "*Just* the four of us," she scoffed. "You mean us and our army of butterflies."

The redhead shook her head. "I didn't mean that." She was looking at Jaxon as she said it. "The four of us are enough." Jaxon answered with a small nod, knowing that she meant that he was enough too, without more green stones. It was the closest Quinn would ever come to admitting to him that she was wrong, but it was good enough for Jaxon.

The faint sound of Pima's roar made them turn their heads. Her distant figure was chasing the barely visible Kit. They'd wasted time arguing, Jaxon knew.

Without another word, the group moved toward Pima and Kit, in the direction of the Red Forest.

# CHAPTER 15

# The Ruins

Quinn lay in the grass, her head propped against Pima's stomach. The bear was resting belly-up, moving her head as Mae tossed apples into her open mouth. In the distance, Lukas and Kit ran in circles as a stream of butterflies followed in their wake.

Lukas's wrist was now wrapped in yellow stones, thanks to Jaxon. All week, the three of them had taken turns giving Lukas lessons. Quinn knew it would be more difficult for him without a yellow stone bearer to teach him, but her best lessons about the red stones had been taught to her by a green stone bearer. So, she focused on trying to pass along the knowledge that Gwen had given her.

The lessons were a good distraction during the day, but as soon as they laid down to sleep, there was nothing to distract her from her own mind. Each night, Quinn stared at the starry sky for hours. Beside her, the purple glow of Mae's stones would dance in the darkness as the siren tried again and again to see from afar, to repeat the magic that Jaxon helped her perform when he amplified her power. Quinn would occasionally try to help talk Mae through some of the struggles she was experiencing, but she mostly lay in silence and tried not to dwell on the fact that she had no idea how they were going to save Annabel.

She felt a twinge of lingering guilt for yelling at Jaxon. A flicker of pain had crossed his face when she claimed they'd only saved him so he could make more stones. It wasn't true. They needed him, with or without the stones. An image of Gwen's face crossed her mind as she remembered the old lady's insistence that Jaxon balanced her out. *I know, I know,* she grumbled to the Gwen that forever lived in her head.

The closer they moved to Viridis, the more she thought of her father. Once they were near the army, it was likely she would see him. The last time they'd spoken, he'd yelled at her for not listening to him. Since then, she'd run away from home, kidnapped a prisoner of Viridis, and traveled to another kingdom. The corner of her mouth twitched.

Pima took a deep breath, and Quinn slid off her belly. Next to them, Jaxon was sorting through the contents of his satchel. She watched with interest as he removed a small golden object from it.

"What's that?"

He tugged on one end of it and the other end sprang open. He held an eye up to it.

"A spyglass," he said. "My mother kept it in her library—above what is now Jasmine's war room. You use it to see things that are far away. She used to watch people at the market. When she knew we were expecting company, she'd find them with the spyglass before they crossed the castle's bridge." He tossed it to her, and she examined the intricate markings decorating it. One of the symbols looked vaguely familiar to her. She ran her fingers over it. It was the mark of a shield enclosed by a circle, but she couldn't quite place where she'd seen the symbol before. She held it up to her eye as Jaxon had, taking in the landscape around them, which appeared a hundred times closer.

Beside her, Pima growled in disappointment as Mae stopped tossing food to her. Quinn turned the spyglass toward her as the siren came closer and laughed.

"Mae, your nose is enormous!"

She scanned the land again, this time looking for Lukas. A burst of yellow light blinded her. She cried out, dropping the spyglass in the grass.

"What is it?" Jaxon rushed over, alarmed. He held out his hand, but Quinn stopped him.

"I'm okay." She rubbed her eye. "The yellow stones on Lukas's wrist just blinded me a little." Jaxon picked up the spyglass and tried it himself, pointing it at Lukas. He also jerked away, rubbing his own eye.

"That's strange." He frowned. "My mother explained how it reflects light, maybe the stones produce too much light for it?" Quinn shrugged, not sure what that meant.

Mae was testing the spyglass now, though she didn't make the mistake of seeking out Lukas.

"I love this," she said. "I like the idea that your mother used this to spy on people. I think I would've liked her."

Jaxon scowled. "She wasn't spying," he protested, looking unusually irritated.

"Maybe she used it to search for a new husband," Mae said. Quinn snorted.

Jaxon snatched back the spyglass, stuffing it into his knapsack once more.

"I wasn't trying to say—I didn't mean—"

He cut Mae off. "It's fine, I know my father wasn't a good man." He stood. "We should start moving, we've lingered here too long."

Quinn began packing up what was left of their lunch. She kept a close eye on Jaxon, but he was no quieter than usual and had returned to his normal demeanor. They weren't walking long before dark red trees appeared on the horizon, expanding as they drew closer to them. There were no paths into the forest. Instead, there were wooden signs urging travelers to take heed or turn back. Though it took a lot to scare Quinn, and it wasn't even her first time in the Red Forest, the warnings made her uneasy.

The wall of trees towered over their heads. Red leaves punctured the ceiling of the forest and layered its floor. Pima barreled forward, crossing into the forest without a second thought, scattering fallen leaves as she did. Kit emerged from the bag on Lukas's back, leapt to the ground, and ran to Quinn's side. She knelt so that he could climb up onto her shoulders, where he sniffed at the air excitedly. Taking his enthusiasm as a sign that the forest would treat them well, Quinn relaxed.

Mae looked at them. "Remember, as long as we don't disturb the peace of the forest, she'll let us pass." Silence followed. She smiled reassuringly and took the first steps forward.

Pima circled back to walk beside Jaxon, already munching on something she'd found on the forest floor. Jaxon put a hand on the bear cub's fur. Beside Quinn, Lukas was looking around in awe. He seemed as happy to be there as Pima was.

As the trees grew thicker around them, the forest became quieter. The loudest sound was their own footsteps as they navigated a terrain of fallen leaves, rocks, and twigs. Quinn found herself more at peace surrounded by trees than she had been out in the open. Here, she didn't have to worry if they were being watched. Jaxon, however, appeared to feel differently. His eyes darted from one direction to the other, his brows furrowed in concern.

She waited until Lukas was distracted before she fell into step next to him.

She didn't have to ask. "Something is following us," he said. "There's someone here."

The words had barely left his mouth when a deer emerged from the trees on their right. Its round eyes spotted them and stopped. It stared right at Jaxon, who held its gaze. There was a moment of silence before Pima growled softly and the deer darted away, disappearing once again between the trees.

Purple stones ablaze, Mae held her hand over Pima's head. "Only happy thoughts, Pima," she whispered, rubbing the bear's head affectionately.

"I'll protect you from the deer, Jax," Quinn grinned.

Jaxon ignored her. "I had the same feeling yesterday, like we were being watched," he said. Quinn's smile vanished, remembering how he'd taken to Mae's comment about his father. He did seem more on edge than usual.

"Mae would've noticed," she said. "She knows when there's danger close."

Jaxon nodded, but his gaze lingered on the space where the deer had vanished.

"I'll keep an eye out too." Quinn pulled her sword from its sheath and fell back behind Jaxon again.

The sky darkened earlier than usual that night, the sun struggling to reach them through the thick trees as it dropped toward the horizon. Quinn shivered, but it wasn't just from the darkness. The farther north they moved, the more it became clear that autumn had settled in. She was grateful for the cloaks they'd bought in Verbena Pool's city center. Even with the extra clothes, Lukas's arms were wrapped tightly around his body. She thought about recommending they stop soon so she could warm them up with a fire, but Mae had come to a halt ahead of them.

The siren stood in front of an archway almost completely obscured by vines. Behind it, an old wall made of red clay bricks protruded from the ground. It looked as though it'd been decaying for thousands of years. Next to it, more fragments were sticking out of the ground, evidence that it had once been a rather large structure.

Quinn studied the markings on the archway. They were faded, and the darkness of the forest wasn't helping with visibility. There was a crack at the top, splitting a circle in the center. Was that a shield?

Mae had noticed her staring. "What's wrong?" she asked.

"I've seen that symbol before," Quinn replied, not taking her eyes off of it. She touched her chest, where she still wore the necklace from Riley under her dress.

A half smile graced Mae's face.

"Riley gave me a necklace with that symbol on it. I used it in the library to enter the tunnels under the castle—to save you, Mae."

She pulled out the necklace, and Jaxon's eyes lit up.

"The spyglass," he said. "That symbol is engraved on my mother's spyglass."

"It's an old symbol," Mae said. She touched the stone archway and her eyes glazed over as though her purple stone was seeing into the life of the stone. "A long time ago, the symbol was used by the guardians of the stones. If you wore that symbol on your robes, it signified a great honor. It meant you were chosen to guard one of the three stones. The guardians were held in high esteem, respected above kings and queens. And maybe that was part of the problem." Mae removed her hand and pulled her gaze away from the archway.

"There were some guardians that were corrupt, hungry for power. It's possible some were just naïve, oblivious to the problems they were creating by withholding the stone from some while others had an abundance. I'm not sure; I wasn't there to see what happened. A lot of the history is buried now, intentionally so. All I know is that a great war erupted over the rights to the stones, not unlike the turmoil we're seeing in the kingdoms now. To protect the three stones, they were each hidden and guarded by enchantments—like the Twilight Prulane. While many sirens and gnomes hid away in Woodpine Hallows, others stayed behind and swore to continue to protect the red stone. They feared that, in the wrong hands, the red stone could cause irreversible damage to the land. They've lived here in the forest for a thousand years, hiding the stone from humans."

Quinn was silent as she absorbed this information. Beside her, Jaxon was studying the archway, looking lost in thought.

"Who hid the stones?" Lukas asked.

Mae was taken aback. "What do you mean?"

"You said the stones were hidden to protect the land. Who hid them?"

She was silent. "I don't know," she admitted. "Maybe the same lineage of sirens and gnomes that dedicated their lives to protecting the red stone."

"Why didn't you tell us sooner?" Jaxon asked.

"Does it matter?" Mae pushed her straight black hair over shoulder. Her beauty screamed for attention even now, when the corners of her lips—normally turned upward—were pulled into a frown. "We can't stop what's been set in motion. And I've already betrayed my people with my actions. Repeatedly, I might add. Telling these stories they've kept from humans for so long—it's the final dagger in their backs."

Quinn glanced from Mae to Jaxon and back again. A fierce pride filled her. In front of her stood two people who had quietly risked everything, who had lost the respect of their people, in pursuit of what they believed in.

"Thank you for trusting some humans—for trusting us," she said to Mae.

The siren seemed taken aback, and then she threw her arms around Quinn and squeezed.

"Alright, alright," Quinn's voice was muffled by Mae's shoulder pressed against her face. "I can't breathe!" Kit had dodged Mae's incoming arms by leaping onto Quinn's head. He climbed back down and licked affectionately at Mae's face.

Quinn managed to pull away.

"Can we set up camp here, or are these ruins sacred?" she asked Mae. The sun had almost set, and the night cold was moving in fast.

"It's safe here," Mae said, still smiling at Quinn's words.

"Lukas, will you take watch for us?" Jaxon asked his brother. Each night before they set up camp, they checked in on Annabel and the Viridis army. Lukas kept guard while they were at work, using the opportunity to practice his own magic and attempt to camouflage them.

Jaxon looked around uneasily before they sat down, but Quinn suspected his worry for Annabel was greater than his worry that something was following them. Each time they tried to look for Annabel, they were met with complete darkness. Mae had promised them she was still alive, but the darkness worried all three of them.

Quinn built a fire, and they sat to the side of it, forming a small circle. Lukas leaned his back against Jaxon's so that he would feel any movement his brother made. Beside him, Pima lay with her head in Lukas's lap while Kit was curled up on Quinn's leg. The fox's head was resting on her knee, and his round eyes reflected back the leaping flames of the fire.

Mae took one of Quinn's hands, and Jaxon took the other. "Where to first?"

"Let's check on Gwen," Quinn said. "We need to know if the Viridis army has left the city walls yet." Quinn knew once the mass of soldiers was in motion, they'd no longer be able to afford to move at the pace they were traveling. They had to reach the men before they passed north of the Trade Bridge.

Mae closed her eyes, and after a moment, the forest and the fire faded from view.

*Quinn recognized the road Gwen was walking down. It was in the southern end of Viridis, close to the city walls . . . Close to Quinn's own home. Her heart ached as she thought of her mother, just out of reach.*

*Beside Gwen, Greg was chattering nonstop. The lantern in his hand was swinging wildly at the same cadence. Even though Quinn couldn't hear her thoughts, she guessed Gwen was only half-listening.*

*"Old lady, are you even listening to me?" Greg demanded, holding the light close to her face.*

*"No, I'm not." Gwen didn't even glance his way. "Take the hint and stop talking."*

*Greg let out a growl of exasperation. "We're heading for war, woman! Pay attention!"*

*But Quinn was no longer listening to Greg either. Gwen had turned her head, and now Quinn could see her mother's house, not far off the main road, tucked on the edge of the valley that overlooked the Viridis River. She stared. There was a wall of vibrant blue flowers growing around the house that had never been there before.*

*Greg followed Gwen's gaze to the same spot. He let out a low whistle.*

*"Don't you say a word," Gwen muttered.*

*"We're coming back, you know?" Greg said. "We'll make it back. This isn't our first war. We did pretty good the last time."*

*Gwen faced him, jabbing a finger into his chest. "Have you learned nothing from me, squire?"*

*"Come now, I haven't been your squire in fifteen years!" Greg protested, rubbing his chest where she had poked him.*

*"Quit acting like one then," Gwen snapped. "It doesn't matter how well we did last time. Skill only gets you so far. Nothing really matters in war, except luck."*

*"And the ladies that greet you when you get home after."*

*Gwen tried and failed to suppress a smile.*

*There was silence before Greg spoke again. "This time, don't go vanishing for ten years after the war," he said. "I don't think*

Quinn could handle that again. She sat at the Red Ferry Port every day for weeks."

Quinn's chest tightened. She was only seven when Gwen had left, but she still remembered her feet dangling over the water as she sat on the dock waiting, hoping that Gwen would return and continue teaching her how to fight.

Greg put a comforting hand on Gwen's shoulder as he studied her face. "I shouldn't have brought that up, it's long forgotten."

The old lady snorted. "We both know that's not true. Quinn's memory is as stubborn as she is. I only hope that by now, she's at least forgiven me for leaving."

I have, Quinn thought to herself. She longed to say it out loud to Gwen.

Gwen's next words were angry. "Is that why she ran off? To punish me? Will she wait ten years to return to Viridis?"

Greg chuckled. "No, we'll find her when we're storming the Windsor castle. She'll have already freed Annabel and probably murdered the princes."

"I'll still be mad at her for making us walk all that way for no reason."

Guilt caught in Quinn's chest again. The idea of having to face Gwen and Greg and tell them that she had nothing to show for running away, except a siren she freed from a dungeon and a prince she freed from his own kingdom, filled her with dread.

*The two crested the next hill. A full view of the Viridis city walls and beyond emerged. The Kamen Mountains spanned the right side of the road, jagged, gray, and reaching so far up they appeared to touch the sky above. On the left side, the Viridis River wrapped along the valley, glittering as it reflected the faint light of the moon. It might have been a beautiful sight but for the sea of lights that dotted Prasine Road, marking the trail of soldiers, horses, healers, and wagons of supplies. The men holding up the rear of the army were still moving, but Quinn could see that up ahead, they'd stopped to set up camp.*

*"We've done all we need to do here," Gwen said. "The king is safe and secure. We need to catch up to the others. Commander Maxwell asked me to hold up the end of the army, not trail hours behind it." She paused. "He also suggested I could leave you behind to help protect King Edward in case—"*

*Greg scowled as he cut her off. "I'm not leaving you," he said.*

*Gwen stared at the ground. "C'mon," she said. This time her voice was soft.*

*As they hurried down the path toward the army, the vision faded.*

Quinn opened her eyes. Jaxon and Mae were both staring at her as though they expected her to make a sudden movement. They looked relieved when she didn't.

"We can make it," Mae said, still watching her carefully. "Armies move slowly. We'll have to move a little faster, but we can still get to them before they reach the Trade Bridge."

Quinn nodded, painfully aware of the knot in her stomach that had been becoming more and more tangled the last few days. She didn't want to think about how little time they had to reach Greg and Gwen. There was nothing they could do about it now.

She swallowed the anxious bubble trying to escape her stomach. "Show me, Anna, please," she said instead.

The red of the fire faded once again, and black took its place.

*The familiar darkness was punctured by the sound of Annabel breathing quickly and a loud creaking sound, like wheels spinning just slightly off axis. Quinn guessed she was in a carriage of some kind. Annabel kicked her feet hard against the wall, and the sound echoed around her. The carriage stopped abruptly, and she lurched forward. The door opened a crack. A blonde-haired man held a lantern up to the opening. The flickering light gave his brown eyes an amber hue.*

*"Princess, please," Liam said softly. "I'm trying to help you. I brought you with us because I thought it would be safer for you."*

*Annabel spit in his face.*

*Liam was expressionless as he reached a hand up to wipe it off. The crinkles that normally graced the corners of his mouth straightened. Without a word, he pushed the door to the carriage closed.*

Quinn yanked Mae's arm, dragging all three of them back to the present. "Can you try to see what Prince Liam is seeing?" she asked, not for the first time.

Mae frowned. "He's harder to reach. None of us know him well, so our connection to him will be very weak. Jonathan might be easier—" But Quinn gave her a look. Mae sighed and closed her eyes.

A dark and blurry landscape greeted them, cast in the light of a full moon. Voices muttered and then faded. They were back in their own present, sitting beside the fire. Mae scowled in frustration.

"Wait," she said, her face contorted in concentration.

*The countryside appeared again. Though still blurry, Quinn didn't have a hard time recognizing the dark black curls she was seeing now. Her body tensed in rage. She fought to stay calm so she wouldn't accidentally pull the three of them back to the fire.*

*"That's not what I was saying." Jonathan's voice sounded muffled, but she could still make out the anger in it. The two princes were walking side by side. Quinn thought she could see Annabel's carriage being pulled by a couple of horses ahead of them, past some soldiers clothed in the dark blue of Windsor.*

*Liam put a hand on his shoulder. "It's better this way."*

*Jonathan didn't say anything. He pressed his palms into his eyelids.*

*"Is it the redhead, again?"*

*"She's there every time I close my eyes," Jonathan admitted. Quinn froze. Had she heard that right? Jonathan was thinking about her? "In my dreams, there's a sword in my chest. I'm bleeding to death, and she's standing over me, barring her teeth like a wild animal."*

*Liam laughed as Quinn's mouth tightened, and she wished more than anything she was there now to make his dreams come true.*

*"You may want to have one of the purple stone bearers take a look at your head," Liam said, squeezing his shoulder.*

*Their voices faded.*

Mae had lost her grip on them again. She put her hand over her mouth, hiding a smile.

"I think I've woken up from that same nightmare once or twice," Jaxon said solemnly. Mae tried to voice her agreement but couldn't manage it over a fit of giggles.

"What happened?" Lukas asked. He had jumped up from where he sat behind Jaxon and was leaning on his shoulder. In Quinn's lap, Kit's head was cocked, mirroring Lukas's curiosity.

Quinn huffed. "I hope you both have that dream again tonight."

"What was it?" Lukas asked eagerly.

"We saw a man talking about how scared he is of Quinn," Jaxon said. Quinn scowled at him, trying to ignore how hot her cheeks had gotten.

This explanation seemed to disappoint Lukas. "He's right to be scared of her," he said, shrugging his shoulders as though they'd pointed out that grass was green.

Jaxon grinned at his brother. "Yes," he said. "Yes, he is."

Quinn couldn't help it, the corner of her mouth curled up in a smile. She ducked her head, looking down at her lap, where Kit had settled once again on her knee.

"Lukas is always right," Mae said in a melodious voice.

Out of the corner of her eye, Quinn saw Lukas tilt his head forward, indicating that this too was an obvious thing to say.

When she felt her flushed cheeks return to normal, Quinn looked back up and noticed that Jaxon's eyes were on Mae. The siren guessed what he was thinking. "Another?" she asked sweetly.

"One more, if you have the energy for it. My sister."

Mae took their hands once more.

*They were in a large bedroom that reminded Quinn vaguely of the layout in Annabel's room. There was a small sitting area and a balcony overlooking what Quinn assumed was Lake Hyacinth. Over the bed hung a large painting of an Abaia, the creature that marked the seal of Twelve Pools, the one they'd encountered in the lake.*

*Unlike Annabel's room though, this room felt cold, designed for use, not for comfort. Everything in it was made of a dull metal, allowing for only the occasional pop of purple. The windows were wide open, and a steady breeze blew cold air into the* room. Quinn could just make out a large map stretched out on the table in the sitting area. The corner of the map kept lifting as the wind threatened to blow it away.

The room flickered in and out of focus, and Quinn felt Mae's hand tighten around hers. She thought for a minute that they might be pulled back to the fields, but Mae held her ground. When the flickering stopped, they were in a new room. A large table in the center of it was surrounded by a circle of stained-glass windows. Quinn recognized it as the war room in the Twelve Pools castle, where they'd seen Jasmine when they last spied on her.

There was a short, muscular man bent over the table, studying the exact same enormous map they had seen in Jasmine's bedroom. Quinn was struck by the man's familiar features, his tussled brown hair and freckled face. Even his eyes were the same color as Jaxon's, but harder somehow.

"Come," he said to Jasmine. "I'll show you." He motioned for her to join him at the table. As she walked forward, Quinn registered the height she was seeing from. Her suspicions were confirmed. This was a shorter Jasmine, a younger one. They were in one of Jasmine's memories.

King Alexander put an arm around his daughter and pulled her closer. He pointed at Twelve Pools on the map and then followed the route north and over the Trade Bridge, up the mountains past Viridis. He grabbed both of her shoulders and searched her face. Quinn could just make out the reflection of Jasmine's dark hair, decorated by purple stones.

"This is why we can't trust anyone from outside of Twelve Pools, isn't it, little one?" the king asked. She nodded firmly, and he looked past her, over her head, his eyes twinkling. "Except Kiernan, of course."

Jasmine turned her head, and Quinn was surprised to see Kiernan standing there. She hadn't noticed him before. He bowed his head in response to the king but said nothing.

"There you are!" A woman had arrived. She was wearing a floor length violet gown, and her chestnut brown hair neatly framed the golden crown perched on her head. Her cheeks were flushed pink. She glanced at Kiernan standing there and nodded at him, but seemed too excited to let his presence stop her from speaking.

"I've been looking for you both. I have good news from the healer," she said.

Younger Jasmine folded her arms and held her head high. "You're pregnant," she said. Her voice sounded indifferent to Quinn, almost cold.

The king made a sound halfway between a gasp and a shout. "Is it true?"

Queen Sophia was undeterred by Jasmine spoiling her news. Her smile eclipsed half her face, and Quinn saw Jaxon's kindness in the folds of her wrinkled eyes.

*King Alexander picked her up and twirled her. "Another baby!" he cried. As they celebrated, Jasmine stood still, unmoving. Finally, Queen Sophia seemed to notice her sadness. She moved to Jasmine and squatted in front of her, one hand resting on her own stomach as though protecting the new, growing baby. When she reached for Jasmine's face with her other hand, the young girl pulled away.*

*"Jasmine!" King Alexander's voice was sharp.*

*The queen looked hurt. She bowed her head and was still for a moment before she retreated. Something told Quinn this wasn't the first time Jasmine had been unkind to her mother.*

*"I think I might lie down," she said to the king. He let her leave before turning to Jasmine.*

*"Apologize to your mother immediately," he demanded. "Tell her you're excited for the baby, and that you'll love him."*

*Jasmine didn't budge. "No," she said. "I won't love him. He's going to kill her! The goddess of clarity told me so."*

*Mouth agape, King Alexander stared at her. He commanded Jasmine to tell him what she meant, but the room was flickering again, and then they were back in the present, inside Jasmine's bedroom. In two quick strides, the grown Jasmine glided to her bedside table. Resting on it was a small hand mirror, the sides decorated with intricate flowers. She picked up the mirror and held it up to her face.*

*Dark green eyes with impossibly long lashes stared back at them. Quinn was struck by how beautiful she was. Her sharp jawline and high cheekbones looked to be carved from stone. Though Quinn saw hints of Jaxon's features, there was a softness to him that was absent in hers.*

*She stared into the mirror so intently Quinn thought she was trying to use her mind to crack it. Her lips thinned, and her eyes narrowed.*

*"Get out," she hissed. A shiver ran up and down Quinn's back. Was she looking at them? Suddenly, she wasn't sure if she was in Jasmine's mind or if Jasmine was in hers. "GET OUT!"*

They were thrown backwards, into the hard forest ground.

"*Jaxon!*" Lukas, who had been propped against Jaxon, had also been pushed back. He was now kneeling beside Jaxon in concern.

Quinn lifted herself off the ground, brushing off her dress. "Did she just—"

Mae sat up, her hand over her mouth again, this time in shock. "It's not possible." Her face was pale, and her hand shook. Quinn imagined the vision must have taken a lot out of her.

Jaxon was assuring Lukas that they were okay, but Quinn couldn't help but notice that he didn't seem okay. He was just as pale as Mae was.

"Were you trying to look into her past?" Quinn asked.

The siren shook her head. "I think she must have been looking at her own past when we entered her brain, and that's why we were in her memory. Jaxon amplifies me, but it's still much harder for me to see and understand what I'm seeing from afar like this." She tried to stand but seemed to think better of it. A concerned Jaxon hurried to her side, his stone glowing as he worked on her. Some color returned to her face almost instantly.

Quinn watched him. "Did you know?" she asked. "Did you know that—" She stopped midsentence and glanced at Lukas, worried about the words she chose next. But the boy was still concerned with Mae's well-being, busy trying to make her laugh as Jaxon restored her energy. Quinn didn't want him to know what Jasmine had said and done. She hoped Lukas never found out that his sister blamed him for the death of their mother.

Jaxon frowned and shook his head at Quinn, seeming to understand her question, even though she hadn't finished asking it.

Rage bubbled inside of Quinn. She was overcome with a mad desire to journey back to Twelve Pools and attack the queen for what she'd done to the boys that were supposed to be her brothers, neither of whom deserved her cruelty.

"We can't go back ever," Jaxon said, and Quinn knew he was referring to Jasmine's mind. She nodded in agreement, along with Mae.

It wasn't until they were roasting mushrooms over the fire sometime later that they told Lukas some of what they'd witnessed. Quinn listened but didn't join the discussion, staring at the flames as they flickered and jumped, creating a trail of smoke up through the trees and obscuring the stars above. The shock of Jasmine seeing them had worn off. Instead, her mind kept going back to the creaky carriage and Annabel. Where were they taking her friend? And why?

# CHAPTER 16

# The Forest Guardian

Jaxon's eyes snapped open as Mae's scream yanked him from sleep.

A hooded man hovered inches from his face. The light from the fire revealed gray hair and a scarred face. *The assassin.* A ripple of terror coursed through his body. He flipped himself over, almost rolling into the fire pit. He leapt to his feet and drew his sword, his shaking hands struggling to hold it up. Where were the others?

A blur of red pushed past him, screaming. Quinn's sword moved effortlessly back and forth as she countered Kiernan's attack.

"Jaxon!" Lukas yelled. "*Divoff!*"

The enormous lizard's claws were tearing into the ground as it scampered toward a defenseless Mae. She held up her hands, her head glowing purple. Jaxon sprinted at her and dove, knocking them both out of the way of the lizard. It closed its mouth on air as they tumbled across the ground. Jaxon grabbed Mae's arm and yanked her up. Lukas ran to them, and Jaxon held up one hand, shielding him behind his own body.

"He won't respond to that!" Jaxon yelled to Mae, whose head was still glowing purple.

"No, but he might respond to *that!*" Mae said. Pima, who must have wandered from the campsite while they slept, was now bounding toward them. She spotted the lizard and rose onto her hindlegs. Her roar echoed throughout the forest. When she fell back to all fours, her paws ripped at the lizard. Divoff screeched, but his skin was unmarked, protected by thick scales.

Kiernan must have heard the lizard's cry. He was sprinting toward them. Behind him, Quinn had been knocked to the ground. She rolled to a stand and chased after him. Jaxon reached for the roots in the ground as the assassin ran at Pima, pulling a dagger from the strap on his chest. A wall of vines grew in front of the cub, blocking the dagger that came flying at her.

Quinn was seconds behind him, she slammed a blast of fire into Kiernan's back. He tumbled past the bear as the fire seared his cloak, his sword inches from scraping Pima's back. Quinn flew past Jaxon, her sword engulfed in flames as she advanced on Kiernan. The assassin had ripped off his cloak, which was still on fire, and flung up his sword as Quinn attacked. They disappeared from Jaxon's line of sight.

In the distraction, Divoff had moved in on Pima. He whipped his tail at the bear, and it made contact, ripping the fur from her leg. A small pool of blood trickled to the ground. Pima didn't seem to notice; she was already attacking again. She slammed into his side, her head under his belly as she tried to flip him. He didn't budge, but turned, mouth open to bite her—

Green clouded Jaxon's vision as he called on the tree roots beneath the lizard. He wasn't quick enough this time. The lizard's teeth sank into the bear's leg, and Pima roared in pain. The roots that Jaxon had called on burst from the soil, but the lizard had vanished. Fear gripped Jaxon as he searched for him. Divoff's camouflage was even more effective in the dim firelight. Jaxon scanned the ground for any glimmer of movement as he backed up, holding his arm out as though that might be enough to block Divoff from attacking Mae and Lukas. Distant yells and flashes of fire came from the trees Quinn and Kiernan had disappeared into.

He ached to help Quinn. But right now, Pima needed him more. The bear was struggling to shake off the effects of the bite as she moved toward them, a wobble in her step.

"Jax, look out!" Lukas yelled.

The dirt on the ground shifted as Divoff's camouflaged feet moved through it. There was a flash of movement as the lizard leapt at them, his mouth open as he prepared to bite. Jaxon threw up his hands, a wall of roots springing up in front of him. The lizard dropped to the ground, skittering to a stop and slammed into the wall. Jaxon felt the roots strain as the enormous lizard collided with them.

Divoff tore at the roots with his claws, creating a giant gash through the lower half of the wall. Pima was following his movement. She charged toward him, and Divoff sensed her too late, turning just as Pima barreled into him. The collision sent both of them tumbling into the root wall where they broke through to the other side. Jaxon dove out of the way, dragging the other two with him.

The bear and lizard tumbled to a stop. Jaxon looked for an opening in their movement, his green stone glowing around his neck. He heard Quinn scream from the forest and itched again to help her, but both creatures had returned to their feet. Pima's claws swiped at the lizard's throat, but Divoff ducked under her outstretched paws. He thrashed his long tail as he moved sideways, leaving a deep gash across the bear's belly.

Pima roared in rage and charged once again. She lowered her head and pushed it beneath Divoff, between his legs, driving her body under his stomach with such force that she flipped the enormous lizard onto his back. Her claws ripped into the underbelly of the lizard, this time successfully puncturing the skin and leaving behind four long, red marks.

Jaxon didn't hesitate. He called on the roots beneath Divoff. They erupted from the ground, and Jaxon wrapped them around the top half of Divoff's open mouth, obscuring his teeth and fastening him to the ground, upside down. Beside him, Pima was retreating, her growls turning to whimpers. She collapsed some feet away, and Jaxon tried not to focus on her cries of pain.

Mae and Lukas ran to Pima's side. Jaxon fought the urge to join them and heal the bear. He needed to make sure Divoff was trapped before he helped Quinn with the assassin. He searched deeper in the ground and pulled up more roots, circling the upper half of the lizard's mouth and pulling it tighter to the ground. Divoff tugged his head from side to side, attempting to free himself. A loud screech escaped him and echoed through the trees around them as he chomped his jaw together. The roots held strong even against his sharp teeth. His forked tongue slithered, searching the air fruitlessly. Jaxon wrapped Divoff's tail in roots and then his belly, until he was almost entirely covered. As he squeezed the roots tighter, blood escaped the wound across the creature's belly, dripping blood onto the dirt beneath him.

Kiernan seemed to have sensed that Divoff was in trouble. He had backed Quinn closer to them, out from the cover of the trees. He ducked beneath her next swing, but instead of countering, he slashed at the roots binding Divoff. Quinn cried out in rage. She stepped onto the lizard's root-covered body and pushed off him, her sword flying to block Kiernan from cutting the roots. The assassin growled in rage, and there was a flash of metal as he dislodged one of his daggers. The blade made contact, burying into her chest mid-air. Quinn fell backward, tumbling on the ground.

"No!" Jaxon screamed. He couldn't think, couldn't see straight. He had to get to her, he had to make sure she was okay.

He ripped up at vines beneath Kiernan's feet, but the assassin dodged them before they emerged from the dirt, as though he could feel the rumbling of their movement beneath him. He danced across the ground and then swiped again at the vines binding Divoff, this time slicing through some of them. It was clear Kiernan's focus was on freeing Divoff. As the assassin hacked at the roots, Jaxon abandoned them and rushed to Quinn's side, his neck glowing. She had already ripped the dagger from her chest. It was on the ground beside her, stained red with her blood. The small blade seemed too large to Jaxon, knowing it had just been buried in Quinn's chest.

He held shaking hands over her and reached inside with his magic, feeling the depth of the wound as he pulled it together as quickly as he could. Kiernan had missed vital organs. Relief flooded him.

Mae joined them. She was out of breath, but she leaned in close to Quinn to examine her wound.

"She's alright," he promised her. "Bleeding has stopped. Stay still!" he barked at Quinn as she fumbled with her gloves. Light obscured his vision, a flame now nestled in her palm. He jumped to the side, and she pushed her hand forward. The assassin, still hacking at the roots to free Divoff, spun to the side just in time. The edge of his sleeve had caught fire, but he ignored it. Mae pulled Quinn to her feet.

Jaxon stared at the wet blood on her tunic. "Quinn, let me finish healing—"

A flash of metal and another dagger whistled through the air, straight at him. Jaxon's vision was clouded by red light. He felt the air move, as Quinn pushed the dagger aside. It narrowly missed his face and buried itself in the tree over his shoulder.

Quinn let out a growl of rage not unlike Pima's and shot another fireball at the assassin. Jaxon's stone lit up as he pulled at the roots beneath Kiernan's feet. The assassin, already dodging a series of fireballs from Quinn, didn't move his feet in time. The roots connected, and Jaxon used them to grab Kiernan's foot. Kiernan lost his balance and fell, throwing out his hand to brace himself. Jaxon reached into the ground, and the next roots that sprang up latched onto the assassin's arm.

Kiernan drew a knife with his free hand, slicing at the roots around his bound hand and freeing himself in time to send another dagger at Quinn. She swiped it to the side with a gust of air and flung another ball of fire.

Jaxon was calling on his magic again when something moved just over Kiernan's shoulder. Round, black eyes were watching him. It was a deer. The same deer that had been following them as they journeyed through the forest. Jaxon blinked and the deer vanished.

Beside him, Divoff screeched and broke free from the roots. Jaxon tore his attention away from the assassin and rushed at the lizard, his neck glowing green.

"Get back!" Mae's yell was loud and terrified. "Jax, Quinn, run!"

An enormous golden creature leapt from between the trees and landed feet from Jaxon. He froze as the wolf snarled, saliva dribbling between its fangs. Its thick fur glistened in the light of the moon. Jaxon wanted to move, to run, but the wolf's immense golden eyes locked onto him and seemed to stare into his soul.

Divoff didn't hesitate; he snapped at the wolf's legs. The golden creature bounded over his open mouth and onto the lizard's back. Divoff spun, trying to dislodge him. The wolf lowered his head and tore his fangs into the lizard's throat.

Blood sprayed outward as Divoff's mouth opened wide but no sound came out. He collapsed as all the air went out of him.

The wolf's bloody snout pointed up at the sky as it emitted a loud, eerie howl. Someone grabbed Jaxon's arm and pulled him backward.

"We need to get out of here," Quinn hissed. As he turned to follow, he saw Kiernan rushing toward Divoff, a rare glint of fear in his eyes. The assassin didn't seem to notice they were retreating.

Mae and Lukas were running up ahead. They had picked up Jaxon and Quinn's packs. Kit was in the bag on Lukas's back, watching them as his little head bounced up and down in tune to Lukas's footsteps. The group darted between trees, putting as much distance between themselves and the giant wolf as they could. Pima was keeping pace but barely. Her wounded leg trembled, nearly buckling under her weight every time it connected with the ground.

When they were sure they had left the others long behind, Mae stopped and they all dropped to the ground, panting. Pima collapsed onto the dirt and lay still, her breathing labored. *Hold on a little longer, Pima,* Jaxon silently pleaded. He needed to check on Quinn's wound first. It had opened up again, and she looked like she was having trouble sitting upright. Jaxon suspected she was about to faint. He hurried to her side, guiding her head to the ground. He knew by her lack of protesting that she had lost a lot of blood. As his magic worked to repair the small hole in her chest, the color returned to her face. She pressed a hand to her closed skin and muttered her thanks.

Mae was watching, waiting patiently. "I need everyone to let me into their minds," she said, once Jaxon had helped Quinn sit up. "I'm going to calm us."

"There's a giant wolf out there, and you want us to stay calm?"

"Quinn, please," Mae said. The redhead pursed her lips but didn't protest further. Mae's head lit up in a crown of purple, and Jaxon's heartbeat slowed as his adrenaline dipped. Next to him, Quinn's scowl softened. His head now clear, Jaxon hurried to Pima's side and focused on her wounds, basking her in the soft green light of his stone.

"That was an ancient guardian of the forest," Mae said, when her purple light had faded. "We disturbed the peace; it didn't like that."

"Won't it come after us?" Lukas asked, peering anxiously through the trees.

"If we stay calm and our intentions are to be peaceful, I think it'll let us be."

Jaxon stopped moving his magic through Pima to look up at Mae. "Was Divoff—is he dead?" He had felt the life go out of the creature but still couldn't believe it. He had spent his whole life avoiding any room Divoff was in.

"Yes," Mae shuddered. "I still feel Kiernan's anguish. It was . . . powerful."

"And Kiernan?" Jaxon asked, tentatively. "Is he alive?"

Mae frowned. "I'm not sure. His grief may have spared his life. I don't think there was any fight left in him after Divoff passed. The forest guardian only attacks those who threaten the forest, and he was no threat to anyone in that state."

Jaxon focused on Pima again. He had closed all of her wounds except for the mark where Divoff had bitten her. He tried to push through it, but the wound fought back, resisting his magic. He pushed harder, forcing the nurture stone's magic deeper and pulling the flesh closed. Pima grunted softly, and Jaxon could hear the pain her voice. The marks where Divoff's tiny teeth had pierced Pima's skin reopened, sprouting beads of fresh blood. Alarmed, Jaxon tried again and again. Each time, it was as though his magic were entering the wound and then disappearing.

Quinn put a hand on his shoulder, stopping him. The others were looking on with concern.

Mae's head was shrouded in a haze of purple. "She's in a lot of pain, and she's scared," the siren said.

"I can't heal her," Jaxon said. "The wound won't close . . . It's resisting my magic. I think there's venom in Divoff's teeth."

Pima growled, and Mae put her hand on the cub's snout, trying to soothe her. Lukas threw his arm around the bear's neck, squeezing it in what Jaxon thought was probably not a helpful way. Kit emerged from his bag and was sniffing at the bear's fur. He leapt from Lukas's back and found the bite marks on Pima's leg, where he sniffed again, this time cautiously. He looked up at Jaxon, his head cocked to one side, as if to confirm with him that this was where the problem was.

Jaxon scratched behind the fox's ear in thanks, before returning his hands to Pima's leg. The bear's skin was hot to the touch. Jaxon again wove the skin together near the wound, and again, it came undone almost as soon as he had finished.

"What do we do?" Quinn asked. Her eyes were creased in worry as she knelt beside the bear, allowing Kit to climb onto her shoulder.

Mae was staring into the black of the forest. "I might know someone who can help." Her voice was calculated, hesitant. "An old friend."

"Are they close?" Jaxon asked.

"Close enough." Mae stood and faced the other way. She pointed in the direction they'd been heading. "Keep walking that way for as long as you can. I'll find you." She glowed purple as she placed her hands on Pima again. The bear's response was a soft snort of air.

"Find us?" Quinn frowned. "Shouldn't we go together?"

"I need to move quickly and quietly," Mae said. "And you're very bad at one of those things." She secured her bag on her back.

Lukas took a break from hugging Pima, to hug Mae instead. "Hurry back, Lady Mae," he said. She wrapped her arms around him and pulled his head into her chest.

"I'll be back as soon as I can," she promised, before letting him go. The three of them watched her dart through the trees and vanish into the night. From Quinn's shoulder, Kit squeaked loudly.

Pima stood and hobbled forward, with Lukas keeping one hand on her as he walked at her side. Jaxon and Quinn exchanged worried glances before the two of them followed Pima and Lukas farther into the forest.

Moonlight trickled through the branches overhead, giving them just enough light to navigate the uneven forest floor. The less light and noise they created, the better. Without Mae to guide them, the Red Forest was considerably more intimidating. Even Quinn was more on edge than usual, glancing over her shoulder, though Jaxon wasn't sure what was making her more nervous: the absence of their companion or the thought of Kiernan lurking somewhere out there.

They continued onward, with the occasional stop to let Pima rest. Jaxon had lost all concept of time, but it felt like hours had passed and still Mae was nowhere to be seen. He was unsure how long they had slept before Kiernan and Divoff had woken them and even more unsure of how long it had been since the attack. After one particularly long rest, they tried to move again, but Pima refused to even open her eyes. Her breathing was shallow, and her skin was so warm it almost hurt to touch her. Jaxon did what he could to push his magic through her body, fighting back against the toxins spreading farther throughout her.

"We have to rest," Quinn said. Even in the dark, the bags under her eyes were visible. Lukas had already fallen asleep against the bear's stomach, Kit curled up in his lap. "I'll start a fire."

Jaxon nodded and set up their fur skins. Quinn gathered a few nearby branches and piled them close to where Jaxon was making their beds. He took off his cloak and draped it over Lukas, who was shivering.

When Quinn had finished putting together a small pyramid of wood, she pulled one of her gloves on and crouched down next to Jaxon.

She hesitated before she spoke. "Will you let me try something?"

Too exhausted to worry about what she was about to do, Jaxon nodded. She put her gloveless hand on his shoulder. A weird, familiar sensation swept over him, the same drain of energy that happened when Mae used him to amplify her visions. Almost immediately, a flame flickered persistently in the palm of Quinn's hand. Her eyes glowed red in the light of the fire as she smiled at Jaxon. He looked back in astonishment. He'd heard rumors of stone bearers materializing the elements from nothing, but he'd never seen it done.

Her hand still on his shoulder, Quinn grew and shrank the fireball cupped in her hand.

"Mae was right," she said. "She told me if you could amplify her power, you could probably amplify any stone bearer's power. You're just like the source of the stones, except you're not just the source of one stone, you're the source of all of them."

*Creator of the stones.* The banished seer's words echoed in his head, causing an avalanche of other questions. He had avoided thinking about it all as much as possible, but it kept resurfacing in different ways. How was he able to create stones? How was he able to amplify the power of others' stones? He, of all people, who barely knew how to wield his own magic. He wished he could give the abilities to Quinn instead. She wouldn't be shy about using them.

Quinn lit the pile of sticks she had gathered. She seemed to notice that Jaxon wasn't as thrilled as she was.

"This is a good thing," Quinn said, shaking his shoulder. "This'll help us."

"What will?" Jaxon protested. "I have no idea what this even is."

"Well, that doesn't seem to be stopping you from being able to use it, does it?"

Jaxon smiled weakly and searched her face. He'd never tell her this—he knew it would pain her to be compared to her father—but her eyes were the same icy blue as Commander Maxwell's.

"You think too much." Quinn smiled back at him. The ice of her eyes turned to water as they crinkled at the corners. "Go to sleep before I decide to make you take first watch."

Jaxon went to lay down next to Lukas when he heard the faint rustle of leaves. He called on his stone as Quinn drew her sword beside him.

A dim purple light illuminated the darkness, and a wave of calmness washed over him. Jaxon let the light of his stone die out as Mae moved closer to the fire.

She was dragging her feet and her eyes were red, but she was clutching a small glass vile filled with a murky looking liquid. Without a word, the three of them gathered around Pima's injured leg. She applied the ointment, and Pima kicked her leg out, nearly connecting with Jaxon. Quinn moved to Pima's head, rubbing her snout and whispering words of comfort. The bear grunted softly, and her head relaxed in Quinn's lap.

Jaxon called on his stone and closed his eyes as he reached into the wound. The ointment was pulling at the toxins. He pulled with it, feeling it drain from Pima's leg. When he was sure the last of it was gone, he wove the skin back together. He opened his eyes to find Mae using leaves to clean away the black ooze the ointment had extracted from Pima's leg.

Quinn smiled over at him as Pima stirred in her lap. Jaxon ran his magic through Pima once more, feeling for any lingering aches and pain. The bear lifted her head and grunted a puff of air in his direction, as if to reassure Jaxon that she was alright. He rubbed her belly in acknowledgement. A wave of relief washed over him. Mae offered a hand to pull him to his feet, his relief reflected in her tired eyes.

The three of them finished setting up their mats and laid down beside Lukas, who hadn't even stirred. Kit, however, had woken in the commotion. He found his way to Quinn and curled up near her chest.

Jaxon tried not to think about Kiernan, out there somewhere, probably hunting them once again, but it was no use. His body was tense, and he was afraid to close his eyes. He peered over at Mae, who was still awake, staring at the stars.

"Is he near?" Jaxon whispered to her.

She shook her head. "We're safe for now. You can sleep for a little. I won't let him get close again."

Pima began to snore. The gentle rumblings of her breathing were loud in the quiet of the forest. Jaxon felt oddly comforted by the sound. It felt almost like a lullaby creating a protective bubble around them. Jaxon lay listening to it as he stared up through the tree line until his eyelids became heavy and he drifted to sleep.

# CHAPTER 17

# The River Crossing

Quinn was relieved to see the trees thinning as they neared the edge of the forest. She wasn't sorry to leave it behind. They'd only slept for a few hours and hadn't taken time to eat breakfast that morning. Jaxon was still jumping at every snap of a twig or rustle of leaves, and Quinn was sure he hadn't stopped thinking about Kiernan. She knew that the sooner they crossed to Viridis, the safer they'd be. Pima, on the other hand had made a full recovery and kept bounding ahead of them, Lukas at her heels.

"We should stop soon for lunch," Quinn said when she noticed Lukas's pace had slowed. They needed energy. Mae had been leading the way through the forest and, unlike Jaxon, had not once looked around at their surroundings. Her unusually grim expression set Quinn on edge more than Jaxon's nerves. Mae hadn't told them who had given her the ointment that healed Pima. Had she stolen it? Could the person who gave it to her be following them now?

"A quick lunch." Mae didn't turn to look at Quinn but continued to fixate on the path ahead. "We're getting close; we can rest once we cross the river."

Jaxon had dropped back to listen. "First, we need to find out where Gwen and Greg are so we can find them when we cross."

Mae frowned but gave him a curt nod of agreement.

Quinn couldn't help it. "Do you not trust your friend?" she blurted.

The siren pursed her lips together, and for a moment, Quinn thought she might not answer. "I trust her like you'd trust Sir Greg with a secret," she said. "He might not share it intentionally, but he'd forget to be quiet about it."

"What's her name?" Jaxon asked.

The question seemed to catch the normally unfazed Mae off guard. "Adelina," she whispered. Something gave Quinn the impression that this was more than just a friend, but she didn't press her. "She's a skilled healer, one of the best in the siren clans. I knew she'd have what we needed."

"The reunion was painful," Jaxon stated as he eyed her. Quinn guessed he'd reached the same conclusion she had.

Mae's smile was shaky. "Our friendship is better left in the past," she said.

Quinn wanted to ask what would happen if the other sirens found out she was here, but Mae was clearly uninterested in continuing the discussion. Quinn was used to Mae sharing her emotions and thoughts eagerly and often, even when Quinn insisted that she didn't want to hear any of it. It was strange to be prying information from her.

Mae didn't say anything about Adelina again, and the group continued through the forest in silence. When Quinn was just about ready to stop for lunch, they came across an enormous tree. Layers of long, thick stems were covered in dark red leaves and wrapped the tree like curtains. Quinn followed the others under the tree, ducking beneath the lower layer to enter. Pima was less graceful, snapping one of the branches in half in her attempt to leap through them.

It was quiet in the shelter of the tree. Quinn looked up at the hundreds of twisting branches above and around her that were now locking them securely behind their layers, hidden from the rest of the forest.

"It's a copper beech tree," Jaxon said. He was holding Gwen's Guide open in his hands, and his eyes were darting across the page in a way that reminded Quinn of Annabel. Next to them, Mae snapped a small, fuzzy-looking object from a nearby branch and broke it open, revealing an oval-shaped brown nut. Lukas had taken interest in what she was doing and hovered over her outstretched hand, examining it with an eyebrow raised.

Mae put it in his hand. "It's a beechnut." She'd barely gotten the words out before Lukas had popped it into his mouth and chewed.

Jaxon looked up from the book. "Be careful," he said. "Gwen wrote something about not eating too many of those."

Quinn leaned over the book to scan the page. She laughed. "That's not all she wrote," she said.

"What? What did she say?" Lukas asked, hurriedly wiping his tongue with his hand to try to get the rest of the nut out of his mouth.

"She said not to eat too many of them if you don't want to spend quality time with your butt," Quinn grinned, poking Lukas in the stomach.

Lukas's golden eyes were wide in alarm. Mae smiled and popped another of the beechnuts into her own mouth. "Gwen must have eaten a hundred of them for her to get sick like that," she said.

"It wasn't her," Jaxon said. "She wrote here that Greg ate a bucketful and she had to listen to him groaning and farting all night."

Quinn snorted. "Even better."

Jaxon pocketed the guide and pulled a loaf of bread from his knapsack. "Eat this instead," he told Lukas, forcing it into his hand. "We don't need to risk it, especially since you sleep next to me."

Lukas's smile stretched from ear to ear. He took the bread from Jaxon and a heap of hard cheese from Mae. Smiling to herself as she watched him run off with his goods, Quinn cleared a small area to sit in. Mae and Jaxon joined her, forming their usual circle.

"Keep watch," Jaxon called to Lukas, who was busy sharing his cheese with Kit and Pima. The boy relayed Jaxon's instructions to the dire bear and fox.

Mae took both their hands. "Annabel first?"

Quinn nodded and closed her eyes.

*Annabel pressed her ear against the door, enclosed in the same moving wooden box she had spent the last week in. Voices faded in and out on the other side of the door. A very familiar voice came into sharp focus.*

*"To be on the sea again!" Jonathan cried.*

*Liam chuckled. "Soon enough," he said. "You'd think there were rocks in your shoes with all your complaining about walking. Shall I fetch a horse for you?"*

*Annabel banged a fist hard against the wood, and the boys fell silent. The sound of footsteps neared and someone fumbled with the lock and cracked it open. Sunlight streamed in.*

*"Do you need something, princess?" Liam asked. "You've been knocking at this door for hours now. Your hand must be sore."*

*"Let me talk to him." Annabel's voice was firm.*

*"My brother isn't interested in talking to you," Liam said. "I don't know if you remember, but you leapt at him that first night in Windsor. He hasn't quite forgiven you yet."*

*"I'll be better this time, I promise." Quinn was surprised to hear pleading in Annabel's voice.*

*Liam peered in through the open crack of the door, a move Quinn thought was rather risky after Annabel had spit in his face only a few days ago. "When we reach our destination, I promise I'll let you talk to him all you want."*

*There was silence, and then Annabel threw her full weight at the door.*

*"Jonathan!" Her scream was desperate and angry. There was a flash of light and glimpses of an open road as Annabel pushed the door open. And then she was thrown back into the dark carriage.*

*"What was that about?" Jonathan's voice was closer. Annabel pulled herself up off the floor of the carriage and returned to the door. She continued banging on it and demanding to speak with Prince Jonathan.*

*When she finally paused for air, there was only silence.*

The bleakness of the carriage walls faded, replaced by the barrier of red leaves they were sheltered beneath.

They were still traveling. Quinn shook her head, confused. She kept hoping they'd catch a peek of Annabel's surroundings to get a better idea of where they were taking her, but the wooden box she was trapped in and the small glimpses of the outside offered no clues.

"Gwen, now," Mae said.

Quinn and Jaxon nodded, and the tree faded as a road opened before them and a clear sky stretched above them.

*As far as Gwen's eyes could see, soldiers spread out in front of them, lining Prasine Road. Beside her, Greg was grumbling. "We're going to be on the road for months at this pace," he complained. "You and I could make it to Windsor and back before this lot even gets to the Trade Bridge."*

*"You've suffered worse than this, Sir Greg," Gwen said, and Quinn could hear the smile in her voice. "At my hand, I might add."*

*Greg strummed his fingers over the hilt of his sword. His brown hair was pulled into its usual sloppy bun, but he looked more formal than usual, the green linen of his undergarments poking out from beneath his plate armor, emphasizing his large build. The dire bear insignia on his sleeve marked his allegiance to Viridis.*

*Greg dragged his words. "It's the second day of many long days to come." He paused, straightening as though an electric bolt had run through him. "Wanna do something fun with me?"*

*There was silence and then, "Why not." Quinn wasn't sure who was more surprised by this response, a gaping, open mouth Greg or herself.*

*Greg quickly closed his mouth. "Bubbles, Beers, and Butts is not too far off route," he said as though trying to get the words out before Gwen changed her mind. "We could go right now, soak our feet in the hot springs, drink some beer, and be back before Commander Maxwell even notices we're not holding up the rear."*

*Gwen was silent.*

*"C'mon, Gweny." Greg hit her on the arm. "My brother Dregg owns the place, you won't even have to pay."*

*"You have another brother?" Gwen sounded genuinely surprised. "How many of you are there?"*

*Greg ignored this. "Are you listening to me, old lady? Free beer!"*

*Gwen sighed. "Lead the way." She motioned in front of them. Greg glanced around to see if anyone had straggled behind them, before heading toward the foot of the Kamen Mountains. As Mae pulled them back to the present, Gwen's fading voice said, "But seriously, I need to know how many Wellington brothers there are. That's the fourth one you've mentioned—"*

"They're moving farther north," Quinn scowled, rubbing her temples as her eyes readjusted to the present. While the visions drained the energy from Jaxon and Mae, they seemed to have a worse effect on Quinn. She was not used to this type of magic, and it felt unnatural and intrusive to her. "We're going to have to cover more ground to reach them."

"It seems like they'll be away from the army for a couple of hours. I think that's good," Jaxon countered. "We'll be able to talk to them alone."

She hadn't thought of this. "We won't have to avoid my father if we meet them at the hot springs."

"Are the hot springs the best place for us right now?" Mae's eyebrows knitted together in worry. "I'm not sure we should go there. All of us have bounties on our heads."

Kit squeaked as he climbed up onto Quinn's shoulder. He cocked his head at the siren, as if to say not me. "You're not innocent here either," Mae said, rubbing the fox's head.

Quinn smiled. "Don't worry your pretty head, Maelyn Mori. Your past doesn't matter at Bubbles, Beers, and Butts. Their motto is '*Mind yourself or we'll mind you.*' As far as I know, it isn't governed by any town or kingdom. The normal laws don't apply. I've always heard rumors that Dregg is ruthless if he finds out you hurt the sanctity of the hot springs. The fact that he's Greg's brother makes me confident that's true."

"Do *you* know how many brothers Greg has then?" Jaxon asked.

Quinn shrugged. "Didn't know he had *any* before we met Kraig."

"By the time we make it over there, it'll be dark," Jaxon said. "We should be able to keep a low profile. Maybe Lukas can practice some illusions on us."

"He'll have to focus on disguising himself," Quinn said. "Children aren't allowed at the hot springs."

Lukas scowled at the word "children" and stuck his tongue out at Quinn, who stuck her own tongue out in response. On her shoulder, Kit pressed his nose to her face and licked her cheek, clearly misunderstanding their exchange.

"Can you two eat and walk?" Mae tossed chunks of bread to Jaxon and Quinn. "I want to make it to the Viridis River before the moon does."

Quinn took a hearty bite of the bread, ripping it in half with her teeth. "Let me go first," she mumbled through the mass of bread in her mouth. Mae would have probably sensed if something was off, but not being able to see what she was about to walk into made Quinn nervous. She pulled her sword out with her free hand and peered through the low branches of the tree, scanning their surroundings. Seeing nothing, she motioned for the others to follow.

As Mae charged ahead, Quinn dropped behind the rest of them to keep watch. Everyone had picked up the pace, eager to leave the forest. Even Kit had stopped chasing Lukas's butterflies, instead settling into Quinn's bag for a nap. Pima was walking beside Jaxon, who was feeding the bear some of their rations.

Alone with her thoughts, Quinn wondered how Gwen would react to seeing her. Would she even speak to her?

How would she feel that the banished siren and the prince of Twelve Pools were with her?

She tensed at the thought. She had missed the old lady almost as much as she missed her mother. The idea that she'd be met with anger filled her with dread. Doubt crept in. Maybe it would've been easier to tell her father about the waiting Twelve Pools army. No, she thought fiercely. Nothing would be worse than that.

The soft red of the setting sun coated her face, forcing her to squint. They had finally emerged from the Red Forest. In front of them, a small house stood close to the water. It looked like it had been standing for centuries, and Quinn could make out the faded mark of shield engraved in the decaying wood.

A boat swayed in the water at the end of a long dock. On it sat a gray-haired man, holding a fishing line that had been cast far in front of him. He was staring at them with his mouth half open. Quinn couldn't think of any other word to describe him except adorable. He was the first older siren she had ever seen. His good looks had not faded, but they were different than Mae's. Instead of being drawn to the siren, she felt drawn to protect him.

Mae caught her staring. "Don't be fooled," she whispered to Quinn. "Siren magic is at its strongest at his age. He could con you into anything, if he were to try. Let me do the talking."

"My Maelyn!" the old man cried, abandoning his fishing line and jumping to his feet. His small facial features scrunched into one giant wrinkle.

Mae moved forward to hug him. He stood on his tippy toes to kiss both her cheeks, squishing her face together with his small hands.

"I was afraid I'd never see you again," he said. "I'm getting old, you know? I could go at any second."

"Gramp!" Mae laughed. "You've been saying that since the day I was born."

"Well, that's how you know I'm getting close, isn't it? I hope it's the Clarity God that comes to take me to the other side, so I can tell her all about my granddaughter, the purple stone bearer."

Quinn exchanged a glance with Jaxon, who looked as surprised as she felt.

"You brought along some friends?" The old man had noticed the others. He hobbled over to Jaxon and squeezed one of his cheeks.

"I like the look of this one," he said. "He's got kind eyes. And look at this one's hair, white as a cloud!" He looked from Lukas to Quinn. He didn't reach for her cheeks but instead took a step back. "This one looks like she'd help me meet the Clarity God quicker than I'd like." Pima moved to sniff the old man, and he took the bear's snout in one hand and searched her face.

"Are my eyes going or is this a dire bear?"

"It is," Jaxon said, watching nervously. But Pima just snorted air at the old man, sending his gray hair flying backward.

"Gramp, we need your help," Mae said. "We need to cross the river—quickly."

The smile fell off her grandfather's face. "I know that look. Come along then." He hurried back toward the dock. It groaned beneath their feet, and Quinn tried not to wonder when it was last repaired.

Pima sniffed tentatively at the dock before opting for the river instead. She charged into the water head-on and the current tugged her downstream. Quinn ran to the end of the dock and nearly jumped in after her, but Pima managed to gain control and successfully steered herself toward the other side of the river. Kit fidgeted on Quinn's back and found his way onto her shoulder to watch the bear's bobbing head fade into the distance. Quinn murmured words of reassurance to Kit and ran a hand over his fur.

"Get in, get in." Mae's grandfather waved at them to join him on the boat.

Quinn motioned to Mae to climb in after Lukas and Jaxon, but the siren was watching the shore. Her body had gone rigid, and her head was ablaze in purple.

Three very tall men stood near the edge of the river. The fabric of their shimmering maroon robes reminded Quinn of

Mae's silk scarf. Past them, shadowy figures intermingled in the wall of trees.

The man closest to the dock didn't shout, but his voice rang out as clearly as if he stood beside them.

"I heard you were here—with humans," he said, his words slow and meticulous. Quinn fought the urge to yank Mae onto the boat before he could finish his sentence. "I didn't want to believe it."

Mae's grandpa moved as though to confront the man, but Mae held her hand up, signaling him to stop.

"Let us go, Father," she said. "We're just passing through. We have the right to cross the forest freely, as long as we don't disturb its peace."

His eyes narrowed. "Those are the laws of the forest, not of our people."

"I'm not *your* people anymore; you've made that clear."

The councilor was quiet for a moment, and when he spoke again, his voice was softer. "Come back," he said. "Come back and all will be forgiven."

Without taking her eyes off the man, Quinn unlatched the bow on her back, pulled it over her head, and cocked it with an arrow. Mae didn't stop her. Her head was still glowing, and her eyes were still locked on her father.

His words had turned Quinn's blood to ice. She knew exactly how Mae must be feeling, imagining her own father saying those words. Was she considering his offer? Quinn couldn't tell, but she held her bow straight anyway. Councilor Mori looked from Mae to Quinn and shook his head.

"Your mother trusted humans once."

Mae flinched. "May my execution be as swift as hers," she said firmly. She gave him a small curtsey before she stepped backward into the boat.

Quinn kept her gaze on the man as she followed her friend.

Mae's grandfather hesitated.

"She's as stubborn as your daughter," Councilor Mori growled at the old man. "Take her, if you must, but she won't be granted a return trip."

Anger flashed across the old man's face, so brief that Quinn almost missed it. He opened his mouth to reply but seemed to think better of it. Instead, he climbed into the boat with the others and paddled toward the other side of the river.

Widening her stance to steady herself, Quinn kept her bow aimed at the shrinking figure of Mae's father as they moved away from the shore and the sirens faded into the distance. All the while, Quinn was painfully aware of Mae's quiet sobs and Lukas's whispered attempts to comfort her.

# Chapter 18

## The Hot Springs

Jaxon scanned the wooden sign, illuminated by the full moon overhead. *Bubbles, Beers, and Butts. Mind yourself or we'll mind you.* In front of them, a small archway was sandwiched between lines of tall, thick wood logs sticking straight up from the ground. They stretched outward, ending where they met the sloping stone that outlined the narrow mountain gap in front of them. A sea of stars punctured the sky overhead, dimmed by the strength of the moon's light.

Mae's scarf glowed a hazy purple as she touched Pima's head. She was humming, but the bear was unaffected by her attempts to coax her. Jaxon was glad to see that the siren had returned to her normal bubbly self. He guessed that the encounter with her father hadn't been easy. Jaxon wanted to ask her more about what her father had said and why her mother had been executed, but Mae seemed intent to leave behind what had happened in the Red Forest. Each time he or Quinn brought it up, she said something cryptic about the past belonging to the past. The more distance they put between themselves and the Viridis River, the more she relaxed.

Pima growled at Mae and pulled her head away, out of reach. Mae tried again, but the cub dodged her once more, burying her head in the dirt. Jaxon knelt beside her and extended his own hand, surprised to find that the cub let him touch her.

"It's just for the night." Jaxon said it quietly, so that only she could hear him. Pima buried her face farther and then flipped her body forward in a graceless tumble, coming to land on her back. She tilted her head to look at Jaxon, barring her growing fangs at him. He covered his mouth to hide a smile.

"She won't leave us." He looked up at Mae and Quinn. "Maybe there's somewhere beyond the wall she can hide?"

Lukas pushed himself between Mae and a scowling Quinn before he sprawled out on top of the bear's tummy. Pima lurched upwards, launching Lukas off her body.

"I can hide her!" Lukas said between laughs as he stood and brushed dirt from his clothes. He then pulled playfully on Pima's ear. Jaxon did a double take as he lost sight of the bear. He blinked several times, trying to clear his eyes, until he spotted the puffs of hot air that were Pima's breath, visible in the cool evening. Jaxon was impressed. In the last few weeks, he'd seen Lukas's magic grow significantly, faster even than his own had developed. His brother had approached his stones with no fear or hesitation, and they reacted in kind, granting him their power every time he called on it.

"Hold on to me when we go through the gate," Jaxon said. "You'll need to pull extra strength from me to keep the two of you hidden."

"You can't be serious," Quinn said. Kit had woken from his nap and was peeking out of the bag on her back. The fox's ears were alert and upright as he peered over Quinn's shoulder, sniffing the air. His gentleness was a stark contrast to the redhead's furrowed eyebrows and frown. "We can't bring a dire bear in there!"

Mae was grinning. "You said yourself, outside rules don't matter in the hot springs."

"I recognize an unchangeable mind when I see one," Jaxon said pointedly to Quinn. "That bear is as unlikely to stay behind as you are."

Quinn opened her mouth to object, but Mae leaned against her and pushed her forward, toward the hot springs. "Embrace the uncertainty, Quinn of the red stone."

Jaxon took Lukas's hand. His brother's other wrist, already glowing a dull yellow, brightened when Jaxon touched him.

"Do you remember when those men attacked us at Verbena Pool?" he asked Lukas, who nodded. "What made you lose control then?"

"I was distracted," Lukas admitted. "I won't let it happen again, I promise."

Jaxon smiled. "It might happen again, but that's okay. Over time, you'll learn to hold the connection in your mind, even when your attention is needed somewhere else. It'll become as easy as breathing. For now, just remember to hide yourself and Pima, no matter what else is happening, okay? Even if you're worried about me or Mae or Quinn."

"Or Kit," Lukas added.

"Especially Kit, yes," Jaxon nodded. The gate was getting closer. He squeezed Lukas's hand. "Time to blend."

Lukas's face scrunched in concentration, and in the next second, he vanished. Though Jaxon could still make out the shape of him, it was only because he knew exactly where he was standing.

Up ahead, Quinn knocked three times on the large wooden door as Kit looked on from her shoulder. A sign hanging from the door rattled at the force of her knock. Jaxon moved closer to read it.

*Undergarments optional.*

*Valoo required.*

The door swung inward, revealing a long thin walkway lined by lanterns hanging from metal poles. At the end of the path a large, two-story building made of white brick extended from one end of the mountain pass to the other. Round wooden windows lined the upper story of the building. Some of the windows were propped open, emitting flickering candlelight. A man sat sideways on one of the windowsills, his right leg dangling from it. Puffs of smoke traveled from the man's mouth toward the night sky.

Two women stood on either side of the path, bent over in deep bows. Their silky black dresses were freckled with thousands of yellow stars, which matched the sky overhead. The hair that fell to their waists was so blonde it looked indistinguishable from the white of the moon. The women each held up an arm, motioning the group to move forward.

Jaxon followed the others to the door at the end of the path. He felt as though they'd stepped into another world. Even the air felt different, warmer and heavier than it had on the other side of the gate.

As they entered the building, Jaxon let the door close behind him, forgetting about Pima. Lukas's hand tightened in his as the door caught on the invisible bear, momentarily flickering Pima into view. Jaxon quickly grabbed the handle, trying to pretend like he was simply closing the door and not freeing an invisible bear from it.

He felt and heard Pima brush past him, and he scanned the room, hoping no one had seen. His worrying was wasted. The only person in the room was standing behind an enormous desk, counting multiple teetering stacks of coins and occasionally scribbling on the book of parchment under his elbow.

The man was shorter than Greg, but there was no mistaking their likeness. As he counted the coins, he ran a hand through the mess of brown hair on his head. Jaxon got the impression that he was very confident in himself.

"Finished!" he said, finally looking up at them. "You all have no idea how much meat this'll buy me. I'll be eatin' well for weeks."

The corner of Jaxon's mouth twitched, and he avoided catching Mae's eye. Quinn plopped their remaining valoo onto the desk in front of the man.

"Add another day of meat to that," she said.

"Now, that's an entrance." The man smiled. "Dregg at your service," he said, bowing his head and flourishing his hand. "What are you looking for? You three are a little younger than my usual crowd. I assume you aren't trying to soak in the nudity pools."

The normally confident Quinn flushed a red as deep as her hair.

"Actually," Mae stepped closer to the desk. "We're looking for your brother, Sir Greg Wellington. He's a friend of ours."

"I mean, who isn't a friend of Greg's? That doesn't mean much, does it?" Despite his objection to Mae's word choice, Dregg's entire demeanor had changed. He pushed the pile of valoo back toward Quinn. "Friends of Greg soak free. Otherwise, I'd never hear the end of how it's *the least I could do* after he saved my life that *one* time. Truth be told, I'd rather have died than listen to him remind me about that again."

Dregg pointed to the archway on their right.

"That's the side ye want, spring number six. You'll need to keep your clothes on. Or we can have ye fitted, if ye want something lighter to wear. Someone will search ye when you enter the room, to make sure you leave every weapon behind." He paused here to look Quinn up and down with raised eyebrows. "I do mean *every* weapon. Any suggestion of violence and I'll put ye on my wall."

He motioned over his shoulder. Jaxon had been so distracted by Lukas's sweaty hand and the persistent drain of energy that he hadn't given much attention to their surroundings. He looked closer at what he had thought was just a very busily decorated wall. It was covered in a hundred slips of parchment, the faces painted on them scowling back at him. One or two words were scrawled over the top of each of the heads. Jaxon read "peeper" and "snitch" over a number of the faces.

"Do you make them pose for a painting before you kick them out?" Quinn asked with what Jaxon felt was a suspicious amount of curiosity.

Dregg tilted his head forward, his eyebrows raised. "How else would ye do it?" he asked. "The humiliation is the most important part. I invite everyone to watch. 'Course some are added to the wall later, and the artist—who just happens to also be my very attractive wife—has to paint them based on my memory. Greg's been up there once or twice too." Dregg beamed with pride and stared at the wall for a moment before turning back to them. "I have dinner to cook, but if ye decide to stay in one of the rooms upstairs, you'll check in with my replacement here at the desk. He's a bit rough around the edges, so bring Greg along."

Dregg stopped talking, and the others stood motionless, waiting to see if there was further instruction.

"Do ye all need an invitation?" Dregg asked. "Door's there." He pointed.

Looking amused, Mae went under the archway first. Jaxon released Lukas's hand so that he could move easier into the room. He'd no sooner let go when they were accosted by more of the white-haired maidens. Jaxon didn't have time to react before one of them had unclasped the belt around his waist and removed his sword. He glanced around the room, searching for Lukas, but his brother had managed to keep himself and Pima hidden.

A weaponless Mae put her hands in the air and twirled as they finished searching her.

"May I have something to swim in?" she asked sweetly. One of the maidens handed her a long white cloth and instructed her on how to effectively wrap it around her body. To Jaxon's surprise, Mae pulled her dress up over her head without hesitation or warning. He averted his gaze so fast it caused a sharp pang in his neck. His cheeks burned. On his other side, Quinn was still being searched for weapons. She was complying, but not without the occasional grumble. Finally, the maidens retreated from the room, taking their weapons with them. Jaxon was relieved that they were allowed to keep their stones.

Outside, the ground beneath Jaxon's feet felt harder. The grass and dirt had been replaced with layered stone and the occasional patch of vegetation. In front of them, candlelight flickered as it branched off from the main path into the individual springs. Each path leading to a spring was higher than the last as the ground rose up into the mountainside.

Jaxon was still doing his best not to look too closely at Mae. She had wrapped the bathing cloth between her legs and crisscrossed it over her breasts, finishing in a knot behind her neck. Quinn seemed almost just as naked without her usual weapons.

"Is it wrong that I want to make it onto Dregg's wall?" she asked the other two. Jaxon and Mae both laughed.

Jaxon felt pressure on his hand as Lukas slipped his small fingers back into place. His brother's hand was burning up, his grip not as strong as it had been. Jaxon could only imagine how exhausted he must be. He tightened his grip on Lukas's hand.

"Just a moment longer," he whispered.

As they got closer to spring number six, worry began to bubble within. He'd been so focused on finding Greg and Gwen, he hadn't stopped to think how they'd react to him. How had they felt about the Prince of Twelve Pools showing up in their kingdom? He knew Gwen at least wouldn't be happy that the son of the king who had caused the War of Isabela, had been living under her nose all that time.

Jaxon heard the unmistakable hearty laughter of Greg. Quinn must have heard it too. She caught his eye. A mixture of his own apprehension and excitement flickered on her face. A small wooden sign with a six on it indicated a path that jutted right, zig zagging farther up into the side of the mountain. Under the cover of the secluded path, Jaxon let go of Lukas's hand. Lukas appeared next to a distracted Pima, who was sticking her nose against a lantern lighting their way, causing it to swing precariously.

"You were perfect," Jaxon whispered. He tugged once on Lukas's ear.

"For the love of stones," Gwen's voice traveled to them. "Orange flavored ale? Branberry ale? *Coffee* ale? It's absurd. I'd like a word with your brother."

"Good luck," Greg scoffed. "He prides himself on those flavored ales. Never wants to change anything about this place. I once told him to stock whiskey, and he added me to his wall for insubordination. Beatrice was not kind with her depiction of me either."

The path twisted once more around a corner. Jaxon caught a brief glimpse of steam rising from two large basins of water before he was blinded by green light. The ground rumbled beneath his feet as the roots of nearby trees shifted under the ground. And then the green light was gone, leaving them in the faint glow of the lanterns. Jaxon's eyes adjusted, and the faces of Greg and Gwen swam into view. They were both staring with their mouths agape.

Gwen was standing with her hand outstretched. She lowered it, and the roots at Jaxon's feet recoiled. The silver haired woman looked around as though searching for whomever had crafted this illusion. Beside her, Greg was submerged in the upper pool, his arms propped on the basin wall behind him. Just enough of his body was exposed to reveal a shirtless, hairy chest. Unlike Gwen, Greg hadn't moved to attack them.

For a moment, the only sound was the rushing of water from the upper pool into the lower one.

"Do the stones deceive me?" Greg said. His huge smile stretched from ear to ear. "My favorite group of trouble-makers."

Gwen seemed marginally less excited to see them. "This can't be good," she grunted.

A brown blur bound past Jaxon.

"Pima, no!" But he was too late. The bear dove belly first into the second pool and hit the surface hard. Hot water flew in every direction.

Gwen glowered through water-coated eyelashes.

"This was peaceful while it lasted," she said.

"We're going to need more beer," Greg added as water dripped down his face.

"Sorry about Pima," Lukas said, unconvincingly. "Bears don't really know about manners. I'm Lukas, by the way. Can I swim in there with Pima?"

Greg chuckled. "Go for it, kid."

Lukas joined Pima in the lower pool, and Jaxon followed Mae up the small set of steps to the upper level. She lowered herself into the water next to Greg.

"Not going to sing, are you?"

"Depends," Mae said sweetly. "How many valoo do you have on you?"

Greg grinned and lifted his mug in a mock toast.

Jaxon pulled his boots off and sat on the edge of the pool, sliding his legs in. The hot water soaked through his pants and immediately soothed his tired muscles. The heat was a welcome reprieve from the crisp cold of the evening air.

Relief washed over him. They were safe. They'd made it in time. Greg and Gwen would know what to do. He glanced at Quinn, but she hadn't moved. Her eyes were locked onto

Gwen. On her shoulder, even Kit was motionless as he stared with Quinn, both of them hesitating.

"I'm not going to scold you, if that's what you're worried about," Gwen said. Her posture suggested otherwise, her arms crossed firmly over her tunic.

Quinn raised her eyebrows.

"Fine," Gwen admitted. "It's not how I would've wanted you to do it. I would've preferred if you talked to me before you broke Viridis law and traveled to a foreign land. But my anger about it turned to worry weeks ago."

The corner of Quinn's mouth twitched. She climbed up the short set of stone stairs to stand in front of Gwen.

Gwen scanned Quinn's face. "You've grown."

"I've dimmed my fire, just like you wanted."

Gwen closed her eyes, put her hands on her temples, and shook her head. "That's not what I wanted, Little Red, that's never what I wanted. I wanted you to learn how to control your fire so it stopped burning you."

Quinn ducked her head.

"Well, I didn't learn. I'm still burning myself," she said. "And I still need a teacher. I still need you."

In one swift motion, Gwen reached forward and pulled Quinn into a hug. "I'll never be done teaching you," she said into Quinn's shoulder, almost too quietly for Jaxon to hear. "But you've never needed me." Kit licked Gwen's cheek, then scurried from one of her shoulders to the other, moving under her loosely braided gray hair before returning to Quinn.

After a moment, Gwen released her, and Quinn swiped at her cheeks.

"Sit down and make yourself comfortable." Gwen's voice was firm again. "We have a lot to talk about. I assume you're not here for the bubbles or beers."

"The butts then," Greg said. "They must be here for the butts."

Jaxon couldn't see Lukas, but heard his giggles. Quinn and Gwen sat down on either side of Jaxon as Kit hurdled himself over the edge, into the hot spring. The size of his splash was significantly smaller than Pima's. His head popped back above the surface. His wet fur, flattened around his nose and ears, made him look even smaller than usual. He was kicking his legs furiously, but despite his efforts, he drifted across the pool, spinning in circles.

Chuckling, Greg lifted him from the water and rubbed his head affectionately before setting him back on solid ground. Kit shook his body, spraying water into Greg's face.

"You're welcome," Greg grumbled. He jabbed a finger in his ear and jerked his head up and down, presumably to clear water that had lodged in it.

Unbothered, Kit scampered back to Quinn and settled beside her, his head resting on her thigh.

In the pool, Mae kicked her feet up and floated on her back, staring up at the sea of stars overhead. Jaxon envied how at peace she looked.

Gwen had also noticed Mae's comfort. "You just had to free the siren, didn't you?" she said to Quinn.

Mae lifted her head from the water, smiling. "Someone had to watch over Quinn."

Quinn's face was screwed up as though trying to look annoyed, but the corner of her mouth twitched.

"And *you*," Gwen said, turning toward Jaxon this time. He suddenly had the mad desire to drop into the spring and bury his head under the water for an undisclosed amount of time.

He stuttered as he tried to find the right words. "I didn't mean to deceive—"

Gwen stopped him. "I knew who you were." Her tone was gentler than he expected, and his shoulders relaxed, realizing he wasn't in trouble. "Not at first. But I got there, eventually. You remind me of your mother. Though, from the way the men of Twelve Pools rumble about you, I would've expected you to look like—and be as intelligent as—an ogre." Jaxon knew he should be more upset by her last comment, but being compared to his mother had made his heart swell and ache at the same time, and the rest of her words felt unimportant.

"Gwen, there's something we need to tell you," Quinn said.

The silver-haired woman closed her eyes for a moment as though preparing herself for whatever was coming.

Quinn took a deep breath. "Queen Jasmine has an army waiting for Viridis near the Trade Bridge," she said. Greg spit out the beer he'd just taken a sip of. In unison, he and Gwen both turned to scowl at Jaxon.

"I don't have control over my sister!" He protested.

"It's true," Quinn said. Her confirmation somehow made him feel worse.

Mae returned to an upright position. Her black hair stuck to the sides of her face in the same way Kit's fur was sticking to his.

"Queen Jasmine is powerful. She might be the most powerful purple stone bearer I've ever encountered." Jaxon knew she was remembering how Jasmine had sensed their presence in her mind and pushed them out.

"You can't challenge her in some way?" Greg demanded. "A fight to the death or something? Isn't that the Twelve Pool way—just to be more violent than the next person?"

Gwen ignored him. "What does she want from us?"

"She's working with the Windsor princes," Jaxon said. "Our men have been instructed to cross the Trade Bridge once you've reached the Way of Light, and then ambush you. The goal is to weaken your forces. She didn't send a full army. She's not worried about winning the battle. Her goal is just to make sure you arrive in Windsor with less men than you left Viridis with."

"She knows about the green stone," Gwen said, her face hardening.

Jaxon thought about mentioning that the princes had wanted him as part of their plan, but decided not to. He still wasn't sure what they wanted him for, and it felt almost absurd to say it out loud.

Gwen and Greg exchanged a glance. "This means Windsor never had any intention of making this trade," Gwen said.

Greg shrugged. "We never did either."

"What do we do?" Quinn asked. "How do we stop them?"

"We can send a messenger back to King Edward," Gwen said. "Ask for more men."

"Is there another route the army could take?" Jaxon asked.

"We'd have to go north through ogre territory, the way the Windsor princes traveled when they kidnapped Annabel." Gwen stared off in the distance. "It's not impossible, but it's risky." The creases around the corners of her mouth were deeper than usual, the lanterns casting shadows across her pale skin. On Jaxon's other side, Quinn stared off in the same direction. The flickering light of the candles was dancing in her auburn buns, making them look like the balls of fire she usually threw at people. Her expression matched Gwen's, and Jaxon was reminded of how alike they were. He glanced at Greg, whose eyes twinkled back in amusement.

Quinn shook her head, breaking from her trance. "What if they never make it over the bridge? The only other crossing is hours away, and there's only one boat there. It would take them weeks to rebuild that bridge. We'd be long gone by then."

"What are you suggesting?" Gwen sat up straight.

"I think she's saying . . . *boom*," Greg said, his hands mimicking the burst of an explosion.

Quinn grinned. "That's exactly what I'm saying."

"That bridge has stood for . . . thousands of years," Gwen protested.

Mae's smile matched Greg's. "So, then, it's overdue for maintenance," she said.

Gwen looked at Greg as if expecting him to back her, but he leaned further back on the basin wall and downed the remainder of his beer.

"Count me in," he said, slamming the empty mug down beside him. "It's not every lifetime you get to witness something like that."

Gwen groaned. "Be reasonable," she protested. "The Trade Bridge connects the three kingdoms. It's essential to the peace of our land."

Jaxon frowned. "What peace?" He wasn't sure about Quinn's idea—it sounded unhinged to him—but what he found even more absurd were Gwen's words as they marched toward battle.

Beside him, Quinn straightened. "He's right," she said. "You're walking toward a war with all three kingdoms right now, there's no peace to protect."

"The war hasn't started yet," Gwen said. "There's still time to prevent that."

Greg leaned forward. "Who's being unreasonable now?" he grinned at Gwen.

Mae's stones lit up, submerging the pool in light. Jaxon looked around at the others' faces, all soaked in purple. He felt a small tug of his magic. The siren wasn't touching him, but the water seemed to connect them as she pulled more power from him. After a moment, Mae opened her eyes, and the purple light dimmed.

Jaxon was surprised to see Gwen glowering at Mae. "I don't need to hear it," she said to the siren. "You can't see a future without a war, I'm guessing. Those purple stones aren't fool-proof, you know? You purple stone bearers always think you know the answer. People are more complicated than that."

Mae smiled at her. "The stones are often wrong because people like you refuse to let them decide your fate. You've taught Quinn that, and now you doubt her when she finds a way to carve out a new path—one that the stones didn't see?"

Quinn beamed at Mae, but Gwen's scowl only deepened.

"Eventually, they'll rebuild the bridge," Gwen said. "We'll have to deal with Queen Jasmine, one way or another."

"Tomorrow's problem," Greg shrugged. He stared at his empty beer mug longingly. "Our priority is getting Annabel back, isn't it?" Gwen was tight lipped as she stared at him. Jaxon could practically see her thoughts fighting themselves in her head.

He knew that his sister would be calling on her stones to see the future, too. But Mae often told him that if you didn't ask the stones the right questions, you wouldn't get the answers you needed. Would Jasmine have a question that prepared her for something like this? As powerful of a stone bearer as Jasmine was, would she be humble enough to even consider that her plans could be thwarted?

Finally, Gwen shook her head. "The king might banish me for this."

"Oh no," Greg said, his tone dripped in sarcasm. "You'd have to go home to your tree house and never speak to anyone ever again." She glared at him.

A leg flung itself up over the side of the wall that separated the upper and lower pools, and Lukas's head emerged as he pulled himself up.

Panting, he smiled at them. "Jaxon, can I jump from here?" He barely waited for Jaxon's nod of consent before he flung himself over the ledge.

His cry of, "Pima, watch out," was followed by a loud splash.

"Who is that?" Gwen's voice was level, but she was staring at Jaxon.

"Lukas, isn't that what he said?"

Gwen ignored Greg and continued to stare at Jaxon.

"My brother," Jaxon said, though he suspected Gwen had already figured that out.

Greg let out a shout of joy, flinging his arms out, and spraying water at them. "Ye cured 'em!" His huge smile dropped nearly as soon as it appeared. "Wait . . . You cured Lux Pox? No offense, kid, but I always thought you had a few stones loose thinking you could cure him of something incurable. That's the kind of blind hope someone has after drinking too much Seven Sisters."

"He's wearing yellow stones on his wrist," Gwen said quietly.

Jaxon nodded. "He's a yellow stone bearer," he said. "I drew on power from the God of Light and used it to create a stone. Once Lukas had the stone, the magic trapped in him had somewhere to go. It stopped destroying him."

Neither Gwen nor Greg looked like they knew what to do with any of this information.

"This is impossible," Gwen whispered. "There is no yellow stone. Someone would've known if another stone existed. There's no way to keep that hidden."

Mae, who had resumed her floating, righted herself once again. "A lot of our most ancient history is long gone. My people have the longest memories, and the knowledge is lost even among us."

"Traces of it were in our own history books," Jaxon said. "Annabel was able to put the pieces together. Once I realized what she was trying to tell me and I healed Lukas, I began to see evidence of it everywhere. She'd given me the *Book of Stones,* and when I reread it, I caught references to the stone almost immediately. I suspect there are even more hints of it in the books that fill the Viridis library."

"This means every case of Lux Pox can be cured," Greg said slowly.

A knot formed in Jaxon's stomach. He'd been so focused on saving Annabel and stopping his sister, it hadn't even occurred to him that there were more people out there just like Lukas who needed to be saved.

"One thing at a time." Gwen's voice was surprisingly gentle.

"What power does a yellow stone bearer possess?" Greg asked.

"Invisibility," Quinn said.

Lukas's faint voice became louder as he emerged over the rock and onto the ledge of the upper pool once again.

"It's not really invisibility," he corrected Quinn. "It's more like I can trick your eyes." His wrist glowed yellow, and a small trail of golden butterflies fluttered in a circle around the spring before disappearing into the sky above. "I change the direction the light is bending. It seems like invisibility, but that's because you aren't looking hard enough. No one ever really looks hard enough, even at the things right in front of their face. I used to hide in plain sight without my stones. It's just like Divoff did in the Red Forest. He wasn't invisible, he just changed his colors to match his surroundings."

He looked at Jaxon questioningly, and Jaxon nodded his yes. An excited Lukas jumped backward off the rocks into the lower pool.

Gwen's gaze hardened. "Divoff?" she asked, as Greg grunted in anger. "The Komodo lizard?"

"*Keirnan*." Greg's fists were clenched.

Jaxon was momentarily surprised to find that Gwen and Greg were familiar with Kiernan and Divoff. Then he remembered the rumors about Kiernan after the War of Isabela, and the conversations he'd overheard about Gwen when he was hidden in the queen's tower. He wasn't sure if Gwen knew that Kiernan was responsible for Queen Isabela's death, but she'd been charged with protecting the queen, so he imagined their paths must have crossed at some point.

"He was tracking me," Jaxon said. "My sister sent Kiernan to retrieve me."

"Let him come," Greg grumbled.

Gwen tensed up, scanning her surroundings as if expecting to see him pop out at any moment.

"You said you saw him in the Red Forest," Gwen said. "How did you lose him? Do you know where he is now?" Her knuckles were white as she clutched the side of the pool.

"Divoff is dead," Quinn said. Greg's whoop was so loud Jaxon thought people in nearby springs must have heard him. "We think that might've slowed Kiernan down. We think he stopped to bury the creature instead of chasing us. He also can't use Divoff to track us anymore with that strange forked tongue. Nose. Nose tongue?"

Gwen's body relaxed, but she put her head in her hand.

"He can track you without Divoff," she said after a moment. "But it doesn't matter. The assassin doesn't matter. I feel the same as I did before the war of Queen Isabela. Tension so tight a gust of wind could break it. There won't just be a fight over the green stone." She was focused on Jaxon now, her words meant for him.

"I assume that Lukas is Queen Sophia's son, and that he did not die along with his mother during his birth as we were told. The people of Twelve Pools may not be happy to find out their queen has kept his existence secret. Queen Sophia was as beloved across your land as Queen Isabela was in Viridis. While Jasmine has tarnished your name, she'll have a harder time rallying the people against someone they all believed was dead. Another male heir, no less. Jasmine uses fear and lies to control the people of Twelve Pools. It's more fragile than she knows." Gwen paused again. Her eyes continued to bore into Jaxon's. "More importantly, if this news spreads about the yellow stone . . ."

Jaxon's heart sank, understanding for the first time how much danger he was in. If no one knew where the source of the yellow stone was, that meant he was the only source of it. People would hunt for him to cure their loved ones. *The paper from Annabel.* He dug in his bag, found her note, and passed it over to Gwen.

"The source of the stone is near Windsor," he said. "At least, that's where Annabel believes it is."

Gwen squinted at the scribbled stars.

"When we get Annabel back, she can help us find it," Quinn said.

Looking less convinced, Gwen handed the paper back to Jaxon. He held it out for Greg, who'd pulled himself out of the pool, but Greg waved his hand in dismissal.

"I'll take a look in a second, gotta do something important first," he said as he made his way toward the other side of the pool.

"Incoming!" he called down to Pima and Lukas before he flung himself over the edge. Lukas's shout of laughter was drowned out by Greg's yell as he tumbled into the lower pool with as much grace as Pima had.

Gwen ignored him, scanning Jaxon, Mae, and Quinn's face as the splash of water from Greg narrowly avoided soaking them.

"Start at the beginning," she said. "Tell me everything."

# CHAPTER 19

# The Trade Bridge

Quinn watched the Viridis army shrink as the last of the men moved farther down the road, past the intersection that led south to the Trade Bridge. From where she was crouched on the roof, she could just make out the trailing row of emerald clad soldiers, poking out over the sea of copper-colored rooftops. They continued west toward Windsor, not knowing the danger that would soon approach from the south.

Quinn clenched her fists. This was their only chance to stop the Twelve Pool army from crossing the Trade Bridge. The better they protected the Viridis army, the better chance they had of making it to Annabel.

Below, the village was showing signs of life. A few men in leather vests made their way through the center of the village, where a wide road led to two white towers standing on either side of the bridge entrance. She guessed they were on their way to swap shifts with guards who'd worked through the night.

Kit, who'd been trying desperately to get Quinn's attention, gave up. He raced to the other side of the rooftop and climbed up on top of the stone chimney, where he circled the opening.

The shingles beneath Quinn's feet creaked as she hurried across the rooftop to join him, staying low to avoid being seen. She leaned against the chimney and studied the other side of the village.

Between the two white towers, the stone bridge stretched into the distance. She squinted but couldn't see across the great expanse to the other side. It seemed impossibly large and indestructible in the fortifying glow of the morning light. Doubt nudged at her.

The expanse of the valley that the bridge stretched over was even more daunting. The rock walls descended hundreds of feet below to the rushing Viridis River. The sunlight hadn't reached the river yet but bathed the walls of the valley in a soft orange glow, calling attention to sharp patches of green shrubbery. She knew if she were closer to the valley edge, she could look left and see the enormous waterfall dumping water into the valley. If she were to follow the river to her right, it would eventually lead her to the Endless Sea.

"*Quinn.*" Gwen was hissing at her from the ground. Kit squeaked and jumped to hide in Quinn's bag. As soon as he was secured, Quinn swung around the side of the chimney and scaled the stones, dropping to the ground next to Gwen.

"We don't have time for sightseeing," Gwen said.

Quinn didn't respond. She looked over Gwen's shoulder, but the others weren't in view.

"What is it?" Gwen demanded.

Quinn struggled to put into words the feeling in the pit of her stomach. Kit pushed his nose against her neck in an effort to comfort her. "What if I can't do it?" she finally settled on. It felt painful to admit, but the sight of the bridge had made her feel small.

"Then we'll figure something else out." Gwen paused and studied her face. "You've pushed the limits of the fusion stone's magic your entire life, this is no different. There's no one I'd trust more to do this than you."

Heat flushed Quinn's cheeks, but Gwen's words had given her something else to worry about.

"This will put us all in danger," Quinn pressed. "Maybe I should tell the others to leave."

Gwen gave her a rare smile. "I don't think they'd listen to you, Red."

She gripped Quinn's shoulders with firm hands.

"I can't believe I have to say this to you but *stop thinking*. It's time to do what you do best: fight for the people you love."

Gwen held her gaze, fierce and unblinking, and the doubt clinging to Quinn dissipated. Gwen was right. She was here to save Annabel, she had to focus all of her energy on that. She didn't have time for doubt. Gwen released her and pulled a small round glass bottle of sandy colored liquid from her cloak.

"Be careful with this," she said. "I stole this from our supplies. It's a flash bomb. Even the smallest amount of heat will set it off. The ancient rock of the Stone Bridge will be stubborn; it'll fight you. This will help you fight back a little harder." Quinn nodded and tucked it safely in her belt, alongside her red stones.

"You lot coming or what?" Greg's voice carried from the other side of the building. They moved to join the others. Mae's silk scarf was tied loosely over her head, and Quinn thought she might have already tapped into her siren magic; she looked as though she were floating above the ground, and her skin was shimmering. Beside her, Jaxon and Lukas were wearing their dark cloaks, their stones hidden from view. They had left Pima not too far from the village, but Quinn had a sneaking suspicion she was closer than she was supposed to be. The thought brought her comfort, though she knew it shouldn't.

Mae smiled sweetly. "Ready?"

"Ready," said Quinn.

The siren's wordless tune was soft at first but grew louder. Mae's hair shifted with it, and her features softened. It felt like all of the energy around them was pulling toward her, even the sunlight.

Quinn pushed out the sound of Mae's voice, weaving it through the village like a gust of wind. The siren stepped from behind the building and walked down the main road, away from the bridge. The soldier's eyes followed her first, and then their feet followed too. The stones under her scarf began to glow, and Quinn knew that Mae no longer needed her help.

She pulled back her own magic. Behind her, Jaxon instructed Lukas to stay hidden. On her shoulder, Kit squeaked. She reached up to scratch his head.

"Stay with him," she said to Kit. He leapt off her back and sprung toward Lukas, crouching next to the boy. Both of their heads poked out from around the corner of the building. "If anything goes wrong, go back to Prasine road and we'll meet up there," Quinn said to them. She motioned for the others to follow her to the center of the road.

The towers appeared to be empty and the bridge stretched out in front of them, unguarded. Quinn thought she could see the smoke of campfires rising on the other side. Jaxon pulled his golden spyglass from his bag.

He swallowed as he stared across the bridge through it. "They're moving," he said. "We don't have much time."

Greg pulled his axe over his head and stood at the edge of the bridge. Instead of facing the other side of it, he turned toward the village.

"Light it up, Lil' Red," he said. Gwen joined him, the green from her stones reflecting against the metal blade in her hand.

Quinn and Jaxon hurried onto the bridge.

"Where do we need to be?" Jaxon asked as they walked.

"The middle of the bridge is the weakest point," Quinn said. "The very center of the arch. But that's a five-minute walk, and if the soldiers are already preparing to cross . . ."

Quinn trailed off. Smaller arches flanked either side of the main arch, supporting the part of the bridge carved into the side of the valley before its legs stretched all the way down either side of the river. It would be more difficult to break the smaller one, but Quinn suspected this might be all they had time for. She knelt on the bridge and touched the stone.

Focusing hard on her breathing, she reached into the stone. As she did, she thought about how long the bridge had stood for and about those who'd first built it with their red stones. Rock was the hardest element to move, and Quinn knew it must have taken many red stone bearers to construct the bridge. She thought about the amount of goods and people who'd crossed it since then. With respect for its history,

Quinn eased herself deeper into the stone and met no resistance.

"A few more steps," she said to Jaxon, leading him forward. She again knelt to feel the rock beneath their feet and knew this time, she was in the right place. Quinn closed her eyes, breathed deeply, and then searched for cracks in the bridge. Once she found them, she pushed as much air as she could into them, stuffing each crevice with more air than they could hold. She pushed hard, not allowing any of it to escape. A large cracking sound echoed across the valley below, but the bridge remained otherwise unfazed.

She glanced at Jaxon. "Give me a boost?" she asked, as she pulled on her gloves. He put a hand on her shoulder, and this time, she reached for fire. It sparked almost instantly in the palm of her hand. She directed the ball of flames to the bridge, and instead of pushing air through the cracks, she pushed the fire. She felt Jaxon's magic amplifying her own, and she took hold of that power and used it to bury the fire even deeper into the bridge, heating its insides and weakening the structure. She repeated the cycle of air then fire a few more times.

"They've reached the bridge." Jaxon's voice was surprisingly steady as he peered through the golden spyglass with his free hand.

Beads of sweat rolled down Quinn's neck. Jaxon's words didn't help. She abandoned her attempt at cooling and heating the bridge and instead moved some of the stone in the center, digging a hole into it.

Jaxon was watching her with furrowed eyebrows. "Uh, Quinn, I don't mean to—"

"Jax," Quinn hissed through gritted teeth. "For the love of the stones, if you're about to say something dumb—don't!"

Quinn continued to dig in the silence that followed. When she thought she was deep enough, she lowered the murky liquid Gwen had given her into the hole, using a light gust of air to keep the glass from breaking when it hit the bottom. Beneath her hands, she could feel that the stone had weakened. Even digging the hole was easier than it should've been.

"They're almost halfway," Jaxon said. "Not sure if they've seen us yet—"

Quinn stumbled to her feet, and Jaxon caught her arm, helping her up. Her vision grayed as the world spun around her. Jaxon looked drained too. She'd exhausted them both of their magic.

"We have to move back," she said, unsure if her legs would support her.

Jaxon propped her up under his shoulder and began to lead them away from the bridge. She vaguely registered surprise at the strength of his small stature.

They reached the edge of the bridge, where Greg and Gwen still stood, watching the other direction.

"How are we doing back there, Lil' Red?" Greg asked cheerfully as though she'd just returned from a leisurely walk.

"About to find out," she said, unhooking her bow from her back. "Jax?" Without question, he clasped a hand on her shoulder again.

Her mind raced as she calculated the distance to the hole she'd created and the height she'd need to hit for it to land just right. She took a deep breath and lit the end of an arrow before she nocked it in her bow, aimed high into the sky and released. The arrow arched up before it lost momentum and plummeted back toward the earth. Quinn threw all of her concentration into keeping the arrow lit and using wind to pull it to the ground. In the distance, she saw a blur of purple uniforms as the army moved closer.

The arrow disappeared into the hole. A deafening boom echoed around them, the sound never-ending as it traveled the valley below and returned to them. Debris and clouds of dust flung out in every direction. Quinn threw up her arms, causing a massive gust of wind that blocked the four of them from the shower of debris. It cost her the last of her energy.

Jaxon helped her to the side of the road as her ears rang. They both collapsed, their backs propped up against the guard tower.

Dust from the stone had coated the air. Shapes and light swam into her view and then a green-glowing Gwen and axe-carrying Greg were standing in front of them.

"We can't stay here," Gwen said. "We need to leave." She touched her hand to Quinn to restore some of her energy.

A guard was running toward them through the haze behind Gwen. His waist of red stones was glowing as he dispelled the cloud of dust.

"What did you do?" he shrieked, spit flying from his mouth. "Arrest them. Arrest them now!" Quinn wasn't sure who he was talking to; there were no other guards in sight.

Greg tilted his shoulder toward the guard as though to put emphasis on the Viridis seal that was engraved on his armor plate.

"Sorry, but what exactly are you arresting us for?" he asked.

The guard threw up his arms. "Are you blind?" he shouted, motioning toward the bridge. "The—" He stopped midsentence, gaping at the bridge. Using all the energy Quinn could muster, she followed the guard's line of sight. The bridge appeared in the same shape as it had before, unbroken.

"You were saying?" Greg asked, cheerfully.

The guard continued to stare, mouth agape, at the fully functional bridge. The dust had almost cleared, and they could now see soldiers in purple tunics marching across it, nearing the end. Quinn's heart sank. And then, almost as quickly as the soldiers appeared, some of them seemed to vanish before her eyes. Screams echoed up from the valley below as Quinn realized what was happening. She glanced toward the house that Lukas was hidden behind and saw the bright yellow of his glowing stones.

The guard, who was still staring at the bridge, did a doubletake and then glared at Greg.

Greg shrugged. "Strange," he said, the corner of his mouth twitching. "Might want to get that checked out."

Lukas seemed to lose control of his magic, and the illusion of the bridge flickered once more before disappearing. The Twelve Pool men on the bridge were fleeing back to the other side, as what was left of that section of the bridge crumbled farther. Faint yells filled Quinn's ears. A part of her registered that there was yelling coming from the other direction too.

"Sir, come quick!" A man in the same uniform as the guard trying to arrest Quinn and Jaxon was running toward them. "There's a siren . . . She's tied up our men, and she summoned . . . She's with . . . She's got a . . . *There's a dire bear!*" He keeled over, hand over his stomach as he panted.

The other guard looked from the broken bridge to their group and then off in the direction of the siren, seeming to decide that the bridge couldn't be destroyed more than it already had been.

"Stay here," he barked at Greg and Gwen, before following the other soldier down the main road. There was a moment of silence as he sprinted away from them.

"Follow him," Gwen said to Greg. "Make sure Mae isn't harmed. I'll restore energy to these two and meet you back on Prasine Road. If he gives you trouble, tell him we're un-der orders." Greg didn't need to be told twice. He ran after them, his wide figure wobbling and clanking. He stopped after a few steps to readjust one of the plates on his leg.

"I'm built for comfort, not for speed!" he shouted over his shoulder.

Gwen knelt beside them once more and touched her hand to Jaxon, who already seemed to be returning to his usual self. Movement over Gwen's shoulder made Quinn tense up.

"Gwen, look out!" she screamed.

Gwen moved her head just in time. A dagger flew past her and struck the guard tower behind them, falling to a clatter between Quinn and Jaxon. In one motion, Gwen sprung to her feet and pulled her sword from its sheath, knocking the next dagger from the air. Quinn tried to stand on unsteady legs. Jaxon grabbed her wrist, his magic racing through her as he worked to restore her energy.

Kiernan was standing in front of Gwen. There was a deranged smile on his face, and he appeared almost manic. Divoff was nowhere to be seen. Did this mean he was truly dead? She scanned the ground, half-expecting to see the flicker of his camouflaged scales, but there was nothing.

"Lady Gwen. Raiser of the dead. Woman who talks to trees." The scars on his face stretched as his mouth moved. "So nice to see you again after all of these years."

Gwen spat at his feet. "I won't say the same to you, *Queen Killer*," she snarled.

This seemed to give Kiernan pause, a satisfied smirk on his face. Beside Quinn, Jaxon shifted at the words, but he continued to work his magic on Quinn. Was Gwen saying what Quinn thought she was saying? Was Kiernan responsible for the death of Queen Isabela?

"You finally figured that out then?"

"I always knew it was you," Gwen said. Her stones glowed, but the rock road was thick below her feet and there were no trees close by to draw on her stone's power. Quinn tried to move again, to help Gwen, but again Jaxon held her back.

"You let me live. Why?" Kiernan demanded.

"The war was over. Spilling your blood would've prolonged the end of it."

"You were always weak. And look what that's done! You let me live, and I've raised a woman who will not hesitate to bring an end to the greed of Viridis. Now, continue to prove your weakness and hand over Prince Alexander so I can put my sword through his heart in the name of my queen."

"You didn't raise her; you took orders from her—you're no more than her puppet, Kiernan. She's not your daughter."

Kiernan snarled in rage and drew his sword.

"You mean nothing to her," Gwen continued. "You're a fool if you think you do. And you're even more of a fool if you believe I'll let you take Prince Alexander's life."

Kiernan's scream sounded like the roar of a wounded animal. He swung wildly at Gwen, who blocked his attack with her own sword. They whirled around one another in a flurry of clashing metal. Quinn fought Jaxon again. This time he released her, and she jumped to her feet. She cupped two balls of fire in her hands, ready to launch them at Kiernan, but Gwen and Kiernan were moving too fast and she didn't know where to aim. She watched helplessly, waiting for an opening.

Gwen ducked under one of Kiernan's swings. He sliced at her head, and as she blocked him, he swung his leg up and slammed his foot into her chest, sending her flying. She hit the rocky ground hard and didn't get back up.

Quinn unleashed the fireballs in her hands. Kiernan pivoted, narrowly avoiding taking the full force of the flames. They seared his shoulder, and he furiously patted out the flames with his other arm. She tried to call more fire, but Kiernan was faster. He pulled new daggers from beneath his cloak and flung them at her, one after the other, forcing her to fall sideways as she threw up her arm, pushing hard at the air in front of her and sending the daggers clattering to the ground.

She jumped to her feet, scrambling for her sword. But Kiernan wasn't paying attention to her anymore. The assassin had turned his attention to Jaxon, who managed to pull his sword from his sheath and was brandishing it in front of him.

"*You!*" Kiernan screamed at Jaxon, spit flying from his mouth. "Divoff is dead because of *you!*"

Quinn threw herself in front of Jaxon. Teeth bared and eyes bulging from his head, Kiernan snarled as he raised his sword to attack her. The ground rumbled below Quinn's feet, and roots ripped upward through the stone like it was water, wrapping their way around Kiernan's body, from his feet all the way up to his neck. Kiernan was frozen mid-movement as if time had stopped, the roots pressing deeper and deeper into his skin as they squeezed, turning his face white and his eyes red until he went completely limp. Gwen released the roots, dropping him to the ground.

She stood over him, chest heaving, as she surveyed his lifeless body.

"For you, my queen." Her voice was surprisingly soft and calm. "I should've been there; I should've saved you. I'm sorry."

Something flickered in her eyes, and when she turned away, Quinn suspected that Gwen would never again spare Kiernan another thought.

"Let's move," she said.

Jaxon froze as he stared down one of the alleys. "Lukas," he said. Fresh worry washed over Quinn. In the flurry of movement and attacks, they'd forgotten him. She raced with Jaxon to the other side of the building, followed closely by Gwen. Lukas and Kit were nowhere to be seen.

She searched the ground where Lukas had been crouched, looking for clues as to what direction he'd gone in. "Look!"

she said. Someone had written in the dirt with a stick. *Pima*. Quinn guessed Lukas had followed Greg when he'd heard them saying Mae and Pima were in trouble.

"We'll find him with the others," Gwen said, seeming to have the same thought. "You told him to meet us at Prasine way if we were separated—hopefully they've all made it there by now." The three of them headed north, weaving between the houses and side alleys to avoid the main road.

Quinn tilted her head to one side. Were her ears still ringing or was that a chorus of screams? In front of her, Gwen stopped and motioned to them to hide behind one of the buildings. She peered out from behind the house toward the main road, where the screams were coming from. Quinn leaned just a little farther, trying to look around Gwen.

Men were running away from Prasine Road, toward the trade bridge. One of the soldiers had climbed up the side of a house and was dangling from the windowsill. Another man was trying to break down the door, looking over his shoulder with terror in his eyes.

"Let me in. Let me in!" she heard him shout.

Gwen turned and nearly collided with Quinn. Glaring at her, she motioned the others to keep moving. "C'mon," she said. They ran through another row of buildings before they emerged at the intersection between the three roads.

Greg, Lukas, Mae, and Pima were waiting for them.

"'Bout time!" Greg exclaimed, as Pima sniffed Jaxon and Kit leapt into Quinn's arms. "Was about to send a search party!"

"What happened?" Quinn asked. "We saw some of the guards running. They looked terrified."

A huge smile stretched across Greg's face. "A mama dire bear came out of nowhere, started chasing them," he said, ruffling Lukas's hair affectionately. "I expect they don't see a lot of those out here. Especially not one six times as big as me like Lukas conjured up."

Quinn turned to smile at Lukas, but Mae caught her eye instead. The siren was biting her lip as she stared down the road. "There's someone coming," she said. A horse was barreling toward them. The soldier riding it seemed to recognize Greg and Gwen, and he pulled on the reins, slowing as he reached them but not stopping.

"We're under attack," he said. Quinn was sure her heart stopped beating in her chest. "The Windsor army rode to meet us. They were waiting to ambush us. Commander Maxwell sent me to warn the king."

"Go," Gwen said, but the soldier was already moving at full speed again, toward Viridis. "Kids, listen to me, stay here. As long as you're together, you'll be safe. We'll come back for you."

She didn't wait for an answer, racing with Greg toward the Viridis army. As Quinn watched them vanish over the crest of a hill, a sudden realization hit her: Mae's visions had shown Annabel being taken somewhere. The princes had brought her with them. She was there. She was with the Windsor army.

Quinn turned to the others. They seemed to be waiting for her to do something. She searched their faces and, without a word, led them in the direction of Greg and Gwen.

## CHAPTER 20

# The Black Fog

Jaxon knelt in front of Lukas, who was avoiding his gaze. Instead, his brother was watching the chaos unfold over his shoulder. Soldiers bringing up the rear of the Viridis army were scrambling to gather fresh supplies as healers tended to injured men. Jaxon tugged Lukas's ear, forcing him to focus.

"Pima can't follow us," Jaxon told him gently. "If she comes with us, she could be hurt." Lukas's round golden eyes finally met Jaxon's. "Can you find a safe spot and hide her?"

Lukas nodded reluctantly, his mouth a thin, straight line. Mae swooped down and kissed Lukas on the cheek. Quinn lifted up the side of her dress and unstrapped a small knife secured to her thigh.

She handed it to him. "To protect Pima," she said.

Lukas ran a hand over the blade's red hilt before fastening it to his belt. Kit squeaked loudly from Quinn's shoulder, and she lifted him up and pressed her nose against his, before placing him gently on the ground. The small fox sniffed Lukas's boot and then took a running leap onto Pima, where he eventually settled between her ears, curled up like a red crown on her head. Pima swiped a paw playfully at Kit's fluffy tail as it swung in front of her eyes.

"Kit said he wants to look after Pima too," Quinn said. This seemed to finally appease Lukas, who smiled.

"I'll protect them," he said, searching the landscape. To their left, a few trees dotted the hillside; to their right, farmlands stretched out for miles. Lukas climbed the hillside toward the valley and the Viridis River, which stretched onward to the Endless Sea.

Jaxon watched Lukas run up the hill, Pima's stride overtaking him within seconds. "Don't go too far!"

Quinn pulled on his sleeve, and he tore his eyes away from Lukas to follow the other two toward the sea of blue- and green-clothed soldiers. As they descended the final stretch of hill, they were engulfed by confusion and chaos, Virdis soldiers running in every direction around them.

"Jaxon! Quinn!" A familiar face appeared in front of them. The healer Shay was inspecting them with wide eyes. "What are you doing here? I thought you were both dead!" Her green tunic was padded and covered in a thin layer of chain mail.

There was a splash of blood across her chest and dotting her hair. Her small, mousey features were shadowed in their usual worry.

Quinn clutched her arm so tightly that Shay winced. "Have you seen Gwen?" she demanded.

Shay nodded and pointed straight through the center of the scuffle. Quinn and Mae ran ahead.

Jaxon put a hand on Shay's shoulder. "Stay safe," he said, before following the girls.

Ahead of him, Quinn held one gloved hand up, cradling a flame. Mae's head lit up purple, her silk scarf had fallen, forgotten, to her shoulders. They pushed through the thick of soldiers, managing to duck errant swords and the occasional arrow. Screams and clashes of metal rang in Jaxon's ears.

For a moment, he swore he heard someone screaming Quinn's name. Then, the scream became louder and Quinn's expression soured. Commander Maxwell stood some feet away, yelling for Quinn, anger and confusion at war on his face. Quinn kept her focus straight ahead as she pushed forward, leaving Commander Maxwell behind them. His yells for Quinn became commands as his attention returned to his m en.

The throng of soldiers was so thick now, the three of them found themselves being tussled back and forth. Jaxon tripped over a root in the ground, causing him to narrowly miss a poorly aimed attack from a Viridis soldier.

"We're never going to make it," Quinn yelled back at them, as she helped Mae avoid being squished by soldiers. Jaxon stared at the root he had just tripped over. Even if they managed to follow Gwen and Greg, there was no guarantee that they would find Annabel.

He called for Mae and Quinn and they dropped back. "Do you trust me?" he asked them.

Quinn didn't hesitate. "Completely."

"With my life," Mae smiled.

Jaxon sheathed his sword, his stone ablaze. Quinn and Mae stood on either side of him, protecting him, and Jaxon focused on the ground at his feet, finding roots and then pushing his magic through them, encouraging them to grow. He weaved them together beneath the dirt and then tore the solid piece of twisted roots upward. It smashed through the surface, flinging soldiers aside as it created a half dome over the ground and a tunnel beneath it.

He continued to breathe life into the roots, growing them forward and expanding the tunnel straight through the battlefield before them. Still holding tight to his magic, Jaxon ducked under the archway, Quinn and Mae at his side. He closed the tunnel behind them, wrapping the roots until he was sure it would take hours to hack through.

Enclosed in the tunnel, the sound of the battle around them was muffled.

"Both of you hold on to me," Jaxon said. "We need to look for Anna." They each put a hand on one of his shoulders, and Mae shut her eyes.

*Light seeped through the wooden container.*

*A loud bang. And then another. Annabel was kicking at the wall of her prison. Unlike last time, Prince Liam didn't show up to open one of the doors. She hit the wall with her arm in frustration. Jaxon could hear her labored breathing as she paced the small, enclosed space. She ran her fingers over the wood of one of the doors, leaning close to where it latched in the middle. She pushed just below the latch, and the door budged.*

*Annabel took a few steps back and then ran at the door, slamming her shoulder into the spot below the latch. The force of her impact threw her backward. She didn't hesitate, standing up and running again at the door. She connected with the same spot, and the door flew open. She stumbled out, falling into the dirt.*

*Movement and sound exploded around her. Scrambling to her feet, she peered around one side of the carriage and then the other. She was surrounded by a circle of protective guards who hadn't yet noticed she'd freed herself. Beyond the circle of soldiers, there was an endless sea of fighting. She stuffed her hand down the front of her dress, and from her bosom, she pulled out the small glass vial filled with black liquid. Clutching it tightly, she crawled underneath the carriage and crouched there, unmoving.*

Quinn was already tugging them forward before the tunnel of roots fully swam back into view.

"She's so close," she yelled. "We need to get to her!"

Jaxon called on the roots and expanded the tunnel more as they moved through it. He felt the weight of the men above as the roots sprung up below their feet, tossing them aside. He could feel blades poking and prodding and slicing at the tunnel walls from above, as soldiers seemingly tried to fight through the roots, but Jaxon held steady, drawing deeper from the green stone. He was healing the roots faster than the soldiers could slice into them. The root walls were so thick only small patches of sunlight managed to squeeze through.

Jaxon was growing more confident by the second that they could use the tunnel to reach all the way to Annabel. Then, Jaxon felt waves of pain travel through the roots above. Heat licked at them and overpowered Jaxon's magic. He pulled back, his feet slowing beneath him.

"Fire!" he yelled. A red glow flickered across the ceiling of the tunnel. He tried to repair the roots as they burned, but the fire continued to spread. He was sweating and coughing as smoke filled the tunnel.

Quinn's waist lit up in red as she moved the air around them. It only seemed to make the fire grow stronger. Jaxon felt his control of the roots slip as someone else took hold of them.

"There's another green stone bearer up there too," Jaxon said through coughs.

Mae was looking up, squinting through purple light. "There's so many people, I can't see who's trying to get through."

"Let them come!" Quinn said, and Jaxon was terrified by the look that had come over her face and the calm rage brewing in her eyes. "I know exactly who's doing this."

Jaxon stopped resisting, and a hole formed in the roots above them. A young man lowered himself through it, and a woman followed, gracefully swinging from one of the roots. Jaxon moved to stand beside Quinn, in front of Mae.

"Prince Jonathan." Quinn's stance was wide, her fists clenched.

A face framed by unruly dark curls smiled wide at them, and Jaxon's body tightened in anger. Annabel's life was in danger because of him, and he smirked as though this were a game. The red stones around Jonathan's waist were so bright it hurt to look at them. The Windsor prince moved his hands upward, and the fire above quieted.

Jaxon recognized the blonde woman standing beside him as Evelyn, the prince's healer. She was covered in dirt and blood, strands of her blonde hair pulled out from the pins tying it back, but she looked as striking as she had the day of the Suitor's Championship.

"I knew you'd be here," the prince said to Quinn. "Couldn't stay away from me."

The flames in Quinn's palms grew, the red reflected in her narrowed eyes. Jaxon knew it was taking everything in her not to attack.

"You should thank your stones that I'm not here for you," she growled. "Your blood doesn't deserve to stain my blade."

"Was it you three who stopped the Twelve Pools army?" He tore his gaze from Quinn to look at Jaxon. "And betrayed your own sister?"

Jaxon's jaw tensed. It was a strange accusation from someone who'd bartered a deal with Jasmine in exchange for his life. But the prince had already shifted his focus again to Quinn. He didn't seem to want to take his eyes off her.

"Your plan wasn't as smart as you thought it was," Quinn smirked.

"We're still going to win," he said. "You should tell your people to back down. The sooner we get the green stones, the more likely your Annabel is to return home."

The roots above Jaxon shifted, and he noticed that Evelyn's necklace of green stones was glowing. He yanked Quinn out of the way, as a root reached out where her foot had been. Jaxon drew his sword and sliced the growing root in half. Quinn launched one of her fireballs at Jonathan and then the other at Evelyn.

The healer pulled her arms across her body, and roots from the wall stretched out in front of them, blocking the balls of flame. Jonathan slid under the wall Evelyn had created, his sword drawn. Quinn was ready for him. She blocked his swing, and he had to roll away to avoid hers. Jaxon fought for control of the roots as Evelyn attempted to grab Quinn with them.

Jonathan's laughter filled the tunnel. "I'll never tire of you attacking me," he taunted Quinn.

Mae moved closer to Jaxon. "Have some energy to spare? She's resisting; I want to try going deeper."

Jaxon, who was sweating as he fought against Evelyn, managed a feeble yes. She touched his shoulder, and suddenly he was in Evelyn's mind.

*Her vision was cloudy as she pressed her face into a cold body laying lifeless on a bed. The blonde woman's pale face was unmoving as it pointed up at the ceiling. "Please," little Evelyn screamed. "I can't leave her!" Someone was tearing her away from the body.*

A real scream punctured the memory, and they were brought back to the present. Quinn and Jonathan were still circling one another, swords flying, but Evelyn had fallen to her knees, tears streaming down her cheeks, her beautiful features twisted in rage.

Mae looked taken aback. "Might have dug a little too deep for that one."

"Get behind me," Jaxon said.

Jonathan sent a gust of air at Quinn, and she flew backward. Jaxon caught her before she hit the ground.

"Jax," she said through clenched teeth, righting herself as she watched Jonathan help Evelyn to her feet. "Bring it all down."

Jaxon tried to protest.

"I'll hold him off," Quinn insisted. "Find Anna."

Jonathan was reaching for his flames, and Jaxon could sense Evelyn in the roots again. He took a deep breath and closed his eyes, remembering every lesson that Gwen had taught him. He felt the ground beneath him and the air around him. He was connected to everything, all at once. He thanked the tree he was tethered to for the life it had given to the world, and then he ripped it all apart.

The ceiling of the cave collapsed, the fragments of root he'd ripped in half falling around them like rain. The fire that had been smoldering in the thick vines caught on the small, severed roots. Quinn's stones glowed bright red, fueling the fire. The flames licked at the roots, weakening them until the tunnel collapsed, separating Jaxon and Mae from the others. The flames grew taller, as Quinn expanded the barrier.

Jaxon and Mae were standing once again in the middle of the open battlefield, in confusion and smoke. Around them, soldiers were screaming. The battle cries, Jaxon thought, sounded more like cries of terror. For a second, he wondered if it was the destroyed tunnel now laying in ruins and flames that had scared them, but then Mae yanked on his hand and he spun around to see a darkness blacker than the night sky descending on them.

"Don't let go!" he screamed at Mae, squeezing her hand.

The darkness slammed into them. He could see nothing. It had even snuffed out Quinn's fire. An eerie quiet had fallen, as soldiers stopped fighting, blinded in the pitch black. Jaxon fought the urge to yell for Quinn; she wanted him to find Annabel, not waste time looking for her. He tried to call on the light of his stone. It flickered weakly, then went out. Next to him, there was a dim glint of purple before that too was gone.

"Mae—"

"Ready for it," she said, before he could get the words out.

He gave her all the energy he could, pushing his magic into her. Purple light burst outward, breaking through the blackness around them. A soft melody punctured the quiet as Mae began to sing. They moved slowly, stepping over bodies and weaving around soldiers. The men backed away, fear in their eyes at the sight of the purple-glowing siren gliding through the sea of darkness. Her voice was as beautiful and enchanting as always, but there was something ominous about it. Instead of instilling desire, it seemed to be feeding their fear.

Around them, the black fog had lifted a little. Jaxon squinted through it, and then he saw her. Even in the darkness, he recognized the tone of her golden-brown skin, the softness of her body, the gentleness of her being. A rush of affection took root in his heart.

She was beaming at him. In the middle of the battlefield, surrounded by chaos, she was a beacon of light. Her eyes crinkled in relief as she ran to him. Something fierce came over him. He felt no worry, no doubt. He felt more sure than he had ever been of anything before.

Annabel leapt into his arms, and before he had time to consider the consequences, he pulled her close and his lips connected with hers. A rush of warmth overpowered him as the world melted away. For a second, he was in the castle garden alone with Annabel, eating strawberries, staring at the endless night sky and talking about faraway places. He lowered her, and when they pulled apart, their foreheads rested one against the other.

"I knew you'd find me," she whispered.

"I hate to interrupt," Mae's musical voice punctured their bubble. "But we should get to safety."

Jaxon pulled away from her with a good deal of effort. The battlefield, the blood, and the screams came crashing back. The dark had almost completely dissipated, and the fighting had returned in full force. Beside them, Mae was grinning wildly, an almost annoyingly knowing look in her eye.

"Your purple light guided me to you," Annabel said as she moved to hug the siren. "Thank you." But Jaxon saw the princess search past them. He knew exactly who she was looking for.

"She's here," he promised Annabel.

Relief flashed in her eyes but vanished almost instantly as realization crossed her face. "We have to get out of here." Her hand tightened around Jaxon's arm. "You're in danger."

The elation Jaxon had felt since Annabel jumped into his arms deflated. He shifted his attention from Annabel to Mae, who looked as confused as he felt.

"What do you mean?" Mae asked. "Why would Jaxon be in danger?"

Before Annabel could answer, two soldiers battling nearby collided and staggered in their direction. Jaxon pulled Annabel away as the soldiers fell sideways and were swallowed back into the chaos. Annabel squeezed his arm even harder. She was staring wide-eyed at the space the soldiers had created in their absence. A blond man with a haughty smile stood there, as if appearing from thin air.

Jaxon pushed Annabel behind him. He scanned their surroundings, hoping that Gwen or Quinn or Greg or anyone would show up as Prince Liam descended on them with his sword drawn. Jaxon scrambled for his own sword. Even in his fear, he felt a quiet rage at the sight of Liam, who had caused Annabel to suffer and had turned Quinn's life upside down. His sword didn't shake as he held it in front of him.

"Hello, Jaxon of the green stone," the prince drawled. "Prince of Twelve Pools. Creator of the stones. I knew you'd come for her, the princess who stole your heart."

Jaxon froze. Liam's words sunk uncomfortably deep into his brain, where they echoed like the ringing of bells. *Creator of the stones.* His skin crawled. *How could Liam possibly know that title?* With his free hand, he reached for life, any life, near them, but found nothing except the ashes of the tree he had just killed.

Liam smiled. The blue tunic beneath his armor plates was straight and tidy. There was no blood on him, no piece of hair out of place. *Always put together, always confident, always friendly.*

"They can go," Liam said. He motioned behind Jaxon but didn't take his eyes off of him. "It's you that I'm here for."

Jaxon hesitated for a moment, but something in him knew this wasn't a trick.

"Go," he said to the girls.

"We won't leave you!" Annabel's eyes glistened.

"Find Quinn, tell her I need help."

"But—" they protested in unison.

"I'd listen to him if I were you, ladies," Liam said, lazily tapping the hilt of his sword. "The other option ends with you both dead."

"I'll be okay," Jaxon assured them. "Mae—get her to safety. That's all that matters."

Annabel's eyebrows furrowed in worry as her eyes locked onto his own, and he gathered as much strength from them as he could. Her soft hand found his, holding it for a moment before Mae pulled on her arm and they disappeared into the mass of soldiers.

Liam waited until they were gone, his eyes never leaving Jaxon's face.

"You can make this easy," he said. "You can walk away with me now."

Jaxon raised his sword. Liam smiled and shrugged his shoulders.

"I've been busy following your little princess." He stretched his neck one way and then the other. "I suppose it's only fair for me to join the battle I started. At least for a moment." He twirled his sword effortlessly as Jaxon struggled to lift his in time to block Liam's swing again and again. Liam was taunting him, smiling as he pushed harder and forced Jaxon to keep stepping backward. Liam's blade came closer and closer to making contact with Jaxon's skin. His months of training were no match for Liam's lifetime of it.

Liam aimed his next swing at Jaxon's head. As Jaxon side-stepped him, Liam lifted his leg and kicked Jaxon's hand, sending his sword flying. Instead of trying to swing at him again, Liam grabbed Jaxon's wrist, his fingers tightening so hard, Jaxon thought he might snap the bones. A wild smile spread across Liam's face.

"It's true," he said.

Weakness washed over Jaxon as Liam pulled the magic from his body. Confusion and fear clouded Jaxon's brain as his vision blurred. Everything was spinning around him. He fought to remain conscious but lost.

# CHAPTER 21

# The Bloodsucker

Quinn stared through the sea of burning roots that Jaxon had torn apart. The fire had faded when the darkness had spread over them but was now crackling as it caught in the surrounding grass.

A pile of the smoldering debris shifted, and Evelyn emerged, coughing and sputtering. Quinn took a step forward. Was Jonathan close too, or had he gone, vanished in the cover of darkness? A white flash of rage blinded her. She clenched her teeth together as she fought the urge to attack Evelyn and track down Jonathan to finish their fight.

She took a step back instead. She couldn't let herself get distracted. She had to get to the others. In her hesitation, Viridis men descended on Evelyn. Quinn didn't wait to find out if the healer surrendered. She pulled fire into a gloved hand and sprinted in the direction Jaxon and Mae had headed. How was she going to find them?

"I'm fine, ya old lady!"

Quinn heard Greg's voice before she saw him. She elbowed a soldier out of her way and found Gwen with her hand on Greg, attempting to heal him.

"You know me," he grumbled at her. "If I'm suffering, it won't be in silence."

Gwen looked up in alarm as she sensed Quinn approaching. Her expression turned from relief to anger and fear.

"For the love of the stones!" Gwen shouted. "Will you kids never listen to me?"

"Annabel is *here*—they brought her with them! Jaxon and Mae are looking for her." Quinn tried to catch her breath. "I was fighting Prince Jonathan, but he disappeared."

Greg didn't hesitate. "Tell us where to go," he said. "Ye can yell at her later, Lady Gwen, we don't have time for an argument between the two most stubborn people in this world."

A soldier charged at Greg. Gwen stepped lazily between them with her sword pointed, and the soldier didn't stop advancing in time. The blade slid into his gut, and he froze, unmoving, his sword still raised at Greg as blood leaked from his side. Greg put a large hand on the man's head, covering his entire face, before shoving him back. The sword Gwen was still holding the hilt of came free as the soldier slid off of it and crumpled to the ground.

"Lead the way, Red," Greg said as though there hadn't been any interruptions.

The emerald of Greg and Gwen's tunics made Quinn far more of a target than she had been alone, without any indication of whose side she was on. But she knew that even if Greg and Gwen were to dance around and yell insults at soldiers, she was safer with them than she was without them.

As she led them through the battlefield, Gwen and Greg guarded either side of her. The whoosh of Greg's axe was nearly as loud as his battle cries. Chaos surrounded Quinn, but she ignored it all and focused on putting one foot in front of the other. She spun her balls of fire in her palms before pushing the flames outward. Soldiers jumped out of the way, screaming as their tunics caught fire beneath their metal plates.

"Careful where ye aim those hands, eh," Greg said nervously.

Quinn ignored him, pushing the fire forward to carve out a path. She paused to wipe sweat from her brow. As she dropped her hands, she peered forward down the path, now framed by flames.

There was a blur of movement, and then someone was running straight at her, through the tunnel of fire. They collided with her and arms squeezed around her neck so tightly she thought for a second she might pass out. Annabel's face was wet with tears. *She was safe. Annabel was safe.* Relief like she'd never experienced before flooded through Quinn as she wrapped her arms around Annabel and squeezed back.

Over Annabel's shoulder, Mae appeared. She was looking back the way they'd come. An uneasiness formed in the pit of Quinn's stomach. *Jaxon. Where was Jaxon?*

Annabel was crying into her neck. "You have to go to him," she pleaded. "Jaxon. He's in trouble." She tore herself from Quinn and wiped at the tears on her face.

Quinn's heart sank. Annabel's eyes, which normally held all the answers to all the world's problems, looked back at her, filled with fear instead.

"What happened?" Quinn demanded.

"Prince Liam," Annabel said, pointing in the direction she'd come from. "He's going to take him. He wants his magic."

"I'll take you to him," Mae said.

Gwen raised her eyebrows at Greg.

"I know, I know," he said. "Sorry about this, princess!" He scooped Annabel up as easily as though she were an empty knapsack and tossed her over one shoulder, despite her yelp of protest. Soldiers flocked to defend him, and he barked orders at them as he moved away from the battle and toward the healers and safety. In the distance, Quinn swore she could hear her father's voice as he commanded their men to defend Greg and the princess he was carrying.

Quinn fought the urge to run after Annabel and join the men now protecting her. Jaxon needed her more. She started to follow Mae, but Gwen grabbed her arm and held her back.

"It's not safe," she said. "Liam will be protected. That's a fight we can't win."

Quinn pulled her arm free from Gwen's grasp. "I won't abandon him."

She ran after Mae. Behind her, Gwen yelled in frustration, and when Quinn glanced back over her shoulder, she found the silver-haired woman on her heels.

Quinn saw Prince Liam first. His back was to her as he walked toward Windsor camp, away from the battlefield, but there was no mistaking the blond hair, tall stature, and confident stride. She felt the color drain from her face as she took in the sight of Jaxon hanging limp and lifeless as Liam dragged him unceremoniously behind him. A sharp chill of fear raced up her spine. She heard Prince Jonathan yelling before she saw him, emerging from the thick of the battle not far to her right. He was sprinting toward Liam, rage in his eyes.

"What are you doing?" Prince Jonathan yelled. "We don't have the stones! Why are you calling our men back?"

Quinn noticed then that the Windsor men were moving in the same direction as Liam. They were falling back, and the Viridis men were letting them.

Liam turned to face his brother, but as he did, his eyes found Quinn instead. His gaze moved from the fireball in her hand to her glowing red belt and the sword extended in front of her. His smile made Quinn's breath catch in her throat.

"Brother, mind your manners," Liam said with raised eyebrows. "It's not polite to fight in front of company."

Jonathan whirled around just in time for him to swat away Quinn's fireball with a gust of air.

Beside Quinn, Gwen dropped to her knees. Roots sprung from the ground, chasing themselves up Jonathan's leg. Jonathan pulled the remnants of Quinn's flames to the roots around his feet. They recoiled, and he yanked his leg free. He scrambled to dodge more roots as he moved the air behind Quinn and Gwen, the stones glowing around his waist.

The sharp tug pulled Quinn's legs out from under her, and she fell backward in unison with Gwen. Jonathan plunged his sword at Quinn's chest, but Gwen had rolled to her side and swung her blade backward, blocking the sword before it could connect with Quinn's unprotected chest. Quinn scrambled to her feet as Gwen and Jonathan flew around her, locked in a tight battle.

"Quinn, he's taking Jaxon!" Mae yelled. Purple light framed her head, her face scrunched in concentration. Quinn guessed she was attempting to get into Liam's brain. Liam was retreating, unbothered by the fight that was happening behind him.

Quinn unhooked her bow and pulled out an arrow, lighting the tip of it on fire. The arrow soared over Liam's head. When it hit the ground in front of him, the grass caught on fire. Quinn poured her magic into the flame and the fire exploded outward, creating a barrier of towering flames that cut him off from the other soldiers as it circled around them. She felt some of the red stone bearers on the other side of the wall try to push back on the flames, but she resisted, reaching deeper into her stones than she ever had before.

Liam stopped to face her.

"I gave you back your precious princess." His smile twitched. "The boy is mine."

"I won't let you take him!" Quinn shouted. Her yell distracted Jonathan, and he turned away from Gwen for just a second. That was all Gwen needed. She didn't hesitate, roots erupting from the ground. He hacked at them with his sword, but she'd moved too quickly. They tightened around him, pulling him to the earth and holding him in place. He struggled and twisted, but she only squeezed tighter. Each time he managed to spark a fire, Gwen twisted more roots over the flame, suffocating it before it could fully catch.

Quinn focused on the wall of flames, pulling the fire closer in and tightening the circle around them. Liam's smile faded.

"You think that'll stop me?" he snarled at her.

The stoneless Liam held up his arms and red light poured out from beneath his sleeves. He lit the ground at Quinn's feet. Thin strands of flames lashed out like whips and latched themselves to Quinn's wrists, snaking up her arms. She screamed in pain as the ropes of fire seared at her skin. The parts of her tunic that touched the fire turned to ash. For a moment, she thought the flames would consume her whole body, but they remained tethered to her arm like tightly woven ropes. She desperately tried to snuff the fire out, but it wasn't responding to her stones. Unbearable pain scorched her skin as the fire burrowed into her arms.

Gwen spun around, seeming to hear her screams. Quinn's vision blurred as she watched Gwen abandon her attack on Jonathan to charge at his brother.

"Let her go!" Gwen's yell was heavy in the air. It demanded to be heard. "Let them both go!"

But Liam was ready. Fire leapt from his bare hand and wrapped Gwen's blade in flames, circling to the hilt and then around her hands before moving to her wrists. The shock of heat made Gwen drop the sword. Quinn screamed, trying to break free of the wisps of flame. They buried deeper into her flesh, and she fought to stay upright.

Through her blurring vision, Quinn watched Gwen pull a thick clump of roots from the ground. They crisscrossed over Liam's boots and up his legs. Liam smiled, letting the roots climb and squeeze. As they covered his waist, he touched a bare hand to one of them.

The deep brown of the root turned crimson from heat. The roots were burning. Dark red spread farther through the twisting roots, freeing Liam's waist first, and then his thighs, and then his knees. Gwen's face was screwed up in concentration, and her neck was glowing brighter than ever, but the roots didn't stop burning. Instead, they began to crumble and disintegrate until there was nothing left and Liam stood freely.

Quinn struggled again against the flames. The more she resisted, the more they tightened around her wrists, burning deep into her skin, all the way through to her bone. A rancid smell filled her nose as the fire charred her flesh. Her stomach churned, and she did everything in her power not to retch.

She tried to accept the pain as Gwen had taught her to do, but she couldn't even think straight. It was consuming her. She attempted to move toward Gwen to help her, but she fell to the ground. Her hands shook as her arms struggled to hold her up. She crawled, pulling at the ropes of flame binding her. The world went in and out of focus as she used all her effort to lift her head and search for Gwen.

The silver-haired woman had taken a step back, and Quinn saw something unrecognizable in her eyes. *Fear.*

"Who are you?" Gwen spat the words out. "*What* are you?"

Still smiling, Liam reclaimed the step between them, looking down at her.

"A god," he said.

Liam seized Gwen's neck with one hand and lifted her off the ground. Her short stature was striking now as she hung there with her long, gray braid dangling down her back. She looked more vulnerable than Quinn believed was possible. Quinn extended a hand, yelling her name and yanking desperately at the flames binding her.

Through the glow of the fire on her wrist, Quinn watched Gwen turn whiter and whiter, her skin shriveling. Finally, Liam threw Gwen to the ground.

A horrible, heart wrenching scream filled the air, and it took Quinn a moment to realize that it was her own. She forgot about the fire scorching her body, she forgot about Jaxon, she forgot about everything. She screamed for a green stone bearer, a healer, to come, but there was no one.

Vaguely, Quinn registered Liam crouching over Jonathan, who had finally freed himself from Gwen's cage of roots. Liam put a finger on his chest.

"The green stones," Jonathan croaked. "We need to heal father."

Red light seeped from beneath Liam's sleeves again. The red stones around Jonathan's belt cracked into a thousand pieces as he screamed in pain. Quinn knew it was Liam who'd drained the magic from every single of his brother's stones. Liam, the bloodsucker.

Jonathan collapsed face-first onto the ground.

"You still don't understand, brother," Liam said to the back of Jonathan's head. "Your father never needed a healer. *I* am his illness. And when I return to his side, green stones won't save him. Nothing will."

He turned and walked through Quinn's wall of flames, dragging Jaxon behind him.

The fire around Quinn's wrists loosened, and she pulled free of them, trying not to look at the gruesome marks they'd left behind. Around her, the ring of fire she'd created dimmed and then disappeared. She didn't know who had extinguished it, she didn't care. She dimly registered the pain coursing her body as she stumbled to Gwen's side. There was movement all around her. Viridis soldiers bound Prince Jonathan's hands and carried him away.

Gwen's chest trembled as it fought to fill with air. Quinn stared down at her gaunt face. She didn't look like herself. There was no infinite strength there, no reluctant smile. Her bloodshot eyes blinked once and then twice as they looked up at Quinn, and even in their pain, seemed to smile at her.

Quinn screamed for help again as the world blurred around her.

"I need a healer, *please*!"

Gwen's hand found hers. "It's alright," she said. Her voice was hoarse, barely a whisper. Her lips moved again, but all that came out was a faint breath of air that sounded like, "Red."

Her eyes closed, and Quinn cried out in rage and fear.

The ground rumbled beneath her. Greg was there, pulling her back as the earth split open where she'd just been kneeling and swallowed Gwen whole. Quinn tried to break free, reaching for the woman who'd been like a second mother to her, trying to grab her body so that the healers could bring her back to life. Even though, in her heart, Quinn knew the only green stone bearer powerful enough to do that was laying lifeless in front of her.

Roots were wrapping around Gwen's body, pulling her deeper into the earth. In the center, from where her chest had been, a small tree sprouted.

The tree grew up and up and up, reaching for the sky. Lines of silver intermingled within the dark brown bark. Hundreds of branches grew outwards, spreading out wildly, blocking the sky above Quinn and Greg's heads. Silver leaves erupted from the branches, glittering in the light of the day.

Finally, the ground stopped rumbling and the tree stopped growing and everything was still and quiet.

Beside her, Greg fell to the ground. His large frame heaved back and forth. Quinn couldn't even bring herself to look at him. All around her, the soldiers who had returned to help, dropped to one knee and bowed their heads in respect for the green stone bearer who had brought their king back to life and who had dedicated her life to defending their kingdom.

Quinn stared at the tree that was once Gwen, and her heart cracked in two.

# CHAPTER 22

# The Darkness

Jaxon faded in and out of consciousness. Blurred shapes moved past and around him. Dull pain fired through his body from head to toe, as he was lifted off the hard ground. He struggled to focus his blurry vision. *Intricate yellow designs on black cloth. A long, twisted beard decorated with purple stones. The blood red of a setting sun. The flickering dull green of his stone.* It all faded to black once more.

# CHAPTER 23

# The Silver Tree

Quinn watched the hair on Lukas's forehead fly up and then fall back down as Pima's snores sent puffs of air at his head. The boy and the bear were sleeping face to face, inches apart. Kit was curled up beneath Lukas's arm, his head buried under the boy's chin. A deep, unrelenting weight pressed down on Quinn. She was sure this was the longest day of her life. The battle from that morning felt like a lifetime away. She didn't think she'd even recognize the Quinn she'd been then.

A fire was crackling nearby, casting Lukas's face in dancing light and highlighting the white patches across his skin. His mouth, usually curled up at the corners with a smile, was set in a deep frown. He had hugged his knees into his stomach, making his body look even tinier and frailer than usual. His blanket had fallen to the other side of his body. Quinn lifted it off the ground, dusting dirt from it, and then laid it back over him.

The movement had woken Kit. The fox slid from under Lukas's arm and hurried to Quinn, scaling her body and coming to a stop on her shoulder, where he nuzzled his nose against her cheek.

"I don't need your pity," she whispered to him. Kit just looked at her, unblinking, before he settled in on her shoulder, a comforting weight to balance the heaviness in her chest.

The sadness that had taken over her since Gwen's death squeezed at her heart as she watched Lukas sleep. She wanted to apologize to the boy, tell him how sorry she was that she had failed to protect his brother. But she knew he wouldn't hear it. He was too busy being angry at himself for not following them into battle.

The Viridis soldiers had stayed up late celebrating around them, joyous at the return of their princess, but Quinn knew her friends weren't part of those celebrations. Like her, they were at war with themselves in their own heads. Watching them suffer made her push back on her own guilt. She didn't want to dwell on her mistakes when she knew the task that was in front of her. While the soldiers journeyed east back to Viridis, she would keep heading west to Windsor.

*Stop getting yourself kidnapped, won't you?* she wanted to say to Jaxon. But it would be with a smile as she hugged him tight and vowed never to let him or Annabel out of her sight again.

Subconsciously, Quinn rubbed her wrists. Underneath her green cloak, thin, raised white lines spiraled up to her elbows, where the fire had scarred her. Shay had done her best but claimed it was a different kind of magic that had caused the burns, one that was very resistant to her own magic. Shay had begged her to come back the next day to let one of the more advanced healers work on it. Quinn had agreed, but in her heart, she knew she never would. She wasn't sure if she wanted the marks gone, or even if she deserved for them to be removed.

She walked away from the camp. The dark sky above was bright and cloudless, illuminating the ground in front of her with moonlight. Kit abandoned her shoulder to run through the grass beside her, a pop of auburn in the sea of green.

Quinn watched him as she walked, feeling very far away. She knew she should go to sleep. It was late, but the thought of closing her eyes to darkness terrified her almost as much as the thought of opening them the next morning. She didn't want to begin a new day: the first day in a world without Gwen.

Moving quieted the questions in her brain that screamed for attention, so she kept going. Without her bow on her back or sword at her side, she felt oddly free, like she could walk forever into the night and never turn back.

Quinn crested the hill she'd been heading toward, and with all the courage she could muster, she tore her eyes from the ground and looked up. Remnants of the battle were still strewn about, but in its center, like a beacon of hope, the silver tree glittered in the moonlight.

She ran the rest of the way there, stumbling as the ground sloped under her feet. She ducked beneath the ceiling of silver leaves and collapsed on the ground, breathing heavily. Kit raced around the base of the tree and then ran back to Quinn. He jumped onto her lap, and she fell back into the grass, her arms spread out on either side of her as Kit made himself at home on her stomach. Through wet eyes, the shimmering gray above her twinkled down at her like a million stars. She lay there, unsure if hours or minutes had passed.

"Lil' Red." Greg's gruff voice was calm and quiet. He lowered himself to the ground beside her. "Mind if I join ye for a little while?"

She sat up and opened her mouth to say something, but nothing came out. He seemed to understand. She expected him to start talking. She had never known Greg to let there be quiet. But he was silent too, as he stared at Gwen's tree.

The light rustle of footsteps alerted them to someone else's presence, but neither she nor Greg turned around to see who was there. Mae appeared first next to Greg, her head basked in purple, and then Annabel lowered herself gracefully beside Quinn.

"I woke and you were gone," Annabel said. "I was worried. Mae guessed you would be here." She folded her hands in her lap, her legs straight in front of her and her back rigid. She looked somehow as though she was seated on a throne and not a bed of grass. Even the frayed emerald dress they'd found for her, that hung loosely off her shoulders, had transformed the moment it had gone over her head. It fanned out around her. Silver specs of light danced in the brown of her eyes, reflecting back the leaves around them.

"Wanted to be alone for a little," Quinn said.

Annabel's smile was gentle. "I see that's going well for you."

"Gwen always pretended she wanted to be alone too," Greg grunted. "What a lie that was. Ye spent too much time with her when ye were young; ye turned out just like that stubborn ol' lady."

Taken aback, Quinn scowled at him. "I'm nothing like her," she said.

Greg's laugh was hollow. "Who here spent more than a decade being bossed around by her?" he growled. "Ye didn't know her like I did!"

"I've known her since I was a baby," Quinn argued.

"What are ye, 13 years old? I became her scribe when I was 13. That's 17 years of knowin' 'er!"

"I'm 17 right now, Sir Gregory *the forgetful*."

"Oh." Greg looked like he was thinking hard.

Mae leaned closer to him, one hand shielding the side of her mouth. "That's the same amount of time," she whispered.

"I know," he grumbled, swatting at her hand.

Annabel giggled. She clasped a hand over her mouth, trying to stop herself. "I'm sorry," she struggled to say. "I'm imagining Gwen hearing this and rolling her eyes at the two of you. She loved you both dearly."

Quinn hugged her knees to her chest. The argument had been the most normal part of her day, and for a moment, she'd been able to breathe easy.

Mae stood up and knelt in the grass in front of them. "Will you let me into your minds?"

Greg raised his brows. "What are ye looking for?"

"Memories," she said.

Quinn looked into Mae's deep violet eyes and without question, she put one hand on Greg's shoulder and the other in Annabel's hand. They both took Mae's hands in theirs, completing the circle.

*She was laying on the dirt ground, peering over the top of an enormous round pit. Quinn immediately recognized it as the training grounds, where the Suitor's Championship had been held. Everything looked different, less worn. She knew they were seeing from Greg's eyes, looking at one of his memories.*

*"That's her, that's her!" The blonde boy lying next to Greg hissed. On his other side, another boy released a low, sympathetic whistle.*

*"Maybe you should ask to train under a different knight?"*

*Little Greg didn't respond; he was focused on the arena below. From a distance, a woman advanced on another soldier, her brown braid flying. He kept trying to duck away, but she seemed to know his every move before it happened. Finally, she stepped back. Thinking he'd won, the other man launched himself at her. She threw up one hand, and a tree grew up from under him, wrapped one of his feet and pulled him upward with it. The soldier was flailing around, yelling at her to stop. She spun on her heel and left him there, dangling a hundred feet in the air, upside down.*

*The boys next to Greg laughed and whooped.*

*"He lasted under a minute." The boy on his left grinned. "You're in trouble."*

*"I don't know," Little Greg said, and Quinn could hear the smile in the higher pitched voice of a still-growing Greg. "I kinda like 'er."*

*"It's your funeral, Greg the Stoneless!"*

The memory faded, and a new one replaced it. With each memory that followed, Quinn felt the weight on her chest lighten. Finally, Mae dropped their hands, bringing them back to the present. The siren moved closer to the trunk of the tree and put her hand on the silver-infused bark. She stood there for a moment, humming a soft and slow tune. Tears streamed quietly down Quinn's face, and she leaned against Greg's thick arm. He patted her head awkwardly and blew his nose loudly into his sleeve.

Annabel approached the tree next and put one hand on the bark. She took a step back and bowed low to the ground, where she hovered for a moment.

Greg stood next. He walked to the tree and placed a hand there, seeming unsure of what exactly he was supposed to do. He looked like he might say something, but in the next second, a branch from above fell and smacked him square on the head. He cried out in alarm, rubbing the spot it had hit, before picking up the piece of wood and examining it. He held it out for the others to see. The branch stretched the length of his arm. Up close, Quinn could better see the silver threads interwoven throughout the bark.

Mae touched it but withdrew her hand as though it had stung her.

"That's not an ordinary piece of wood," she told Greg.

He took the other side of it in one hand and applied pressure as though to break it clean in half.

Quinn yelled in alarm, but the branch resisted and didn't so much as bend.

"Thought that might happen," he said calmly, as the others breathed in relief. He lifted the branch up over his head and secured it into the slot his axe usually rested. "It'll make a good walking stick," he said.

Shaking her head like she'd just witnessed him cursing the stone gods, Mae turned to Quinn.

"Do you want to—"

"I'm not ready," Quinn said, firmly.

Annabel took her hand and led her away from the silver tree, back up the hillside.

Greg parted ways with them when they got back to the camp. He said he was off to find a cup of tea, but Quinn suspected he was planning to find something stronger.

She moved in the direction of Annabel's tent, but Annabel stopped her.

"Wait," she said, before releasing her.

Quinn rubbed at her arm where Annabel had gripped it. "When did you get so strong?"

"You need me." Annabel held her head high, looking ready for a fight. "You need both of us."

Quinn scowled, confused. "Of course, I do." She tried again to move toward the tent.

"We're coming with you," Annabel said.

Quinn turned her head so sharply she felt something pull in her neck. She glanced from Annabel to Mae, frowning. "Mae can come," she said. "I was going to ask her to, anyway. My father was too distracted to do anything about her—or me—today, but I know he saw us both. King Edward still wants Mae's head. But I won't take you, Anna, or he'll want my head too."

"If you don't take me, I will call on my entire army to hunt you down, Quinn of the red stone."

Quinn laughed. "Your father will do that anyway!"

"But he doesn't know where you're going, does he? I'll lead him right to you!"

Quinn searched Annabel's face, trying to decide if she was serious.

The princess smiled at her. "I have a plan. Don't worry."

"You're the princess," Quinn said. "You can't run away from your kingdom."

"I don't plan to run, I plan to walk," she said, firmly. "Prince Jaxon left his kingdom to rescue me, now I will leave mine to rescue him. If I sit at home, I'll have to wait even longer to kiss him again."

Mae reached over and pushed Quinn's gaping mouth closed. "I told you," Mae whispered at her through a smile. Annabel seemed to take Quinn's silence not as complete shock but as consent.

"Now that we've settled that, I know what we need to do next. Follow me."

Not waiting for a reply, Annabel dragged Quinn and Mae in the opposite direction of her tent. Quinn shook her head, still trying to process the sentences that had just come out of her friend's mouth. *Annabel and Jaxon had kissed?* She wasn't sure what she was feeling, only that the words had shook her enough to disrupt the pit of darkness that had taken root in her heart.

Annabel stopped in front of a tent that was guarded by two men with red stones around their belts.

"We'd like to speak with the prisoner," she said.

Confusion spread across the guards' faces, but they both stepped aside and bowed.

Quinn followed Annabel into the tent and felt her blood turn to ice as Prince Jonathan came into view. He was sitting in the middle of the room; his chest was wound in chains that locked him to a wood post in the center of the tent. His head was hunched over, but he wasn't sleeping. His gaze was fixed on the ground like he was staring past it—or through it. Beneath the chains, she could see his belt, empty of the many stones that had once decorated it.

The sight of him there, helpless, broken, and pitying himself, caused white-hot rage to flash through Quinn. She curled her hands into fists. It wasn't fair that he was as broken as he was, when she wanted to be the one to hurt him.

Annabel knelt in front of him.

"Prince Jonathan," she said, with more gentleness than Quinn felt he deserved.

He struggled to lift his head. His eyes caught the light of Mae's glowing purple stones. Normally bright and blue like the ocean, they looked gray and empty in the darkness of the tent.

"Our sources tell us your brother has broken off from the Windsor army. Do you know where he might be going?"

He said nothing. Quinn lurched forward, reaching for one of her concealed knives, but Annabel held up a hand to stop her. Quinn shrugged in defeat and stepped back.

Jonathan hung his head again, and Annabel put a hand under his chin and lifted it back up.

"Help us find your brother and I will freely give you the green stones you came for," she said.

"Anna!" Quinn cried. Annabel ignored her, not taking her eyes off Jonathan.

"The Endless Sea," he whispered.

"What do you mean?" Annabel asked.

Mae and Quinn exchanged looks under Mae's veil of glowing purple stones.

"His homeland," Jonathan said. "Across the Endless Sea."

"There's nothing out there," Annabel said. "I've studied every map and read every travel log. There's nothing but monsters and storms and death."

"There's more," Jonathan said. "He told me a long time ago, when we were just children, when he first arrived in Windsor. He doesn't know I remember. He showed up at the castle doors with my—with *his* mother—their boat had crashed there. They were cold and wet and confused. When my father asked where they came from, Liam pointed to the sea. Now he lies and tells everyone he's from Morski. I thought he just wanted a normal life. I didn't know."

Quinn's disgust for Jonathan deepened. Even if what he said was true, how had he been so oblivious? Jaxon was gone, and it was his fault. Annabel stood, but Jonathan grunted. He rattled the chains that bound him as he moved in protest.

"I didn't know," he repeated, this time louder, more desperate. "He fooled me. He fooled us all. I thought my father was sick, but now I know—it was Liam. He's been—he was killing him." Jonathan's voice stretched with pain as he struggled with the words. "How could I have known he was the bloodsucker? How could anyone have known? He has no stones." His entire face contorted with shame. "Take me," he pleaded, his voice cracking as it became louder and stronger. "I need to find him. If he returns to Windsor, my father—and my kingdom—will be in danger. Take me and Healer Evelyn with you. I'll help you find him. I offer you my sword and my crown, Princess Annabel. I will do whatever you ask of me."

The princess paused, looking from his crumpled body up to Quinn, who shook her head in a fierce no. It was bad enough Quinn was going to leave Viridis with the princess; she couldn't take the only prisoners they had with them.

"We'll consider it," Annabel said. Without another word, she exited the tent. As soon as they were out of earshot of the guards, she spun to face Mae.

"Well?" Annabel asked.

"He wasn't lying," Mae said. "At least, he doesn't believe himself to be lying. I read Jonathan wrong once before."

"And should we bring him?"

Quinn froze at these words. She couldn't believe Annabel was considering it.

"I think so," the siren frowned. "I don't know if I'm asking the right questions, but it feels as though the goddess of clarity is pushing me in that direction. I've never seen so much uncertainty in every answer my stones are giving me. There's a murkiness there that reminds me of when I tried to look past the Suitor's Championship."

Quinn was silent. This seemed like the kind of plan Gwen would advise against. She knew Jonathan would have information about Liam that they might need if they were going to get Jaxon back. But was it worth the danger that put them in? Then again, the stoneless Jonathan wasn't much of a threat at the moment. *What would Jaxon do?* She already knew the answer to that. She looked at Annabel, who seemed to be waiting for Quinn to say something. She appeared more certain than Quinn had ever seen her. She wasn't the same person she'd been months ago. Neither was Quinn.

"We're going to need more help," Quinn said. "And we're going to need a boat."

As if on cue, she spotted Greg tiptoeing around tents and sleeping soldiers, a bottle of brown liquid tucked under one arm. The branch from the silver tree was still sticking over his shoulder, shimmering in the moonlight. He stopped moving, as if sensing Quinn's stare. He spotted them and his eyes squinted in suspicion as the three of them hurried toward him.

"Thought you kids went to bed," he said under his breath as they got closer.

"Thought you were getting tea," Mae whispered sweetly, eyeing the bottle under his arm.

Quinn ignored them. "We need your help. We need to find someone who knows how to navigate the waters of the Endless Sea . . . It would help if they had a boat too."

Greg smiled. "As a matter of fact," he said. "I do happen to know a fellow."

Once more, Quinn couldn't sleep. She thought about waking Mae and asking her for help, but both her and Annabel looked at peace in their deep slumber. As if in a trance, Quinn began to walk. She wasn't sure how she made it to the silver tree, only that she was in front of it once more.

She found a nook in the base of its trunk and curled up inside it, folding one arm under her head as a pillow. Sleep claimed her immediately.

When she woke some hours later, she was covered in fallen silver leaves.

# Chapter 24

# The Descendants

J axon woke to gentle rocking. He didn't want to open his eyes. He didn't want to acknowledge his own existence. His body ached with the memories of what his magic had done. Though he was not conscious for it, the power Liam had drawn from him seemed to have left a mark on his mind. Vague, blurry images kept flashing in his brain like the fading memory of a nightmare. Each time these images came to him, his entire body seized in sadness and guilt. Deep down, he knew with certainty that Gwen was dead and that his magic had helped to kill her.

Unable to bear the darkness any longer, Jaxon opened his eyes. He was laying on a small, uncomfortable cot on the floor. Metal bars closed him in from all sides. The dimly lit room appeared to be made of wood. The floor was definitely moving. Or his head was spinning. He wasn't sure which.

Jaxon knew days, maybe even weeks, had passed. Worry for Lukas, Annabel, Quinn, and Mae haunted both his waking and sleeping hours. The only comfort he held onto with certainty was the belief that as long as Lukas was wherever Quinn was, he would be safe.

The gentle rhythm of boots on a wood floor alerted him that he was no longer alone. Through the haze of darkness, someone was walking toward him. As the man got closer, the lantern he was holding lit up.

Eyes Jaxon had once thought were brown, shimmered with specks of red. A strand of the man's blond hair fell from his neatly pushed back hair and across his forehead.

"You've finally woken." Liam smiled at him. The same friendly, welcoming smile he'd tossed around the Viridis castle months ago. The smile he used to get any and all information he wanted. Only now did Jaxon notice how it was a smile too big for his face, a smile that asked for so much in return. "The drugs were a little stronger than I expected, but they were necessary. I didn't want to make it easy for your friends to come looking for me."

Jaxon stood up, holding onto one of the cell bars for support.

"What do you want with me?" he demanded.

Liam held the lantern a little higher. "You really haven't figured it out, have you?" he said, beaming. "You and I, we're special. Our blood traces all the way back to the very beginning. We descended from the stone gods."

Jaxon felt his legs shake, but he held tight to the bar, refusing to lower himself in front of Liam or allow his emotions to show.

Liam leaned in even closer, almost pressing his face against the bars of Jaxon's cell. "Except," he said softly, "you descended from the weakest of the stone gods, the Goddess of the Nurture Stone, who foolishly put kindness above all else. My blood, on the other hand, comes from the God of the Fusion stone. Do you know what this means?"

Jaxon stared unblinking at Liam's eyes, which were flickering with light.

"I can pull magic from others, while you can only give it. You have a limitless supply, Jaxon. And now, that supply is mine. I spent years searching for the source of the red stone, building my following, and practicing draining magic from others. My foolish stepbrother thought I was out exploring for the fun of it. When my travels brought me to Queen Jasmine, I learned that the source of the green stone was in Viridis, a secret that had been passed to her by your father. It wasn't the stone I was looking for, but to be so close to finding one—it was exhilarating."

Liam's eyes flickered in eagerness. He held the lantern higher, and his sleeve fell down, revealing a crimson mark on his skin. Jaxon remembered seeing that same mark the night the acrobats had performed in Viridis. At the time he hadn't thought much of it, but now, he couldn't pretend that it didn't resemble the white marks of Lux Pox. His stomach sank. How could he have missed that?

"I went back to my brother to convince him that we needed to find the sources of all the stones. He wasn't interested—he liked his little carefree life on the edge of the world. I still needed to use him, but he was harder to control than he had been when we were younger.

"I began to drain the magic and life from his father. Jonathan didn't know what was happening to him. He tried everything to save him; he brought in healers from across Windsor. I convinced him that it wasn't enough. We needed more green stones, and I knew where to find them. He was reluctant at first, but as his father's condition worsened, he was willing to try anything.

"He wanted to avoid bloodshed, so he agreed to an arranged marriage with one of the Viridis princesses, hoping this would give him claim over half the stone. As we traveled to Viridis, he was so consumed by himself and his worries that he didn't notice I'd disappear for hours, hunting for answers and amassing even more followers—there are so many hurt by the same cowards responsible for my own suffering.

Even when we were little, care-free Jonathan was oblivious to everything I was doing. He saw my scars every once in a while, of course, but he never questioned them or how similar they are to the mark of Lux Pox. He didn't know I had learned to use the magic of the red stone without the stones themselves.

"At first, I wasn't worried others would notice. I was pulling the magic and life from red stone bearers, and I was able to effectively discard the bodies. But I admit I was becoming more careless. I knew I was getting closer, I knew the answers were just out of reach. The gnome at the Viridis library knew where to find the red stone, but he refused to tell me. The night of the acrobats though, I was handed something far better than the red stone—I was handed *you*. I knew what and who you were as soon as I saw the green stone around your neck, but that annoying redhead confirmed it for me."

Jaxon clenched his hand into a fist, his whole body shaking uncontrollably. Liam was too busy staring at the stone around Jaxon's neck to notice.

"The first man in thousands of years to bear a green stone. I was still trying to move in secrecy. So, I focused on the one thing I knew with certainty that you wanted, that was within my reach: Annabel. You're surprised? Princess Cassandra was smitten with me. She poured her guts out to me. Not many people had the patience to sit and listen to her for hours. I did, though. She saw more than anyone. She knew all of the secrets.

"When I was done with her, I discarded her. Her death forced Jonathan to act. The stupid boy never once questioned why Annabel was slung over my shoulder or why I knew Cassandra had been killed by the bloodsucker. Our backup plan was set in motion. My men were supposed to take you in the aftermath of the battle, but that didn't go quite to plan. Kiernan got to you instead. I was forced to wait. But no matter. You're here with me now, aren't you? Two gods among men."

Liam backed away from the bars.

"Look at me," he said. "Usually, I'm the one listening to secrets. I rather enjoyed being on this side, watching your world fall apart."

Jaxon thought his hand must've frozen to the cell bar. All the warmth had left his body, his mind was numb.

"Now, get comfortable, creator of the stones," Liam said cheerfully. "We have a long road—or rather, a long sea—ahead of us."

He walked away, whistling.

"Where are you taking me?" Jaxon called after him.

Liam stopped. He turned to smile at Jaxon once more.

"My home," he said.

Which stone bearer are you?

VISIT JRGERACI.COM TO TAKE THE QUIZ AND FIND OUT!

www.ingramcontent.com/pod-product-compliance
Lightning Source LLC
Chambersburg PA
CBHW022005310726
48972CB00006B/1519